BAD HAIR DAY

BY

K T BOWES

Copyright held by K T Bowes
writing for the Hakarimata Press

ISBN 978-0-9951190-7-9

DEDICATION

I'd like to dedicate this novel to all women with curly hair.
This is for you.
Trust me, the purple-willy-shaped lube works.

CHAPTER 1

A Curly Bomb

Pop!

"Arghhhh!"

Engrossed with emptying a fresh bag of two-dollar coins into the cash register, Kit's hand jerked in shock. The coins tumbled in every direction but the slot she intended. Groaning, she slapped her palm over an escaping pair and stilled their chaotic tumble. She couldn't prevent the other four coins from bouncing onto the floor and rolling under the counter. "What are you doing over there?" she called.

"You dirty old man!"

Kit froze at the indignation contained in the wavering female voice. She slammed the drawer of the cash register closed and abandoned her post to investigate. Skidding to a halt at the end of the aisle containing personal hygiene products, she barrelled into a mobility scooter with a grunt of pain. The red flag protruding from its rear poked her in the eye. She wailed as the scooter's occupant reversed over her foot. "Stop! Stop!" she squealed. A pair of flashing blue eyes glinted from behind outdated spectacles as the scooter driver jerked on the accelerator handle and drove forward over her foot again. "No! No! Keep still!" Kit dragged her foot clear of the wheels and hopped on one leg, rubbing her instep with frantic fingers.

Pursing her lips, she glared at the scooter driver as a numbing ache blossomed across the top of her foot. "You need special permission from Mr Rashid to ride that around the shop!" she snapped. "Health and safety."

Instead of apologising, the woman pointed a shaking finger at the shop's owner. Mr Rashid stood in a slick puddle of clear goop, the back of his olive left hand rubbing at his eyes. "Oh, my days!" he mumbled through a beard and moustache dripping with shiny moisture. "Oh, my days."

"What happened here?" Kit hopped forward and almost lost her balance on the tiles. A layer of grease covered the aisle floor. "Whoa! Clean up on aisle three!" She let go of her foot and snatched hold of the opposite shelf. A multi pack of toilet rolls tumbled to the ground.

"I can't see." Mr Rashid turned in her direction. He stopped rubbing his eyes and stretched the fingers of his left hand out in front of him as though blind. The mobility scooter driver tutted as Kit spotted the object clutched in his right hand.

"You're not meant to put that in your eyes," she said, drawing out the suggestion as awkwardness shrouded her like a veil.

Mr Rashid's eye rubbing had slicked his eyebrows upward into an alarmed expression. He lifted the tube of purple-willy-shaped lube and waved it at Kit. His blindness meant he turned his body towards the female customer instead. The woman gave another huff of indignation. "This is your fault!" Mr Rashid spat.

Kit dodged sideways as the woman put her scooter in reverse and sailed past Kit at speed. Her wheels caught on the grease and she performed a breath-taking doughnut and spun to face the opposite way. Her wheels scrabbled for purchase and spread the grease around the corner as she took off past the counter. "Disgusting!" she shouted, once out of reach of Mr Rashid's greasy hands. "I'll report you!"

Kit wrinkled her nose at the clatter of the scooter colliding with the newspaper rack. The woman gave a wail of dismay and unhooked herself with much clanging and the screech of metal. The door chime registered her final escape into the sunshine. Kit turned her attention to Mr Rashid. His attempt to shuffle forward in his sensible shoes led to a slippery, arm waving dance. "How is this my fault?" she demanded. "You went to check the stock, not play with the purple-willy-shaped lube. What possessed you to cover your entire body with it? I think it works best if you remove your clothes first."

"Get Mrs Rashid!"

Kit inhaled and took a step backwards. "I will not! Go upstairs if you're planning kinky business!"

"I need her!"

"Oh, please!" Kit placed her sore foot on the ground and frowned at the dirty tyre marks staining her white plimsoll. "That woman ruined my shoe."

"Get Mrs Rashid!" Mr Rashid's voice rose to a wail. "I need help. I can't see!"

Kit took a step towards him and lost her footing again. "The floor is like sheet ice."

"Get my wife!" Mr Rashid shook the tube of purple-willy-shaped lube at Kit and the lid fell off and rolled under the nearest shelf. Then she noticed the crack winding its way around the top of the tube.

"What happened to the tube?" she asked. "Did you squeeze it too hard?"

"It exploded!" Mr Rashid growled through bared teeth. The snarky angle of his eyebrows and his tight lips made him resemble an angry schnauzer.

Kit shook her head. She used the shelf to edge her way back to safety, struggling to avoid the greasy tracks left by the mobility scooter. "Exploded? It can't have just exploded by itself. You must have done something to it."

"It was on its side, so I picked it up and sat it upright and it exploded! In my face! Get my wife. Oh, and you're fired."

"I'm fired?" Kit's head shot upright and her eyes widened. She slithered back towards him and snatched the broken tube from his fingers. "You're firing me because you won't admit you dropped it and now, you're embarrassed? Really?" Kit put her hands on her hips and lube dripped onto her left leg. She groaned and tried to tamp down her redheaded temper. "Don't be ridiculous. I need to close the shop before someone breaks their neck in this mess. Then I'll get Mrs Rashid."

Kit slipped her plimsolls off and tiptoed around the shelves to the front door. She shot the catch and flipped the sign to show 'closed.' The clearing of a male throat just behind her made her jump and scream at the same time. Her eyes narrowed at the man rubbing his chin with nervous agitation. "Is there anything I can do?" he asked. "I'm good at first aid."

"I bet you are!" Snarkiness oozed from Kit's voice and she backed away from the handsome customer. His dirty blond hair showed highlights either from the unforgiving New Zealand sun or an expensive overseas holiday. She didn't care which. His proximity raised a host of conflicting emotions. Kit teetered between wanting to hug him or beat him to death with the remains of the leaking purple-willy-shaped tube. Unable to trust herself, she took another step backwards, her bare feet slippery against the tiles. Never any good at ice skating in her youth, she didn't imagine she'd prove much better at almost thirty.

The man offered a steadying hand and she batted it away, choosing to end up on her backside rather than allow him any further foothold in her life. "You need to stop coming here!" she bit. Her fingers grappled at a nearby shelf, at the same time squeezing the lube. A jet of clear liquid shot down the front of his pants.

"You can't get rid of me, Katharine." Alec Roy frowned at the grease soaking into his expensive pant leg. "Yuk! What is that?"

"Lube." Kit tilted her chin up, giving herself a haughty look. "I'm sure you can find a use for it with your wife. There's more on the shelf, if Mr Rashid hasn't got into that too."

Alec dared to take a step forward. He lifted his hands as though to embrace her and then thought better of it. "When will you forgive me, Katharine?"

She reared back as though slapped. "For abandoning me on the day of my father's funeral? For marrying someone else like I didn't matter?" She pressed a shaking index finger over her chin and pursed her lips as though thinking. "Actually, Alec, I think the clincher was firing me after more than a decade of hard work because you seriously thought I killed your father!" Her voice rose to a screech and she hated the sound of it. Alec blinked against the force of each word, an expression of distaste spreading over his angular features. Hysterical women weren't his favourite kind. Kit considered ramping up the volume and antagonism in the hope he'd leave of his own volition.

"I didn't fire you." His tone remained even and calm, irritating Kit further. "You quit."

Without a suitable response on the tip of her tongue, Kit resorted to her two favourite weapons; bluster and fury. "Go away, Alec. Leave me alone. Never come here again." She pointed the tube of purple-willy-shaped lube remnants at the door.

Alec's strong brow furrowed into a set of neatly crafted lines which disappeared as soon as they landed. "I can't," he began.

"Get out!" Genuine hysteria lodged a lump in Kit's throat as she issued the command.

"I can't!" Alec's voice rose a notch and helplessness descended over his capable veneer as his lips closed into a firm line.

"You locked the bloody door!" Mr Rashid yelled. "Let the poor man out and get me my wife!"

Kit slipped and slid towards the door and fumbled the catch. She pivoted on the hairy coconut fibre doormat to stop herself ending up on her backside. Alec slipped through the narrow gap and collided with a customer trying to get in. Kit slammed the door, shot the catch into the locked position and dropped the blinds in a single fluid movement. She ignored the angry sounds from beyond the glass.

"Help!" Mr Rashid yelled. "I can't see!"

Kit shimmied along the tiles, using the shelves as hand holds. With a glare along aisle three at her furious employer, she nipped behind the counter, lifted the telephone and pressed the intercom for the apartment above the shop. A woman's voice answered, an inflection in her tone. "What now?" she demanded. "You said you'd be upstairs half an hour ago. This body suit is cutting off my circulation."

Kit's eyes narrowed and she tapped an irritated beat on the counter with her fingernail. "So, he wasn't just standing it upright then?" she demanded. "What a liar!"

"Oh, Kit." Mrs Rashid cleared her throat and an embarrassing silence deadened the air between them.

Kit sighed. "Your randy husband had an accident with a tube of purple-willy-shaped lube and he's blind. Oh, and he just fired me."

CHAPTER 2

Curly Placation

"I sat him on a plastic stool in the shower." Mrs Rashid dried her hands on a towel and ignored the knocking on the front door. "He's sulking." Her lips quirked upwards as she gave in to the grin. "His hair has never looked so shiny. Like a Bollywood star."

Kit shook her head and sat the mop back in its bucket. Grease snaked across the water like an oil slick. "I'll finish up and then go. He fired me."

Mrs Rashid inhaled. "Don't even think of not coming in tomorrow. That silly old man needs you."

Kit pursed her lips and smirked. "Not as much as he needs you, apparently."

A flush crawled up Mrs Rashid's neck and intensified her stunning mocha tones. She blinked in a rapid-fire motion. "I'd be grateful if you didn't mention this to any of my sons," she said, lowering her voice. Her fingers strayed to her ample bottom and she grappled around in her voluminous skirt. Kit heard a distinct twang. "Mr Rashid bought me fancy underwear and I need to get it off fast. I've lost an entire seam in an intimate crevice."

Kit closed her eyes, but the mental image stayed imprinted inside her eyelids. She shook her head. Nope, still there. "Okay, but at least put cones at both ends of this aisle until the floor dries. Then we can open the shop before that customer breaks down the door."

Mrs Rashid shuffled off in obedience before returning upstairs to rescue her pruned husband from the shower. Kit shoved the mop and bucket behind the counter and served the distressed man who snatched a tub of baby milk powder from the dried foods' aisle and barrelled towards the counter waving a fifty dollar note. "Don't have kids!" he snarled. Snatching his change from Kit's hand, he ran for the door.

"I don't intend to," she replied to no one in particular.

"Oh, you'll change your mind. Wait until you hit twenty-eight and those hormones start flowing. You'll be popping out bubs with the rest of the crowd." The middle-aged woman adjusted her suit jacket, causing her breasts to bulge against the narrow channel between the lapels. She dropped a jumbo-sized bag of confectionery on the counter and dug in her bag for her wallet. "I'm babysitting the grand-kids tonight. Little buggers. These are for bribery." She missed Kit's wooden smile as she keyed her pin number into the credit card reader. Exiting amid a cloud of lavender and Rescue Remedy, the woman left without realising the offence she'd caused at having dismissed Kit's life choices with a blanket statement.

Kit busied herself in between customer interruptions, using a bucket of soapy water to wash the shelf where the lube exploded. It had coated the underside of the shelf above and splattered other nearby products. She washed those too and put several of the items with soiled labels into a reduced bin near the counter. The floor seemed less of a skating rink by the time she'd run over it twice more with clean water and disinfectant. She spent the rest of her shift in bare feet as her plimsolls needed shoving in the washing machine. They were scarred both by the oil slick on the bottoms and the tyre mark across the instep from the mobility scooter.

Raj breezed in after lunch and frowned at the sight of the cones at either end of the aisle. "You dropped something?" he asked.

Kit communicated her irritation with a pointed glare. "No. Your father did. I've spent the morning clearing up and haven't had time to even Scrunch Out the Crunch from my hair." She waggled her head and ringlets bounced on either side of her face. "And this woman told me I'd change my mind about having kids. She doesn't even know me."

Raj jabbed an index finger towards her bare feet. "You can't have kids. Dad won't grant you maternity leave. Where are your shoes?"

Kit sighed and headed towards the bathroom. "Covered in what your father dropped."

"No, no! Don't leave me here! I just popped in to see my parents!" Raj threw his arms in the air, the drama wasted on Kit's retreating back. "Have kids if you want to! I'm sure he'll give you a couple of hours off just to give birth. He's not an unreasonable man." Raj sniggered at his own humour. The smirk drooped as he realised the statement summed up his father's expectations for his assistants.

"Five minutes," Kit announced, throwing the statement over her shoulder. "I'm entitled to a toilet break."

It took six minutes for Kit to use the toilet, wash and dry her hands and crack the cast formed by the lube on her hair. Her ringlets lost their wooden appearance and sprang into place with perfection. She finger-curled a stray hair into a nearby clump to avoid it frizzing later and admired the final effect. Then she frowned. Raki made the lube she used, crafting two full vats of it in his laboratory. It worked even better than the purple-willy-shaped stuff she'd relied on until recently. As her thoughts returned to her missing friend, a line of anxiety carved itself into her forehead. "Where are you, Raki?" she breathed. Her reflection offered no clear answer and she sighed and turned away.

Raj chatted to his mother behind the counter. They laughed about something and Kit imagined she knew what. Mrs Rashid kept prodding her fingers into the back of her skirt, so Kit figured she still wore the painful body suit.

An hour later, Kit paused with her hand on the door handle leading to the apartment above the shop. Her arms ached from the effort of making a pyramid out of baked bean cans. Mrs Rashid's eyelashes fluttered as she leaned against the counter. "Raj just nipped out to fetch his father's prescription. He won't take long. He's a lovely boy."

Kit ground her teeth in her jaw. "And I've known him since he still wet the bed. I don't see a relationship between us working. Am I safe to get my bag and go home now?"

Mrs Rashid wrinkled her nose. "Mr Rashid is a little embarrassed. Perhaps don't mention 'the incident' to him."

"Okay." Kit gave her a winning smile, while her mind worked overtime. Hell would freeze over before she let her vocal boss off the hook for this one.

"No, seriously." Mrs Rashid raised a hand in warning. Bracelets cascaded along her forearm like tinkling bells. "One exploded last night after you left and we thought maybe it was a one-off incident. He was checking the batch numbers when the second one exploded in his face earlier."

Kit's complexion paled. "The second one?" The event lost its humour. "The ones I got from Australia?"

"Yes." Mrs Rashid nodded, the action jerky and repetitive as she increased the emphasis of her statement. "He just rang and cancelled the next order from your friend. He wants his money back."

"Debbie?" Kit felt the groan building in her chest and fought to keep it there. "Money back?" An accident with Debbie's credit card had led to a thousand tubes of lube arriving at New Zealand customs instead of ten. Debbie hadn't forgiven her. If she couldn't offload the haul filling her garage, she'd excommunicate Kit from the local chapter of Women with Curls and send her back to Frizzy Hair Hell.

Kit took the narrow stairs two at a time. She snatched her bag from the shoe rack at the top and spun around to leave. A wavering voice called from beyond the lounge. "Is that you, my sweet? I'm still slippery."

Kit closed her eyes against the thought of an excited Mr Rashid and almost lost her footing. She reached the bottom of the stairs at a run and blasted through the door. Raj caught her, his upper arms bulging with muscle and sinews. "Where's the fire?" His eyes crinkled in amusement.

"I'm just in a hurry." Kit grabbed her plimsolls by the laces and dangled them in front of her as she ran for the door. "I'll be here bright and early tomorrow," she called.

Raj released a whoop of joy at the thought of not being the one to open the shop for the paper boys at five in the morning. Kit didn't wait for his reply, ploughing across the car park on a mission.

Her phone rang as she settled into the creaky leather seat of her yellow car. She answered it one handed, her tone impatient.

"Kit, Raki didn't come home again last night." Kit heard the strain in Langdon's voice. She shifted the battered mobile phone across to her other ear.

"Where can he be?" she demanded. "He always tells us when he's going away. This is too strange."

"Jerry's back from his visit with his parents and he's concerned too now. He's adamant Raki told him he'd be home for dinner five nights ago. I asked if he could be mistaken, but he says not. Raki said he wanted spaghetti Bolognese, so that's what Jerry cooked specially before he left for Auckland. What should we do?"

Kit sighed and looked at her watch. "I'm on my way. We'll talk about it when I get home. I agree it's very odd and not something Raki would normally do. Does Jerry remember where he was going?"

"The university. He went to pick up something from his lab and said he'd only be half an hour at the most. That was five days ago." Fear leaked from Langdon's voice and infected Kit.

"Give me about twenty minutes," she said. "We'll sit together and work out a plan. I promise I'll come straight home."

"I think we should call the police again." Langdon sounded funeral-serious. "Jerry doesn't stress about much, but he's worried about Raki."

"Okay. I'm coming now. I need to make one more phone call about some exploding lube. I think I have bad news to break to a very scary woman."

CHAPTER 3

A Fast Buck

"You what?" Debbie growled. Kit could hear her teeth grinding through the telephone. "I'm not giving him his money back." She sounded determined and Kit winced. "It's bad enough that he's cancelled the next order."

"It might not come to that. Mrs Rashid just mentioned it was the second one to explode. I wondered if you'd had any other reports?"

"I don't care! I'm not giving any money back. It's not my problem. The tubes were sold as seen."

"But if there's a problem," Kit began. Debbie interrupted her.

"This is all your fault. You can give them their money back for all I care. It was your mistake and now I'm paying the price. I have a garage full of sex lube and that's down to you."

"That's not fair! It was a simple error and I apologised. I intended to get rid of the lube myself. My mother offered me a loan so I could pay you back. You demanded all the product and said you'd take care of it. I tried to help you out by selling a load to Mr Rashid, but I didn't foresee you would hike the price."

"It's supply and demand," Debbie snapped. "There's a shortage, but only for as long as the next shipment takes to get here. I need to get rid of what's left in my garage before that arrives otherwise, I'm stuck with it. Raising the price a little at least means I can cover my credit card bill if I don't sell it all."

"Of course, you're not stuck with it!" Kit argued. "How do you work that out? You'll always be able to make your money back, even if you add on the import duty. But hiking the price too high will make it less attractive. Besides, I thought the Curlies were snapping it up fast."

Debbie's tone became sarcastic. "I told you, I have a credit card bill to pay. You can tell your megalomaniac shopkeeper that he's not getting any money back from me!" A sharp click heralded the end of the call.

Kit gave a sigh and shook her head. Guilt blossomed outward from the centre of her chest. Debbie was right; it was Kit's mistake. Her panic over the lube shortage had caused it. Although she'd offered to put it right, she'd been relieved when Debbie had demanded the lube be delivered to her garage and said she'd take care of it herself. Kit suspected Debbie had seen a way to make a fast buck and hoped it didn't backfire and cover them both in the process.

The journey home took far longer than usual as Kit planned what she might say to the boys. A tractor travelled at a snail's pace despite the queue building behind it. The driver ignored three opportunities to pull to the side until an angry man in front of Kit decided to lean on his horn. Raki's sudden disappearance created a strange knot in the pit of her stomach. A creature of habit, Raki always told one of them his plans. Since Jerry's arrival at the flat, the two boys had bonded enough to start cooking together and sharing the cost. If Raki had requested Jerry's famous spaghetti Bolognese and not turned up, then it was cause for alarm.

Kit used her indicator before turning left off the main road and heading home on the narrow lane which passed her house. She pursed her lips and made a decision.

The officer manning the telephone at the local police watch house answered on the third ring. He breathed out a bored sigh at Kit's enquiry. "As I explained before, Miss Maguire, it's not uncommon for adults to go walkabout for a variety of reasons. It's still too soon for us to start a manhunt. Have you spoken to his parents as I suggested or tried to contact someone at the university?"

"Raki's parents are travelling America at the moment," Kit conceded. "They attended a science conference at the start of the month. They don't have social media and I only have their home phone number. Is there any way that you could contact your counterparts in America?"

The officer masked a snort of hilarity and moderated his tone. "Look, with respect, Miss, he's just your flatmate. It's unlikely he would tell you all his plans. I suggest you try the university or wait for his parents to come home. I'd be more concerned about whether he's paid his share of the rent and bills because if he hasn't, then that's a whole different set of problems."

Kit offered polite noises of thanks, which she didn't really mean before ending the call. She hadn't considered the issue of rent and tried to push the new concern from her mind.

Her Volkswagen bug gave a happy shudder as Kit bounced it up the sloped kerb of her driveway and manoeuvred it around Jerry's old Mustang and Langdon's much newer station wagon. She settled on the gravelled area just under the lounge window and sat with her hands resting on the steering wheel for a moment.

Her driver's door popped open and made her start. A hand appeared in her peripheral vision. "How was work at the chalk face?" Jerry's full lips broke into a smile as he leaned down next to her. His dark hair mussed in the breeze. Tall and imposing, he oozed a sense of safety and competency. "Anything exciting to tell?" He took Kit's handbag from her outstretched arm and waited as she stepped free of the vehicle, then he closed the car door behind her with a click. His eyes narrowed at the sight of her plimsolls dangling from the laces in her fingers. "Oh. That looks intriguing."

Kit waved a hand in dismissal and followed him up the porch steps. "My day involved being run over by a woman in a mobility scooter, a tube of exploding sex lube, and a dirty old man who needs to exercise more self-control." Kit dumped her plimsolls outside the front door and followed Jerry into the house. She blinked against the darkness inside after the bright sunshine which dappled the lawn. "I almost forgot," she added, "I threw Alec out of the shop again. He can't seem to get the message." A sudden yawn occupied her facial muscles and she clapped a hand over her mouth. "Sorry, it's been a long day," she conceded.

Walking to the front window, she looked out at the neat lawn. A young man sauntered past, hands shoved in his jeans pockets and a hood pulled up over his head. A bright red beard glinted in the sunshine. Kit frowned. "That's weird."

"What is?" Langdon appeared from the kitchen, a steaming mug of coffee in his left hand. He'd removed his uniform jacket, but his dog collar and black shirt still marked him as a cleric. A blonde fringe danced against the flick of his eyelashes and the sleeves of his shirt strained against muscular biceps.

Kit shook her head. "A guy walking up the lane dressed for winter." She shrugged. "Nobody walks this far out of town."

"Do you want me to have a word with Alec?" Langdon offered. "His behaviour is becoming more than a little stalkerish."

Kit smiled at the suggestion but wrinkled her nose. She imagined the kind of word Langdon might favour and sensed it involved a lecture on appropriateness and a great deal of talk about repentance. "He'll get the message eventually," she said, though her brain reminded her he hadn't managed it yet. "He's not used to people turning down his offer."

"I can help him with that," Jerry suggested. The underlying growl in his voice sounded ominous and hinted at more than a conversation.

"It's fine," Kit said. "I appreciate both of you very much and if it gets unbearable, I will definitely ask for your help. But we have a bigger problem right now and I don't know where to turn to next." She threw herself into her reading chair and flicked on a lamp beside the tall bookcase. It seemed ridiculous with the bright afternoon sunlight streaming through the front window and glinting off the roof of her yellow car, but it offered her a sense of comfort as she pulled her legs up beneath her. Langdon settled himself on the wide couch opposite and Jerry slumped down next to him.

"Meeting in session," Langdon said. He brushed his blonde fringe from his eyes and blinked as though preparing to chair a meeting of his church deacons. Jerry grinned and bit his lower lip. Kit felt the humour pass her by for once.

"I'm lost," she admitted. "I just tried the police station again and the local cops aren't interested. We need to find him ourselves somehow. His parents are away and no one else cares."

"What about his rent?" Always practical, Jerry used his ex-lawyer's mind to begin with the evidence. "Raki knows Kit's situation with the mortgage. He knows she won't afford the payments unless we stay on top of the rent. If he planned to go away, he would set up an automatic payment, so she didn't fall behind."

"Good point!" Kit's eyes widened. "I didn't think to check the flat account."

"I'll do it." Jerry reached into his jeans pocket and pulled out his mobile phone. His fingers moved across the keypad at speed as he pulled up the shared bank account into which each member placed money ready for rent and upcoming bills. Kit held her breath, only releasing it as Jerry looked up and gave a slow shake of his head. "Nothing," he concluded. His fingers tapped against his thigh. "I know he's absent-minded, but he wouldn't forget this kind of stuff."

"Why didn't he set up automatic payments, anyway?" Langdon shook his head. "It's really easy to do and Raki's cleverer than all three of us put together."

"I told him not to worry," Kit admitted. "He went overdrawn a couple of times last year because his housing benefit or his student allowance hit his account late. I usually give him a couple of days leeway after the due date and he's always paid me back. It's a little tighter now that I need to make the mortgage payment on time, but there's still a week's grace and so I haven't worried. I trust him. In all the time we've lived together, it's never been a problem." Kit's teeth gnawed on her lower lip. She didn't dare contemplate the mortgage payment due at the end of the month.

"We'll help you cover it." Jerry spoke into Kit's thoughts as though he'd read her mind. The horrified look on Langdon's face showed he hadn't discussed it with him first. With a huge effort of will, the prudent vicar forced himself to agree with his curate in the interests of flat harmony. A slight tick in his left cheek told Kit he didn't like it.

She swallowed, reluctant to accept their help but lacking any other possible solution. "Thank you." She lowered her voice and her tone sounded sad. "If for some reason Raki doesn't return, I'll pay you back myself." Her sentence seemed to split the air. All three of the flatmates held their breath as the awful fact presented itself. They hadn't wanted to acknowledge the possibility that their scatty, lovable friend might never come home. Now, she'd said it and the reality hit them like a hammer blow.

CHAPTER 4

A Persistent Itch

"For the last time, please go away, Alec," Kit said with a sigh. Tiredness dogged her tone. The flatmates stayed up late the night before but came to no conclusions about how to find Raki. He hadn't posted on social media since the night he disappeared. A picture of his happy grin still occupied the top slot on his profile with the words, '*Yummo! Spag Bol for dinner. Can't wait.*' It haunted Kit as she moved through her work like an automaton. Bed at one o'clock and up again at four left her ragged around the edges. She wore Mrs Rashid's green scarf over her drying curls and glared at Alec across the counter.

"Have you converted to Islam?" he demanded.

Kit sighed and pushed his cash across the counter towards him, wincing as a ten-cent piece tumbled over the side and bounced on the tiles. She shoved the lemonade bottle serving as his cover after it. "Go away!" she stressed.

Alec righted the tilting drink bottle but didn't bend to pick up the rolling ten-cent piece. His blue eyes held Kit's gaze as he reached for her hand. Kit snatched her fingers back and fought the urge to wipe them on her jeans. "Stop coming here! I don't want your custom and I don't want to see you again!"

"Now now," a male voice interjected. "Let's not drive customers away. Any money is good money." Mr Rashid shouldered Kit aside without care and took her place behind the counter. He held his hand out for Alec's money, an expression of expectation on his face. He twinkled his fingers at Alec's resistance. "You drink, you pay." He bumped the back of his hand on the newspaper covering the counter, impatience in his fiery brown eyes.

With a look of mute appeal at Kit, Alec picked up the coins and laid them in Mr Rashid's palm. The shopkeeper added up the value faster than it took Alec to gather them together. Mr Rashid shook his head. "What is this?" he demanded. "You try to rip off an old man? I am a poor shop keeper!" Kit pursed her lips and turned her face aside to hide the laughter bubbling into her chest. Though he might be old, Mr Rashid was a long way from joining New Zealand's genuine poverty cases.

Alec fumbled around on the floor, looking for the stray ten-cent piece. His blond head bobbed up and down behind the counter as he searched for it.

"Here!" A woman in the queue behind Alec dug in her purse and handed over a shiny silver coin. Gnarled fingers clutched it and made a pecking motion at his face. "Get a bloody move on, young man!" When Alec kept his hands by his sides and refused to accept her offering, she dumped a loaf of bread and a jar of jam on the counter. Shoving a ten dollar note at Mr Rashid, she pushed a stray lock of grey hair from in front of her eyes as she waited for him to navigate the cash register. Happy to accept anyone's money, Mr Rashid processed the transaction with incredible speed and handed across her change. She blasted through the front door without giving way to the man already on his way in and he stepped back in alarm.

"Don't mind me!" he shouted at her retreating back. He moved into the confectionery aisle with a grumpy look twisting his face into a pout.

"See what you did," Mr Rashid said. He pushed the bottle of lemonade towards Alec with a sigh. "I'll let you off this time," he said, his tone heavy and laden with foreboding. "I know you come just to ogle my shop assistant. She told me all about you." He flapped his hand in Alec's direction. "Go home to your wife. This girl needs a nice Indian husband. I know just the man." Mr Rashid flapped his hand again and Alec backed away. His blue eyes flashed in disbelief and he shook his head.

Kit's shoulders slumped, but she lacked the energy to join this familiar dogfight. Mr Rashid slipped an arm around her neck and pulled her close. Alec's eyes widened in horror. He assumed Mr Rashid had designs on her for himself. Kit closed her eyes to avoid both Alec's obvious disgust and the irrational desire to explain herself.

Alec left the drink on the counter and strode from the shop. With a satisfied click of his tongue, Mr Rashid folded Alec's coins into his hand and closed his fingers around them. "He left a donation," he said. "How kind. Perhaps you should marry him."

"He's already married, Mr Rashid. You just said that. I'm not interested in him or any man. It's difficult enough finding my own way in life without having to accommodate someone else." Kit fixed a hand over Mr Rashid's wrist and slid his arm from around her neck.

"I have the perfect man for you," Mr Rashid said. A look of satisfaction settled over his olive features. "I know a man with a good sense of humour and lots of money. He likes nature walks and time spent with friends." His eyebrows waggled. "He's looking for a special lady."

Kit groaned. "I'm telling Raj. You need to stop looking at your sons' online dating accounts. Do they realise you troll their profiles?"

Mr Rashid rattled the change in his hand and pressed buttons to open the cash register. He placed each coin in its designated slot with loving care and closed the drawer. Black eyebrows streaked with grey performed a waggling dance on his forehead as he turned to face Kit with a feigned look of complete innocence. "I have many sons to choose from, Kit. Just pick one. I think Raj would be very happy."

"I think Raj would be horrified," Kit concluded. She shook her head and red ringlets bounced around her face. "I think I might tell him about your newfound mission to marry him off to every woman who walks into your shop."

"Not every woman," Mr Rashid protested. "I didn't suggest it to Mrs Miller."

"Mrs Miller is eighty-three. You gave her special permission to ride her mobility scooter around the shop. And the only reason you didn't suggest it was because you saw she wasn't wearing her hearing aids. You didn't want a conversation involving constant repetition and a whole lot of misunderstanding."

Mr Rashid's head bobbled on his neck. "This is true," he agreed. "And the suggestion might give her heart problems." His face crinkled with amusement.

Kit shook her head. "I think the suggestion might give Raj heart problems," she rebuked. Swallowing, she turned to face her employer. "I don't know what to do about Alec," she confided. "He comes in every day now he knows I'm working here. It's getting embarrassing. Don't you care that he wants me to work for him?"

Mr Rashid bridled and his lips parted in an expression of dismay. "What? What are you saying? He comes because he likes you, doesn't he?"

"No." Kit shook her head. "He wants me to go back to work at the garage. He's offered me a better job as his personal assistant. I've told you that twice."

Mr Rashid blustered and puffed out his chest. "You just got here!" he exclaimed. "You can't leave me already."

Kit rolled her eyes. "Then stop letting him come in here and pester me," she demanded. "One day I might decide to do it just to shut you up." Reaching for the pricing gun, Kit lifted the hatch built into the counter and ducked underneath it. She smiled at the sounds of indignation coming from her boss as she picked up Alec's discarded lemonade and went to put the bottle back in the fridge.

"Where are you going?" Mr Rashid grumbled. "I want to read you Raj's profile. He's a perfect match for you."

"I'll be in the bathroom." Kit tapped the back of her hair through the scarf. "It's time to remove my Plop."

"With my pricing gun?" Mr Rashid called.

Kit shook her head and the laugh bubbled in her chest. "No, but I needed an excuse."

It took less than five minutes for Kit to whip the scarf from her head and gently tease the crunchy cast on her curls. It wasn't time to Scrunch Out the Crunch yet and she inspected them in the mirror for early signs of frizz. Nothing. Perfect coils dangled in their rightful place. Spreading the scarf over the towel rail to dry, she jumped at a knock on the bathroom door. "Just a sec," she called. Her fingers closed over the button to disconnect the lock and twisted. It didn't move. "Hang on, the lock is sticking again." Kit gave it another twist. Still, it didn't budge. "What's so urgent?" she demanded. The question bought her some time as panic blossomed in her chest. "Mr Rashid?"

Raj answered. "Some guy is looking for you at the counter."

"What guy?" Kit stopped fighting the lock and took a step back. She drew in a yoga breath and took a moment to release it by slow degrees. One. Two. Three. Four. The urge to start screaming while smashing her way through the fire door subsided enough for her to collect her thoughts.

"Dunno. Dad sent me. He said you've been ages."

Kit twisted her wrist and checked her watch. "Six minutes!" she groaned. "And I used one of those fighting the door. I can't get out." She heard the desperation in her own voice and tamped it down with difficulty. "What does the guy look like?"

"Business suit. English accent. Not happy." A dull sound echoed through the door as Raj rived on the handle. "I thought Dad fixed this," he said. His voice sounded muffled. "You should use the bathroom in the apartment. Mum won't come in here for this exact reason."

Kit gave a whimper and pressed her spine against the sink. She forced herself to ignore the tiny window criss-crossed by protective bars. "No escape," she whispered, wondering why the fact had never occurred to her before that moment. "Because you've never got stuck in here before," she groaned to herself.

"What?" Raj sounded irritated and Kit sympathised. They both had other things to do. She pulled her tee shirt away from her stomach and flapped it to create a breeze.

"It's getting hot in here," she called. "Please, can you get me out?" Hysteria bubbled and she comforted herself with the promise that she'd always use the upstairs bathroom in the future. Alec's offer of work at the garage started to look like a good idea. Roy's Motors didn't skimp on fittings or force their staff to take two-minute comfort breaks.

"Dad!" Raj's shout carried through the door. "Kit's stuck. Can you help me?" She didn't hear the reply but guessed Mr Rashid had refused by Raj's grunt of frustration. He wouldn't leave the cash register unattended with a customer standing within reach, not even for a million dollars. Kit rolled her eyes. Maybe for a million dollars, although she suspected he already had more than that tucked away in the bank or under his mattress. "Fine!" Raj sounded determined. "I'm breaking the door down!"

Kit thought she heard a muted squeak and felt the light vibration of feet pattering through the shop. Mr Rashid's voice sounded high and raised. "Don't break the door down," he whined. "Who will pay for it?"

"Did you fix this lock?" Raj demanded. "Mum asked you to spray it with some grease last week."

"I did!" Mr Rashid squawked. He sounded muffled, as though he shouted from the middle of the shop. "I put some of that purple lube stuff on it! That's greasy."

"You did what?" Raj sounded appalled. "You put sex lube on a dodgy lock?" He groaned. "Please, stop talking, Dad. I don't want to know why you thought of using that as an alternative to proper maintenance oil."

Kit heard him making retching noises. Fabric brushed against the door and the handle twisted again. Nothing shifted and she remained a prisoner in the tiny space. Using her finger and thumb, she covered alternate nostrils and breathed in and out at regular intervals. Breathe. Hold. Release. Her heart still pitter-pattered in her chest, but some semblance of self-control returned. Then Mr Rashid blew away her dignity in one sentence. "It was Kit's sex lube."

CHAPTER 5

The Price of Regret

"I bet Alec would let me leave early." Kit pouted as she used the pricing gun like a weapon on a line of tinned peas.

Mr Rashid frowned and shrugged his shoulders. "Go then, see if I care."

"Fine!" Kit stuck her chin in the air and gave a series of rapid blinks. Raj had shouldered the bathroom door hard enough to split the frame and Kit had rushed into his arms like a withering damsel. Mr Rashid had looked satisfied until he realised he'd need to replace the frame as well as the lock. They both knew she wouldn't take Alec's job offer and the game continued.

Mr Rashid left her stocking the shelves to serve a customer. He returned moments later pushing a shopping trolley bearing the logo of a local supermarket. He'd filled it with tinned goods from the stockroom. He winced as the front left wheel spun in the wrong direction. "This one's broken," he announced. "I'll take it back at the weekend and get another."

Kit tutted. Mr Rashid didn't steal the trolleys. He called it a long lease and felt no shame about depriving his nearest competitor of their assets. "I'm not using that bathroom until you get the door fixed," Kit stated. "Raj said I could use the one in the apartment." She narrowed her eyes and gave him a haughty glare. "It will take longer."

Mr Rashid's head bobbled on his shoulders as he thought of a suitable retort and failed. Instead, he resorted to childish mocking. "Raj said," he repeated, effecting a high voice that sounded nothing like Kit. "Raj said."

Kit blew out a breath and altered the price on the gun. She gave the next line of peas a five-cent reduction, knowing it would kill Mr Rashid when he saw it in the hands of a customer. Retail legislation meant he'd have to sell it at the displayed price or remove it from sale. Kit pushed the six tins to the back of the shelf and cheered up a little. Karma always felt great. "I'm not marrying Raj, so you can stop that right now." She turned with a flourish and found Mr Rashid closer than she expected as he reached into the trolley. The nozzle of the gun cracked him on the forehead and a sticker released itself onto his olive skin. $1.94 grinned at Kit from the white sticky paper. He'd see the price and realise what she'd done. Karma didn't seem so great anymore.

Indecision created an embarrassing bout of hiccoughs and Kit clapped a hand over her mouth as the first four erupted in a row. Her whole body jerked with the force of their expulsion, making it impossible for her to retrieve the sticker from Mr Rashid's head without poking him in the eye. "But Raj is a nice boy," he complained. "Very accomplished. You should read his online profile."

Kit tried not to stare at the sticker and peeled her gaze from her employer's forehead. "He is a nice boy," she agreed. Another hiccough made her pause. "But you only want me to marry him because then I'd be part of the family and you wouldn't have to pay me for working here."

Mr Rashid gave a great inhale and filled his lungs with fake bluster. "Lies!" he cried. "All lies."

"Just mend the...hic...bathroom door handle...hic...please?" Kit begged. Unable to face the evidence of her attempt to mete out justice, she abandoned the pricing gun in the trolley and ran to greet the next customer just stepping from his car.

Mr Rashid endured a morning of smart comments which sailed completely under his radar. The customers enjoyed the price ticket on his head, making snarky observations without giving the game away.

"Cheap at the price," a woman commented. She smiled at Mr Rashid and waved her carton of long-life milk. He frowned and tried to return her grin, his gaze following her through the doorway.

"Vastly overpriced," a man sniggered. He ran his card through the machine and laughed to himself as he pressed his card number into the keypad to release the payment.

"Where did the man go?" Kit demanded as the thought entered her mind. She glared at Mr Rashid and tried to ignore the sticker on his forehead. "There was no man looking for me earlier, was there? You just wanted to hurry me out of the bathroom."

"Not true." Mr Rashid stuck his nose into the air. "He left when you didn't come out."

"Tall story," Kit growled. "You need a better imagination." Her eyes narrowed. "What did he call me then? Kit or Katharine?"

"Neither." Mr Rashid wrinkled his nose. "He asked for the small, mouthy girl with the carroty hair."

Kit gasped and her eyes widened. Mr Rashid's lips twisted into a sardonic smile, knowing he'd won the round by a hefty margin. Kit fumed behind the counter as she stacked boxes of matches into a teetering tower. She wished she'd priced him lower.

Mr Jim arrived just after lunch for an extra carton of soymilk. His work hours seemed more chaotic of late. "My wife apparently prefers this one," he said as he handed over the exact cash. He leaned across the counter and whispered something to Mr Rashid. Kit frowned but couldn't hear what he said. The effect on Mr Rashid proved devastating. His eyes widened, but he made no reply. Mr Jim tapped the side of his head in greeting to Kit as he left and she gave him a feckless wave.

"What's wrong?" she asked her boss.

Mr Rashid stared at the newspaper headline on the counter in front of him. He swallowed and tapped it with his finger. "I need to go upstairs," he said. His colour paled and his hand shook.

"Are you sick?" Guilt spread through Kit's body like a backwash and she itched to remove the price tag from his forehead. Memories of his sudden heart attack returned to compound her sin. "Is it like last time?"

Mr Rashid's lips turned downward into a look of sadness. "The policeman said someone has taken out a hit on me." He blinked, his expression serious. "I need to get out of sight. We should shut the shop."

Kit's eyes widened in horror. "Shut the shop?" She spat the words with more force than she'd intended. "But you never shut the shop!"

Mr Rashid shrugged like he didn't care. "My cousin is in the mafia. He accused me of cheating him out of some money. When I left India, he promised he'd find me. After all these years, it's finally happened." He gave a sigh of resignation. "I will take my good lady wife and we will go into hiding."

"No, no." Kit flapped her arms like a flightless bird attempting a futile lift off. "Mr Jim would never say that to you in such a casual way. This is serious. Let me run after him and ask for more details. What exactly did he say?"

"It doesn't matter." Mr Rashid flicked up the board which served as a counter hatch and stepped through the gap. "I gift you the shop. You are a good girl." He pressed a hand over his chest and then drew it across his forehead. Sweat beaded there and the price tag fluttered to the tiles without him noticing. "I will go to make my plans." His feet seemed to drag as he used the door to the upstairs apartment. It clicked behind him and Kit spun on the spot.

"But I don't want a shop," she whispered. "I've got enough problems of my own." Thoughts of Raki returned to the forefront of her mind and she slumped behind the counter for the next hour. In between customers, she searched on her phone for a map of the university campus. A look at her watch showed she had another hour before the end of her shift, but Mr Rashid hadn't returned.

The front door beeped as a customer stepped into the shop and Kit saw Mr Rashid's eldest son steer a course towards the counter. "What are you plotting now?" he demanded, his tone half humorous, half accusing. His wink diffused any sense of pique.

Kit shook her head and laid her phone on the counter. "I'm trying to find a map of the university campus. Do you know where the science building is?" She tapped the tiny map with her index finger and frowned. "So far, I've found a cowshed and a cricket pavilion."

Sanjay released a hearty laugh which channelled his mother's genes. He sounded like Raj. "Science and Engineering is in G Block. Use Gate 8 on Hillcrest Road, although you'll struggle to find parking. You might have quite a walk."

"I think I want the chemistry department." Kit twisted her lips into a pout. "Or maybe biology."

Sanjay waggled his eyebrows. "Are you thinking of abandoning my father in his hour of need?" His tone sounded serious, but his brown eyes sparkled.

Kit groaned. "He called you. Good. Perhaps you can talk sense into him."

Sanjay snorted. "I don't understand what this is about either. My mother called me in a panic. Dad is upstairs packing for a long journey as we speak."

Kit rolled her eyes. "It's weird. The Hamilton police chief came in for some soymilk and he said something to your dad. Then Mr Rashid got all strange and told me to shut the shop."

"Shut the shop?" Sanjay's eyebrows shot up into his fringe. "He never shuts the shop."

"I know. That's what worried me. Even stranger, he gifted the whole thing to me." Kit leaned back against the glass enclosing the cigarette cupboard. She let her gaze stray around the neat aisles and the products wearing their sticky prices. She pursed her lips and promised herself she'd redo the peas hidden at the back of the shelf.

"You didn't accept it?" Sanjay's eyebrows disappeared completely behind his fringe and his eyelashes gave a rapid flutter of alarm.

Kit snorted with indignation. "Of course not!" she snapped. "I don't want it!"

Sanjay released his held breath and muttered a naughty word under his breath. "I need to go upstairs and sort this mess out. Are you okay on your own for a while longer?"

Kit shrugged. "I can't stay here after my shift ends, though. I need to speak to someone at the university."

"In the science building?" Sanjay ran a hand through his dark hair and his eyebrows reappeared, giving him a less startled appearance. "Who?"

"That's the problem; I don't actually know."Sanjay stared at the ceiling stained by fly poo and the dent made by the lid of an exploding lemonade bottle. He paused for a moment. "I studied there. Three years of bio-chemistry." He wrinkled his nose. "Professor Kirke was our head of department. I think she's still there." His lips spread into a mischievous grin. "Her nickname is Woolly."

Kit stuck out her bottom lip. "Because she forgets things?" she demanded. "I sometimes feel like my brain is filled with cotton wool."

"No." Sanjay tapped his chin. "Because of her hair. It looks like wire wool." His gaze travelled to Kit's perfectly coiffed curls and he blanched. "Oh. No offence. Yours always look nice." He ignored the irritation burgeoning in Kit's eyes and beat a hasty retreat for the apartment door.

"Wait!" Kit shouted after him. "What did the policeman say that got Mr Rashid so upset?"

"Oh, that." Sanjay pressed the numbers into a worn keypad to unlock the door. "He told my father he had a price on his head."

CHAPTER 6

Curly Academics

Kit tapped her fingernails against the leather of her steering wheel. She stared at a line of fraying stitches along its curvaceous edge and wondered if an upholsterer might be interested in fixing up her old car. She blew out an exasperated breath. "Sorry Bug." She changed the tapping to a loving caress. "My bank account is emptier than my stepfather's head. Let's get the mortgage paid for this month and find Raki, then I'll see what I can do."

Her route south took her past Langdon's church and the traffic ground to a halt at the lights. A crowd gathered on the footpath in front of the angular building. It cheered as one as a bride and groom stepped onto the porch. A couple of wedding guests tossed rice and confetti until the crusty verger appeared to stop them messing up his steps. He limped around behind the crowd like a dog herding rebellious sheep, his broom swishing at the pavement and grass verge with frantic, futile movements.

The crowd seemed to still and phones lifted into hands as though the gathered souls waited for the arrival of a divining angel. The bride proceeded down the steps, lifting her voluminous dress and concentrating on her footing. The action gave her the posture of a question mark. Her suited groom already looked fed up as he conducted a slow death march into married life. They passed through the body of the crowd, ignored as another event occurred at the top of the steps.

Langdon and Jerry stepped through the arched front doors like the brothers of Adonis, one blond and the other dark. The white surplice of each billowed in the gentle breeze. Identical smiles graced their handsome features. They drew more attention than the bride and groom, the crowd clicking photographs like paparazzi. Kit gave a snort of hilarity and patted the steering wheel. "Oh, my goodness," she breathed, "God really does have a sense of humour."

She used the expressway to skirt the busyness of the town centre, pushing her little car up to the speed limit despite the alarming knocking sound coming from somewhere underneath the chassis. The leafy campus of the University of Waikato stretched before her at the roundabout on Ruakura Road, a hive of activity without a single parking space. Kit tried to cruise around the car parks, but the bug developed a case of the hiccoughs and morphed into a kangaroo. An SUV had parked on the grass verge and she contemplated joining it until she saw the infringement notice flapping from beneath its wiper blade. A van with a towing hook trawled for victims and pulled up behind her as she tracked a lone teenager walking to her car.

Kit groaned and followed her at a snail's pace. A snail with a terrible attack of the backfires. "Stop farting!" she snapped and the bug gave a sigh of sadness. "I already apologised for missing your last service," she growled. "I told you; I'll book it when I've got spare money." She puttered along behind the girl, who struggled with a laptop bag and a bulging binder. "Please, lady, get your car and let me have your parking space?" Kit hissed.

The girl half turned a couple of times, the hunching of her shoulders displaying her discomfort at Kit's obvious dogging of her steps. She wore the student uniform of jeans and a hooded sweatshirt. The wires from ear buds threaded through the neck of her shirt.

Without warning, the girl stepped over the kerb at the end of a long line of cars and headed towards a bus stop. Kit jammed on the brakes and the tow truck almost rear-ended her. The teenager turned in a circle and eyeballed Kit with pure defiance. She lifted her right hand and made a vulgar gesture with her middle finger. Kit's brows furrowed with indignation, which turned into laughter as the girl dropped her binder and paper exploded into the wind. "Karma is a bitch indeed," she breathed, rounding the end of the car park and heading towards the exit. She looked in her rear-view mirror and saw the tow truck driver's door open. He performed an interesting dance on the grass with the student as they both grabbed for flying paper in a curious academic snowstorm.

Kit headed for a different gate and another car park filled to bursting. She kept checking her petrol gauge and gnawing on the inside of her cheek. "Where are you, Raki?" she demanded. "If you went off with a random girl, I'm gonna turn you into a eunuch." With the tow truck driver busy with flying paper at the other gate, Kit risked hanging around the new car park. She checked her watch, seeing she'd wasted an hour travelling to the campus and looking for a parking space. "How does anyone ever get to class?" she mused. A thought popped into her mind and she gaped, realising she'd missed an important feature in Raki's disappearance. "Where's your car, bro'?" she demanded. If Raki had reached the campus, the night he vanished, his car would either still be there or the tow truck driver would have taken it.

With renewed enthusiasm, Kit set about combing every car park on the campus with a different goal. Two things happened. The first occurred ten minutes later, when she discovered the ancient Toyota resting under a giant ginkgo tree in the car park near one of the ornamental lakes. In desperation, she'd ventured into an area designated for staff and hit pay dirt. Kit parked behind it and walked around Raki's car, shielding her eyes to peer through the windows. A bright yellow square taped to the inside of the windscreen drew her attention and she gave a huff of understanding. "A staff permit," she said to herself. "Of course." Raki earned extra cash as a laboratory demonstrator for the undergraduates. He'd also started lecturing as a teaching fellow.

Kit checked the car doors and found them secure. She settled back into her bug and turned the key in the ignition. It gave a threatening click, but the starter motor did its job and the engine turned over eventually. Grateful for the small mercy, Kit rolled the car towards the main parking area.

Then the other thing happened. An inaudible bell tolled within the hearts and minds of everyone but her and the campus burst into life. Students appeared from every direction, heading to their vehicles and leaving. Parking spaces emptied and refilled as the hour marked an invisible change over and new students arrived to fill the gaps. Kit swore as she realised what was happening. "Lesson change," she huffed. "Now, if I can just snag a space."

At Gate 5, an older model Mini buzzed from a corner slot in an angled parking space and Kit raced an SUV to occupy it. She backed into the narrow space at speed with a whoop of joy. Several grumpy faces passed her as other drivers continued their journey to find a parking space.

Kit's next hurdle surprisingly enough proved to be an inanimate object. She left her vehicle and followed a group of pedestrians, waiting with growing impatience to pay for parking. Her purse disgorged a couple of shiny gold dollar coins and she clutched them in her palm. The slender grey machine chatted as it released tickets on cheap paper, which curled in the recipients' hands. Kit jangled her coins and waited for her turn.

Fighting a sense of extreme intimidation in the company of proven and wannabe academics, Kit searched the machine's frontage for a slot to accept her meagre offering. The queue behind her became restless and demonstrated its irritation through the shuffling of feet. "Where's the thing?" Kit demanded. She flapped her hand at the machine and her coins jingled. Turning to the next in line, she appealed to him with veiled frenzy in her eyes. "Where's the hole thingy that I put the money in?"

The teenager shook his head. "This one doesn't take cash," he informed her. "Use your credit card."

"But I don't have a credit card." Kit heard a ripple of disbelief move through the queue. The bodies forming a line had curled around her in a curious arc, desperate to peer at the only woman on the planet who didn't put her trust in a flimsy strip of plastic.

"What do you use instead?" The teenager dragged his hood back and popped a bud from his ear. He looked interested, the chewing gum in his mouth laying idle on his tongue. "How do you live?"

Kit swallowed, not enjoying the sudden attention. She sought to banish her celebrity status before it took a proper hold. "I bought a house," she offered. She bounced the dollar coins in her palm. "I have this left."

"That's terrible," said a girl from the back of the queue. "But can you hurry? My lecture is due to start."

"Is there another parking metre which takes cash?" Kit asked. A series of nonchalant shrugs served as a reply. Kit stepped back to allow the other members of the queue to use their plastic and scurry off to their various destinations. The sight of the tow truck lumbering down the slope towards the car park sent her into a panic. Turning, Kit looked back at her car, which stood out like a yellow beacon amid all the beige and grey metal surrounding it.

"Hey!" a male voice called. She swivelled to see a sporty looking student holding out a ticket. "I've put your registration number into the machine," he said, jerking his head towards her bug. "The ticket is good for 24 hours." He looked older than the others and less frayed around the edges. Ginger curls moved in perfect waves from his crown, his style trimmed into an unmistakable Curl by Curl Cut.

Kit ran back to accept the ticket and tipped her coins into the man's open palm. "You're related to a Woman with Curls," she gushed, referring to her secret curly club.

"Yup." The young man grinned. "I've seen you at our house. My mum is the chairwoman." He lowered his voice and leaned closer. "You're the one who got her into lube, aren't you?"

Kit blustered, the answer condemning her whatever she said. "For her hair," she stammered. "Just her hair."

The man threw his head back and laughed. His curls bounced in unison, a few still needing him to Scrunch Out the Crunch. "That's what my dad said." His eyes crinkled with amusement. "She covered herself with it this morning, her clothes and everything. Dad nearly broke his neck on the bathroom floor. She reckoned it exploded in her hand, but Dad thinks she got over enthusiastic." He closed his fingers over the coins and gave Kit a wave over his shoulder. Turning away, he set off across the grass behind the parking metre.

"No!" Kit groaned. "Not another one." She jogged back to her car as the tow truck started cruising for customers. She jammed the ticket between the dashboard and the windscreen, preventing it from curling by wedging two pencils either side. Both looked fluffy from their sojourn in the glove compartment and one rolled off as she slammed the passenger door.

Kit wandered until she discovered the library. An imposing foyer gave way to a cafeteria and an information desk. She waited in line, feeling small and out of place as the receptionist dealt with lost access cards and waved people off in different directions like an air steward. Her enquiry felt trivial. "Please can you tell me where I can find the chemistry doctoral students?" she asked. "I'm looking for my friend."

With a smile which oozed tolerance and infinite patience, the woman pushed a leaflet across the counter and waved her arm towards the main doors. "Go through there and take a right, a right, a left and another left. You'll see the faculty of science and engineering building to your right."

Kit thanked her and accepted the map. She walked outside and took a right, followed by another right turn. Her next left traced a narrow pavement, but things didn't go to plan as the route ended at a building which bore no markings.

Lifting the map, Kit shielded her eyes and tried to read the tiny writing. For the millionth time that week, she wondered if Raki would appreciate the lengths she'd gone to in her attempts to find him.

"You dropped something." The voice made Kit jump in fright and give a ridiculous squeak. She frowned at the slip of paper which the woman held out to her. The flyer bore an advert for the cafeteria inside the library foyer. Kit guessed it had fallen from the map.

"Thank you." Kit took it and folded it in half, shoving it into her back pocket. "This place is a maze."

"What are you looking for?" The woman's voice carried an English accent. The voice didn't match the person, creating an interesting paradox. Though she sounded light and enthusiastic, the woman dressed in frumpy clothing better suited to a nineteen fifties governess. Dark curls crowned her head, glossy and coiled into ringlets.

Kit narrowed her eyes, wondering if she had uncovered another closet Curly.

"I'm looking for the science and engineering faculty," Kit stated. "I'm looking for my friend."

The woman nodded and jabbed a finger behind Kit. "It's around there," she gushed, her voice still not matching her appearance. "Who is your friend?"

"Raki Han," Kit replied.

The woman cocked her head. "How do you know Raki Han?" she enquired.

"He's my flatmate," Kit replied. "He hasn't been home for almost a week and we're concerned."

The woman's head jerked back on her shoulders and she frowned. She stepped closer to Kit, giving the appearance of confidentiality. "We noticed his absence." She lowered her voice. "He's due to submit a chapter of his thesis at the end of this month. I'm also waiting on a journal publication. It's important he doesn't miss his deadlines, or his funding might be in jeopardy."

Kit's eyes widened. "That's terrible," she breathed. "I didn't know things were that bad."

"Yes." The woman stuck out her hand and almost jabbed Kit in the stomach with her sharp fingers. "Professor Aileen Kirke," she said, adding, "with an 'e'."

Kit took the proffered hand and gave it a light shake. The woman's fingers seemed to contain no bones, and the handshake reminded her of the final flick after rinsing a lettuce. Glancing down, she saw knuckles and fully formed digits. The ring finger sported a weighty diamond, proving someone somewhere loved the strange woman. Kit released the hand and took a cautionary step backwards into a welcome patch of sunshine. Buildings crowded either side of them, creating a shaded and sinister corridor. Her shoulders slumped. "I guess I've had a wasted journey," she said with a sigh. "I hoped Raki might have got busy on an experiment and forgotten the time. He's done it before this."

The professor made a sound of agreement, but neither her face nor her body moved to give further clarity. Kit floundered, not knowing if Raki was the good student she believed or masquerading as one. She swallowed, but the gulp morphed into an inner groan as verbal diarrhoea seized her lips and tongue. "Yes, he went missing overnight once and turned up having made me a batch of lube for my hair." Kit's inner voice screamed at her to shut up, but the hatch in her face had got itself stuck in the open position. "Do you have a Curly Routine? You look like you do a version of it. Do you use lube? I use lube."

The professor frowned and reached up to touch one of her curls with a delicate finger. Then she nodded. "I had a meeting. I'm on my way to Scrunch Out the Crunch. Lube?" Her eyes narrowed behind owl shaped spectacles. "You say Raki made lube here?"

Kit took a giant inhale. "Here?" Her mind unravelled her mess of words and she shook her head. "I didn't say here. He just turned up with the lube. He has friends he sometimes works with on different theories. I suspect he was with one of them."

"Friends?" Professor Kirke, with an 'e', removed her glasses and lifted a corner of her tweed skirt to wipe the lenses. She glanced up at Kit from beneath giant, unkempt brown eyebrows. Like two enormous, hairy slugs, they seemed to blink in the daylight before the thick glasses covered them in plastic again. "What friends?" She cocked her head and the action held a degree of threat. Kit took a fortifying step backwards and felt grass beneath the soles of her off-white plimsolls. The washing machine had smudged the tyre tracks into grey sweeps across the laces.

"I don't know them," she admitted. Her left arm gave a feckless wave along the path she hadn't yet covered. "I thought I might find someone in his department who knew him."

"He keeps to himself. You won't find anyone there who knows even the smallest fact about Raki Han." Professor Kirke turned the toes of her sensible shoes towards the building ahead and glanced at her watch. "I'm lecturing soon," she said. A tiny smile lifted her lips. "Why don't you give me your number and I'll call you if I hear anything?"

Kit yanked her tee shirt down over the back pocket of her jeans. Her phone nestled in its usual snug hidey, a little curved from the number of times she'd forgotten to remove it before sitting. "I don't have it with me." She lied outright, an alarm bell tolling in the back of her brain, though she couldn't say why. Disappointment crested the professor's expression and she slipped her phone back into the top pocket of her stiff jacket.

"What's your name?" she demanded. "I could look you up in the university database."

"Katharine Rogers." Kit swallowed as another lie slipped free. Not a total lie as she was unfortunate enough to have Kenny as a stepfather. She prayed Jerry would be willing to dab her forehead with Langdon's expensive oil of frankincense when she got home, to absolve her sins. He'd done it once before, although he'd refused her confession. Her lips twisted into a pout. He got too giggly. Maybe she'd ask Langdon.

"What do you study?" The dark brows knitted, lifting the spectacle frames off the professor's face a little and leaving the nose grips to hang free.

"Law." Kit decided she might as well be hung for a whole sheep rather than just the proverbial leg of lamb. Something about the woman made her uneasy. Her lawyer father had taught her always to trust her instincts. "I should go. My lecture starts in a few minutes too." She jabbed at her swinging red curls. "I've Scrunched Out My Crunch but I could fit in a few more Finger Curls before it starts." Walking backwards, she hauled her phone free and used a cunning sleight of hand to draw it in front of her as she turned. Then she kept walking. Behind her, Professor Kirke enquired about the name of her lecturer, but Kit feigned deafness and kept going until she reached her car.

The bug behaved with unexpected enthusiasm, leaving black tyre marks on the coveted corner parking space as Kit gunned the gas and bolted. She paused at the gate onto the main road and checked both ways for traffic. As she pulled out onto the main road, she recognised an adolescent male strolling across the road. He glanced in her direction and pulled his hood higher to cover a bald crown. His red beard stuck from the front at right angles to his face. Kit swallowed as she recognised him and her brow furrowed in confusion. She contemplated running after him but imagined what Jerry might say to such stupidity. A car behind her honked in irritation as her foot hovered over the brake. When she glanced in her rear-view mirror, the young man had gone.

CHAPTER 7

Curly Cuts

Kit rushed from the university to her meeting of the Women with Curls at Debbie's house. She arrived feeling ragged and disturbed by inner fears which wouldn't lie down so she could ignore them. She found Debbie's house filled with the usual brand of curly chaos associated with the women.

"Hi, Kit." Pam embraced her with a warm hug and narrowed her eyes. "We need to talk about that lube you sold to Debbie." Kit cringed and nodded as her happy metre drooped a little lower.

"Your son told me," she admitted. "He helped me with the parking metre at the uni."

"Cool." Pam's face brightened. "I'm glad he went to class for once." She patted Kit's shoulder and drifted away to clear up a spat about a new brand of conditioner advertised on the television. "Don't even think about it, ladies!" she intoned. "That stuff is loaded with sulphates."

"Here you go, gorgeous." Kit's friend Piper handed her a steaming mug of bulletproof coffee. Heavy cream left a layer of grease around the rim, which wouldn't help her waistline. Kit took it with a sigh and bartered away dessert instead.

"Thanks. What a day!" she breathed.

Piper gave her shoulder a squeeze of understanding but didn't ask for details. A suspicious line of baby sick wove its way up the neckline of her black tee shirt and under her hair. Kit figured she'd return the favour and not ask for a rundown of her friend's day either. She sipped the calorie loaded drink and tuned in to another conversation happening behind her. A look of horror spread across her pretty features as she whirled around to intervene. "Wait, what?" Kit's jaw dropped open and she fumbled the handle of her mug. Coffee slopped over the counter as she tried to set it down again. "Can you repeat that? How much?"

Debbie tossed her greying curls and fixed a hand over her hip. She thrust out her left foot as though in a challenge. Her tone became aggressive. "I'm selling the lube for twenty dollars a tube." Her right eyebrow rose, daring Kit to contradict her. "I need to make my money back, with enough to cover the import tax." She narrowed her faded eyebrows and her body language issued a warning, making it clear she blamed Kit for her lube dilemma.

Kit blanched and dropped her interrogation. Having been the reason for the thousand tubes of purple-willy-shaped lube in Debbie's garage, she didn't feel able to criticise her for doubling the price of each tube. Offering the WWC secretary a faint nod of conciliation, Kit leaned forward and lowered her voice. "Don't forget, we still owe my mother five hundred dollars. She paid the import tax, remember?" Her voice contained a hint of warning, and she saw Debbie's eyelashes flutter. Kit strayed nearer the wasp's nest. "I mean it, Debbie. My mother gets paid back first."

The other woman's eyes narrowed to slits. "I said I would, didn't I?" she snarled. "Even though that scruffy bloke dossing at her place pinched my backside when I collected the boxes."

Kit jerked back in shock. "Kenny Rogers? My stepfather?"

Debbie removed the aggression from her stance and appeared to back down a little. She tossed her head and her fringe of ringlets bounced. "I haven't forgotten your mother's money," she hissed, "but my credit card bill is due in less than a week, so I need to scrape together at least ten thousand dollars before then."

Kit nodded. "You can't be too far off that already. You've doubled the price and the Curlies have bought heaps. If the shortage continues, we should be able to get rid of the rest. How much is left?"

"One box." Debbie relaxed. "Both local supermarkets took a box each and I've invoiced them. I'm just concerned that the tax man might come after me rubbing his hands because he thinks I've set up a little side-line." She gnawed on her lower lip.

"You should." Kit gave her a comforting smile. "You're really good at this."

Debbie humphed and turned away. She embroiled herself in the debate about the new conditioner. It sounded like the scales had tipped and the discussion started on its way towards a full-blown argument.

"I'll take two tubes, please." Piper touched Kit's shoulder. Her eyelashes fluttered and then she looked away. Her lips turned down into a pout and a sudden sadness clung to her like an aura.

"What's wrong?" Kit whispered under her breath; Debbie instantly forgotten. "Don't buy them from her. She's doubled the price. I can let you have some of mine for free if you promise not to tell. I don't want them to find out and trash my house again." Kit jerked a thumb over her shoulder.

Piper shrugged and nodded at the same time. "I don't mind," she murmured. "As long as I get some."

Chairwoman Pam clapped her hands together to get the women's attention, and Kit abandoned her quest with Piper. She shot her friend a sideways glance filled with concern and promised herself she'd get the full story later. A hush settled on the packed room and Pam directed everyone into her lounge. A bottleneck occurred at the lounge door and it took a few moments for the women to funnel through and find a seat.

A tarpaulin covered a square in the centre of the lounge rug and Debbie bounced into the middle of it. Gabby giggled. "Oh, I saw this movie. The assassin stands the victim on a tarpaulin to avoid ruining the decor." Debbie glared at her.

Pam produced a pair of scissors from a nearby coffee table and made a few practice snips at the air. "After the success of Kit's demonstration last month, we thought we'd try one of our own." She glared around the room, holding the gaze of each of the gathered women. "But I do not wish to see a repeat of what happened at Kit's house," she warned. "Debbie and I thought long and hard about whether to even continue this group based on last month's behaviour." She raised an eyebrow and looked at Kit. "On behalf of the Women with Curls Hamilton branch, we apologise that the group's behaviour was bad enough to need a visit from the police. It will not happen again."

Sensing she was expected to contribute, Kit nodded and avoided looking at anyone in particular. "Thank you," she mumbled.

Piper gave her a sideways eye roll and shook her head. She leaned into Kit and whispered in her ear. "Says the woman who ran away from the scene with a lube sample tucked into her ass crack."

Kit smirked and pursed her lips. The superficial damage to her lounge and dining room took less than an hour to put right with her flatmates helping. Because the meeting ended with the appearance of Senior Sergeant Jackson Delaney, the women didn't eat the food they'd brought to share and it fed Kit's household for the following week. And despite the disaster with the lube order from Australia, Kit had managed to shift a quarter of it in less than a week. Mr Rashid had bought ten tubes to restock his shelves, complaining even though she sold them to him at the price she paid. She stole a glance across at Debbie and her eyes narrowed. The woman seemed determined to make a profit, and Kit sensed she didn't intend to share it. Her shoulders slumped and she considered the alternative. Debbie had behaved with surprising calm at the news that Kit had spent ten thousand dollars on her personal credit card by accident.

"Right ladies!" Pam clapped her hands again to silence the gathered Curlies who had begun to talk amongst themselves like naughty schoolchildren. She punctuated each word with the snip of her scissors. "Today, Debbie and I would like to demonstrate the Unicorn Cut." The women hushed and their eyes widened with piqued interest. Snip, snip, went Pam's scissors. The sharp metal blades relayed a veiled warning of what might happen to any Curly considering a repeat of the riot at Kit's house. Debbie snagged a barstool and plonked it in the centre of the tarpaulin. Then she slumped onto it with her legs dangling. Pam stood behind her and proceeded to ready herself for the demonstration, her hands flailing like a maestro. Kit watched in fascination as Debbie hauled her sweatshirt over her head. A roll of fat seeped over the back of her bra strap and oozed over the sides of her jeans like dough left in a warm place to prove. Debbie's willingness to strip off in public pricked Kit's sense of sisterhood and reminded her of the underlying safety of this group of struggling women. She settled onto the floor next to Piper and waited for the demonstration.

With a great deal of huffing and puffing, Debbie stuck her head between her knees and allowed Pam to wrestle her curls into a cloth ponytail holder. The blood rushed to her head and her eyes appeared glazed as she sat up again. Pam held a packet still containing two more cloth ponytail holders. "Curlies do not use elastic bands in their hair," she stressed. "It damages our curls. It's best to avoid ponytails where possible, but I realise that those of you in the food industry have no choice. These bobbles are quite a reasonable price and I found them in the Two Dollar shop at Chartwell Mall." Twang-twang, went the bobble. Snip-snip, replied the scissors.

Debbie spent the next ten minutes wide eyed and sweating as Pam used the ponytail as a guide to layer her curls. Pam paused with the scissors raised above Debbie's head to issue another instruction. "This can go very badly wrong, girls," she warned. "The trick is to get all your curls into the ponytail. Finger curl your hair first and then position the bobble on top of your head. The further forward you position the ponytail, the shorter your front layers will be and the longer the back layers. The ideal place to start for a first attempt is up high at the centre of your head along the midline. That will ensure you get even layers distributed all over your head." Debbie closed her eyes and her lips moved as though in prayer. Pam lifted the fat ponytail and smoothed the curls until they flattened like the bristles of a brush. Then she took the scissors and gave a few delicate snips. Debbie moaned as though experiencing actual physical pain. A few hairs fluttered around her shoulders and drifted onto the tarpaulin.

Shooting her head upright, Debbie's eyes widened at the sight of the smattering of hair dotted across her bare arms. "No more! That's enough!" She flapped her hands at Pam in the exact moment the snipping scissors settled on her ponytail once more.

Pam jumped and the sharp blades chomped at Debbie's grey curly ponytail, removing a chunk from the back. Kit watched as myriad thoughts passed through Pam's head and their eyes met for a fraction of a second. Mutual understanding passed between them.

"Wasp!" Kit hauled herself onto her feet, using Piper's shoulders as a ladder. She jabbed a finger in the air and several of the women shrieked.

"I'm allergic!" Gabby squealed. "Don't let it get me!"

With a look of pure gratitude, Pam used the distraction to aim a few more snips at Debbie's ponytail and straighten the chunk to a gentle taper. Debbie escaped the tarpaulin and blasted through the ranch slider into the garden like an Exocet missile. A number of Curlies followed her. They trampled the tarpaulin and disbursed the grey hair across the carpet. Pam closed her eyes and held her ground until only Kit and Piper remained in the room.

"I don't mind wasps." Piper looked around her, her gaze raking the ceiling for the offending insect. "I can catch it in a glass and put it outside," she offered. "Keep a lookout for it and I'll fetch one from the kitchen." She padded from the room on her futile mission.

Kit pursed her lips and watched the colour drain from Pam's face. "How bad is it?" she whispered.

Pam swallowed and rubbed her sweating brow with the back of her hand. The scissors shook in her fingers and snipped dangerously close to her eye. Her voice wobbled. "As bad as it gets," she hissed. "I'll just stay here on the assassin's mat and you can shoot me now."

CHAPTER 8

Disaster Recovery

Piper showed immense disappointment at failing to locate the wasp. The Curlies filed back inside after sunning themselves in the evening glow or hitting the buffet table in the dining room. Pam looked like a woman on the edge and kept her scissors in her hand as though preparing to ward off an attack.

After frightening the neighbour's children off their trampoline by waving at their father in her bra and knickers, the unsuspecting Debbie plonked herself back on the bar stool. "We'd finished, hadn't we?" she said, her tone cheery.

Pam remained frozen to the spot and said nothing. Kit stepped up to the plate and prepared to rescue her fallen sister. "Actually, Debbie," she said, lifting one of Debbie's wonky ringlets. "I'm wondering how it might look a little shorter. It's not a good demonstration for the girls if Pam snips a few dead ends. Why don't we try to frame your face a little more and show the girls how to make the most of our curls? Yours are on point. You should be proud of them."

Debbie simpered beneath the compliments and wobbled her head. The uneven ponytail swayed from side to side. Kit swallowed and turned to face the women. "When I do a Unicorn Cut at home by myself, I let my hair down and redo the ponytail part a few times. It makes sure I capture those stray curls which escaped the first time. I've found it's the best way to get even layers." Kit patted a red ringlet and it obeyed by giving a gentle boing and settling back into place on cue.

At Debbie's reluctant nod, Kit pulled the cloth bobble from her soft curls. She ran her fingers through them a few times and tried to see how she might salvage Pam's terrible accident.

"Okay." Debbie frowned and nodded, uncertainty in her voice. "Don't take much more off though, please." Kit shot a frantic look at Pam and got nothing. The chairwoman looked welded to the tarpaulin in her flip flops, a slight tremor the only evidence of her still breathing.

Kit pointed to the tarpaulin. "See, there's nothing there," she said. She prised the scissors from Pam's rigid fingers and lifted them in the air like a conductor about to direct a concerto. Then she snipped with the attitude of a prisoner on death row.

"Off, off, off!" the women cried. They got really invested, squealing and chanting like they were at a football match and not encouraging a woman in her bra and knickers to go for the full egg-head design. Kit finished the unicorn cut and released Debbie's curls. Switching to a Curl by Curl cut, she completed Debbie's makeover with shaking fingers.

Debbie hurried upstairs to Pam's shower and washed her hair with sugar scrub and expensive conditioner. She arrived downstairs as the girls polished off the buffet and Kit held her breath. She'd eaten nothing, tapping her foot on the floor in a continual, irritating movement. Piper seemed subdued and confessed how much she hated going back to work after her maternity leave. She intimated she was struggling with someone in the office. Kit made sympathetic noises and tried to show an interest. But thoughts of the garage and Alec made her miserable, so she nodded in all the right places while listening for Debbie's screams of rage.

The girls gasped as a new and improved Debbie skipped into the dining room. She'd changed into fresh clothes and finger curled her hair. Kit detected the scent of purple-willy-shaped lube surrounding her like an aloe vera cloud.

"Wow!" Gabby made a beeline for her while gushing, "You look amazing." The women gathered around a simpering Debbie and the sound of compliments and questions rose to a steady hum.

"I owe you one," Pam breathed. "I thought she'd kill me." She hung her head and slumped onto the sofa next to Kit. "I don't think I can do this anymore," she whispered. "It's all becoming too much for me. I'll nominate you as the next chairwoman."

Before Kit could object, Pam rose and slipped away. She sought sanctuary in the bathroom and didn't surface until after the Curlies left. She offered Kit no opportunity to discuss her unexpected and radical decision.

A telephone call sent Kit outside into the evening sunshine. The caller spoke before she could answer. "Mr Han? We need to talk."

Kit's eyes narrowed at the familiarity of the voice. She took a deep breath and replied, "Professor Kirke. This is Raki's phone."

A long pause stretched between them, punctuated by the sound of exasperated huffs. "Why do you have his phone?" Professor Kirke demanded.

"Mine broke. Raki bought a new phone and gave his old one to me. He got a new number and alerted his contacts."

"Well, he didn't tell me." Professor Kirke's voice sounded gushing and enthusiastic. Kit thought about the incongruity of the woman's physical appearance and frowned. "What's his new number?" she demanded.

Kit held her breath. For some reason, she didn't want to give the professor Raki's number. She had no excuse, other than a deep sense of unease. "I'll have to get it for you. I'm struggling with this phone and haven't loaded all my contacts yet. My flatmate can help me and I'll text it to you."

Kit prepared to end the call, halted by the woman's next question. "You mentioned using lube on your curls," she said. The statement surprised Kit and left her unprepared and floundering. The professor didn't wait for her reply. "I'd like to try it," she said. "I was hoping you could tell me where to buy it and give me instructions."

Kit swallowed. "There's a shortage at the moment, but a friend has managed to stockpile a few tubes. I'm sure she wouldn't mind selling it to you."

"Do you have her number?" Professor Kirke asked.

Kit suppressed a groan. She couldn't pretend not to have Raki's number and produce Debbie's. "Hang on a moment, she said. I'll find her." Kit kept her hand covering the speaker and picked her way through the crowd to find Debbie. "This lady would like to buy your lube." She held her phone out to Debbie, relieved when she took it.

Debbie wandered away and began a conversation with Professor Kirke. It trapped Kit at the meeting as she waited for her phone. She busied herself with tidying Pam's dining room and loading the dishwasher with cups and plates. Piper joined her. "What do you think I should do?" she asked. "What would you do?"

Realising she'd missed hearing the crux of Piper's dilemma, Kit gave a vague answer. "It'll take time to settle in," she said, offering a benign smile. "You've been away a long while."

Piper's head jerked back and her eyes narrowed. Kit tensed, sensing she'd somehow tripped herself up. Piper's expression crinkled into one of pleading. "Why don't you come back?" she begged. "I'm sure it would be better with you there."

Kit found a dishwasher tablet in a box under the sink and set the appliance running. She leaned against the counter and observed her friend. "I can't," she concluded. "Sorry."

"Do it for me?" A sense of hope drifted across Piper's expression and she blinked. "It could be like old times."

"But it can't." Kit gnawed on the inside of her cheek. "Mr Roy is gone and he wasn't the person we thought he was, anyway. Jason and that clown of a salesman are both out on bail awaiting trial. Alec must have employed new people by now. The culture we remember can't be the same. Besides, I refuse to work for Alec Roy. Mr Rashid is an oddball, but at least I know what I'm getting. The minimum wage is a killer, but I'm managing to make ends meet for the moment." Her mind drifted to Raki's absence and the knowledge that she couldn't cover the mortgage without his rent long term. "I need to find Raki. This is getting serious."

Her cheeks pinked as she wondered where her concern really lay; with Raki's welfare or his financial contribution.

"What can you do?" Piper accepted the subject change with reluctance.

Kit sensed something else lurking behind her friend's worries, but thoughts of the garage sapped her energy and she didn't want to think about it. "I don't know," she mused. "I drove to the university today, but his professor hasn't seen him for ages. I've tried speaking to the police and they're not interested. He hasn't been missing for long enough yet."

"What about speaking to his friends?" Piper suggested.

"Tried that. He doesn't have any, according to his professor."

Piper's head shook from side to side with certainty, and her curls bounced against her cheek. "That's not right," she declared. "I've met Raki and he's lovely. I find it hard to believe he has no friends at all."

Kit frowned and shook her head. "I think they all left when they finished their degrees. Only he stayed on to do his doctorate." Her brow furrowed. "I keep seeing this guy everywhere. He's scruffy looking with a red beard and very little hair on his head. He wears a hoody." She blinked as Piper nudged her arm.

"Where do you see him?" she asked.

Kit shrugged. "That's the thing. He keeps popping up in unexpected places. I saw him walking on our street and then again at the university. I wonder if he's a student." She glanced across the kitchen and saw Debbie still nodding into her phone. "What's she doing with the professor?" she groaned. "Swapping recipes or bra sizes. She's been ages."

After another five minutes, Kit pushed her way through the crowd towards Debbie. She found her still chatting to the professor and her tone sounded amiable. Kit held her hand out for the phone and Debbie finished her conversation. To Kit's horror, she gave the professor her address and phone number and the date of the next Curly meeting. "Bye for now," she said with enthusiasm. "Don't hang up because Kit wants a quick word with you."

Kit took a deep breath and prepared her request, careful to sound less fraught than she felt. "Hi, would it be possible for me to speak to your postgrad students?" she asked. "I'm sure someone knows something about Raki which might help the police."

"Are the police involved?" Professor Kirke sounded guarded.

"No." Kit winced. "They're not interested yet, but I need to find him."

"It's not appropriate for you to speak to the students." The professor's voice became hard. "I'll ask them for you and let you know what I find out." Her tone altered to sickly. "I'll see you at the next meeting, Kit. Or is it Katharine?"

A shiver ran down Kit's spine and the sense of foreboding returned. She'd lied to the woman but guessed Debbie had unwittingly given the game away.

Professor Kirke killed the call and left Kit staring at a blank screen. Confusion filled her mind along with the sense of having just been thwarted for reasons she didn't understand.

CHAPTER 9

Bad Unicorns

After another exhausting day in the shop and yet another visit from Alec, Kit sank into the comfortable folds of her favourite armchair with a sigh. Mrs Rashid had coaxed her husband out of his hiding place under the bed and reassured him that his cousin was still safely in India. Kit contemplated making a full confession, but when Mr Rashid timed every bathroom break to the millisecond, her guilt wore off pretty fast.

Jerry hummed to himself in the kitchen, rustling up something complicated involving a loaf of fresh bread. Without Raki at his elbow like an eager puppy, he looked somehow diminished. Kit opened her mouth to raise the familiar and painful topic of Raki's disappearance when her phone chirped. She reached for it and wrinkled her nose. Her fingers moved over the keypad with determination and she pressed the button to send.

"No!" she hissed after pushing her phone into her jacket pocket. She tensed as it vibrated against her keys, creating a rattle like old bones.

"What's wrong?" Jerry's brow furrowed as he studied her, waiting for an answer.

"Gabby wants me to cut her hair." Kit rose and dropped her forearms on to the kitchen bench. She let her chin sink into the folds of her sleeve. "She won't take no for an answer."

"Why you?" Jerry asked. He lifted a serrated knife and continued his mission to cut the thinnest slices of fresh bread ever witnessed on earth.

"Pam had a small disaster with Debbie's hair at last night's meeting. I managed to fix the mess enough to look half decent. There are no hairdressers who understand our Curly Method and it makes it difficult to get a haircut."

"I don't understand." Jerry sliced the bread wafer thin. "There are hairdressers all over Hamilton. Can't you find one suitable and spread the word around your group?"

"It's not that simple. We don't use shampoo and it's hard to find a hairdresser who agrees with that part of our process. Even though it works, we still meet lots of opposition. Shampoo is very much a twentieth century product for women and we've allowed ourselves to be brainwashed into believing it's best for our hair."

"Isn't it?" Jerry paused with the knife poised over the unfortunate loaf of bread. Crumbs scattered across the wooden board in every direction.

Kit shook her head and pressed her face into the soft fabric of the jacket covering her forearms. "No. It's terrible stuff. The chemicals in it claim to do wonders for our hair, when they actually sabotage it."

Jerry resumed his slicing. His latest slice looked almost transparent. "So, now you've excelled at something and they want you to continue?"

Kit shrugged. She studied the motion of his capable hands as he took a sharp knife and cut each slice into tiny squares. "What are you doing?" she demanded.

"Communion bread." He said the words as though they offered an explanation without further embellishment.

Kit blinked, wincing as her phone vibrated against the keys again. "Gabby went to the hairdresser yesterday. The one she used to have agreed with the Curly Routine. She left to have a baby and Gabby let her replacement cut her hair. She cut it wet and made a mess of it. Then she gave Gabby a lecture on the need for shampoo. Gabby is hysterical. She took today off work because she's embarrassed. She started texting me this morning, but the last few came from her husband. He says she has to go back to work because they need the money, but she's threatening to do an LRS. Then

Pam joined in with spamming my number. They're all ganging up on me."

"What's an LRS?" Jerry's handsome brow puckered into thin lines.

"A Last Resort Skinhead."

"Then cut the woman's hair!" He sounded horrified, strains of genuine dismay punctuating his words.

Kit's shoulders sagged. It sounded so simple when Jerry said it. She gave an involuntary shiver and shook her head before resting her chin on her wrists. "I can't. I know nothing about cutting hair. If you knew how many mistakes I'd made with my own curls, you wouldn't let me loose on anyone else's. I have no qualifications in hairdressing."

Jerry scooped the tiny squares of bread into a plastic container. He sealed the lid with a smile of satisfaction. "All the qualifications in the world can't replace bitter experience," he said. His voice softened and he leaned across to clasp both Kit's hands between one of his. He slipped his thumb into the delicate cleft between the bunched fingers of her left hand and rubbed until her fist uncurled. "I don't feel qualified to lead my congregation. Yet, they look at me in expectation because they need me to serve them. It seems to me this group of women are desperate for help and you're able to give it. Isn't it our duty to help when we can?"

Kit groaned. "Now you've made me doubt myself," she whined. "If I cut Gabby's hair, then I'll have to cut all the others' too. Bad things happen to people who pretend to be something they're not. What if it all goes wrong? It's not just that they might sue me, it's the misery of having ruined someone's hair." Kit looked up to meet Jerry's gaze. He blinked and his expression flooded her with empathy.

"We're all impostors, Kit," he whispered. "None of us really knows what we're doing. I understand why you don't trust other people, but you don't even trust yourself." He scooped the rest of his bread squares into two more plastic containers and sealed the lids. His strong fingers mirrored the care and consideration with which he would place each bread square onto the tongue of one of his congregation members as they sought spiritual healing. Kit observed him move around the kitchen as he swept up his mess and rinsed the bread board and knife. He gave her a wave as he stacked the containers on the kitchen bench for later and jogged upstairs to get ready for his evening table mass.

Kit's phone continued to buzz in her pocket. When she pulled it out, she discovered twelve missed calls and twenty-three waiting texts. She bypassed them all and pressed the buttons to access the Internet with a sigh. "Okay Aunty Google," she said. "Show me what you've got."

Kit's fingers worked on the ancient phone's keyboard as she surfed the Internet. She watched a couple of videos showing how to perform unicorn cuts on other people. Her phone rang in her hand and she almost dropped it. She paused the video showing a woman leaning over a bath semi-naked with a pair of deadly looking scissors pointed at the end of her ponytail.

A voice issued from the speaker phone. "You have to help me," it pleaded.

Kit sighed at the realisation she'd answered the call. "I'm just doing some research," she replied. "I'm not sure I can help, but I'll bring my scissors."

"What?" The male voice sounded horrified. "Is that all you've got?"

Kit frowned. His texts had verged on desperate, but Gabby's husband sounded suicidal in person. She swallowed and ground her teeth. "No. I've got hair clips and I've seen a couple of videos."

"What are you talking about?"

Kit stared at the unknown number on the screen and gulped. "Who is this?" she asked, her voice wavering.

"It's me, Raki!"

Relief flooded through Kit's body and left her with a peculiar weakness which extended to her fingers. She dropped the phone and scrabbled to retrieve it. "Raki! I've been so worried. Where are you? Why didn't you warn us you were leaving? I went to the police and everything, but they wouldn't help me."

"The police?" Raki's voice notched up to a level of hysteria Kit had never heard him use. "You can't involve the police! Please tell me you didn't call them?"

Kit swallowed. "They're not interested. You haven't been gone long enough yet."

"You can't involve them! I'm using a burner phone, Kit. I can only use it once and I need you to do something for me."

Raki's urgency infected her and she placed her ear closer to the phone speaker. "Where are you, Raki?" she demanded. "What's happened? What do you need me to do?"

Birds twittered in the background against the backdrop of Raki's heavy breathing. He hissed and sighed into the phone. Kit heard the honk of a single horn and Raki spoke to someone, his voice muffled. Then he said, "Gotta go. Don't tell anyone anything, Kit. That's what I need you to do. It's important."

She inhaled and released a groan of irritation as silence greeted her. He'd disconnected the call. When the phone rang again, Kit jabbed her thumb over the button to answer and lifted the phone to her ear. "I need to call the cops! This is just too weird."

Silence. Then the clearing of a throat. "I'm sorry for harassing you like this," a stranger's voice said. "But she won't come out of the bathroom. She's taken my beard trimmer in there with her and I don't know what to do."

CHAPTER 10

Curly Coercion

Kit arrived at Gabby's house armed with her wash bag of hair equipment. Gabby's husband relieved her of the additional bulging carrier bag bumping against her shin. "I'm sorry about this." He winced. His bushy black beard reached as far as his chest and offset the nakedness of his bald head. A toddler with enormous brown eyes and skin the colour of a perfect mochaccino blinked up at Kit, dragging on a fistful of her father's trouser leg. She pointed at the carrier bag and grinned.

"For Mummy, baby." Gabby's husband lifted the child with practiced ease and dangled the carrier bag in his free hand. "I'm Kev." He waggled his dark eyebrows at Kit. "And this is Keisha."

"Hi Keisha." Kit smiled at the child. A line of dribble tracked down Keisha's baby suit. Kit managed to disguise her reluctance to touch the child. A distinct waft of manure emanated from the bulge which began at the child's hips. It seemed inappropriate to mention that her future didn't contain children, so Kit fixed the smile onto her lips and asked after Gabby. Keisha made a grab for the wash bag and left a globule of spit on Kit's sleeve. Kev hung his head and for one frantic moment, Kit thought he might be about to place his precious daughter into her reluctant and incompetent arms. She took a calculating step nearer the front door, in case she needed to escape.

"She ran into the bathroom when I got home and won't come out. Keisha missed nursery because she refused to leave the house. She was quiet for half an hour, but I heard her using my beard clippers. What's LRS?"

Kit swallowed and her fake smile wilted. "You don't want to know." Her voice wavered. "Take me to Gabby, please?"

Kev carried the bag and the baby and led Kit down a dark hallway to the rear of the house. He stopped outside a closed door and an expression of helplessness drifted onto his face. "Gabs!" he called through the door. "Your friend is here."

"What friend?" Her voice sounded muffled and devoid of hope. A hitch indicated she'd spent at least the last hour crying. "Don't come in or I'll do it." The beard trimmer whirred again to emphasise the threat.

"It's Kit!" She leaned closer to the door and waited as silence greeted her. Frowning, she looked up at Kev and gave him a reassuring smile. Then she called to Gabby, "I hope you haven't cut off those stunning Afro curls." Kit added a note of threat into her tone. "Last Resort Skinheads are a myth. Nobody actually does it."

A sniff preceded a sob. "She wouldn't listen to me," Gabby cried. "She used shampoo and then cut it wet. It's lopsided and I've got this weird step thing at the back. My hair feels like wire and my self-confidence washed down the plughole with the foam from her special shampoo for black curls." Gabby screamed the last part of the sentence. She swallowed halfway through as hysteria took hold.

Kit closed her eyes and plotted a suitable course of action. The plastic bag in Kev's hand contained a bottle of apple cider vinegar to do a clarifying wash, but she imagined the Afro products contained silicone. It wouldn't work. She leaned towards Kev and avoided Keisha's grabbing fingers as the child lurched for her auburn curls. "Do you have any dish-washing liquid?" she whispered.

"No!" With the sonar of a fruit bat, Gabby heard her and ramped up her wailing. "I can't start again. I just can't!"

Kev's eyes widened in horror and he laid the carrier bag at Kit's feet with great reverence. Trying not to drop the baby, he jogged back towards the kitchen.

Kit leaned against the door with a sigh. She lifted her wash bag and clutched it under her left arm. The backs of her fingers tapped against the door and the contents of the carrier bag slid themselves onto the floorboards. Kit's favourite conditioner rolled out and hit the skirting board. "Gabby, I'm here to help. There are a million things I should be doing right now and unless you open this door, I'm leaving."

Click.

Kit jumped as the door disappeared behind her and she almost fell through the opening. Jerking upright, she turned to see an almost unrecognisable Gabby peering through the gap. A towel covered her head, masking the damage caused by a professional who hadn't performed the biggest part of her role, listening to the client. A dressing gown covered the rest of her body in a fluffy pink haze. Kev arrived waving a bottle of detergent, having deposited the child somewhere on route. "Will this do?" he asked. He shot a nervous glance at Gabby and she disappeared back behind the door. Spreading his arms wide, he gave her a virtual hug despite the barrier between them. "It doesn't matter, Gabs," he urged. "I saw you pop out a baby. Nothing could be worse than that."

Kit inhaled and stared at the clueless male. She shook her head as Gabby wailed and slammed the bathroom door. "Not helping!" she hissed. She flapped a hand towards the direction he'd come and shook her head. "Just give me an hour," she demanded. "Don't come back until I call you."

Kev's shoulders rounded and he dug his hands into his trouser pockets as he turned. His socks swished along the floorboards and Kit heaved a sigh of relief as the lounge door closed.

"He's gone." She tapped her fingers on the door and it opened enough for Gabby's swollen eyes to peer out. "We can salvage this," Kit promised, hoping if she said the words enough they might become true. "Just give me an hour. If not, I'll let you do an LRS and sweep up the curls myself."

The door opened enough for Kit to squeeze through the gap, but Gabby slammed it behind her. "Here we go then," Kit whispered under her breath.

Kit realised she'd underestimated the time required. She spent the first twenty minutes persuading Gabby that doing another Final Wash with dish-washing detergent didn't constitute starting again. Calling in reinforcements, she dialled Pam's number and handed the phone to Gabby.

"It's just a Blip," Pam confirmed over speakerphone. "Let Kit wash the silicones out and we'll count it as a Minor Blip. MB. In fact, let's not count it at all. Nobody needs to know."

Kit screwed her eyes tight shut at Pam's lie. Gabby's phone kept vibrating itself off the windowsill as the other Curlies blew up her number with commiserations. Kit opened her eyes and sighed as she checked her watch. Her patience thinned as she thought of poor Raki, holed up somewhere in danger. She squeezed the bridge of her nose between thumb and finger before holding her hand out for her phone. "I don't have time for this." Impatience leaked through her tone. "Just give me my phone back, please. I need to make a call." Raki asked her not to call him back, but she couldn't just do nothing.

"She's leaving!" Gabby's wail notched up and a bump against the door betrayed Kev listening behind it.

Kit rose from her perch on the side of the bath, her temper fraying around the edges as Pam's voice echoed through the speaker. "She won't leave you, Gabby. We're a sisterhood. We're all there with you." The theme tune for an English soap opera sounded in the background and Kit ground her teeth as it signified her evening disappearing. It also explained Pam's obvious reluctance to continue the conversation. Kit snatched the phone from Gabby's outstretched hand.

"You're not all here with her. I am. And I'm leaving. She won't let me help her and I can't do this right now."

Gabby uncurled herself from her foetal position on the bathmat and glared at Kit. A curious frenzy back-lit her brown eyes. "You have to help me!" She gripped Kit's ankles. "Don't leave me here. Kev doesn't love me. He said I looked ugly giving birth!" She screwed her eyes shut and giant tears leaked down her cheeks.

"I didn't say that!" An apoplectic Kev hammered on the bathroom door, the sound echoing along the narrow hallway. "I love you, Gabby. I don't care what you look like, babe."

"Again! Not helpful!" Kit shouted through the door. She killed the call with Pam and while Gabby's hands busied themselves clawing at the hem of her jeans, she bent forward and lifted the towel clean off her head.

Gabby let go of Kit's ankles long enough to cover her hair with her arms. "Don't look at me!" she wailed. "It's a mess!"

Kit pursed her lips and stared down at the ball of frizz gracing Gabby's head. She inhaled and released a long yoga breath of patience and calm. "It's not that bad," she lied. "Not bad enough for an LRS, anyway."

CHAPTER 11

Curly Close Encounters

Kit yawned and rubbed her eyes. Black streaks of mascara dotted the back of her hand. It took until midnight to fix Gabby's hair, and she'd crawled out of bed four hours later to open the shop.

Mr Rashid leaned across and dragged her arm away from her face. He shook his head and tutted at the makeup on her hand. "No wages for you this week," he announced.

"What?" Kit gasped. "Why?" Her lower lip turned down in dismay.

Mr Rashid shook his head. "I don't employ animals." He waved his brown hand at her. "You are a panda face."

Kit groaned. "Let me go to the bathroom and wash it."

Mr Rashid looked at his watch and grinned. "Two minutes. Downstairs bathroom."

"No way!" Kit stamped her foot. "You just want me stuck in there so you can dock my wages."

Mr Rashid feigned indignation, although Kit saw a spark of an idea flash behind his eyes. She cursed herself that tiredness made her put thoughts in his head. "I mended the lock," he said. "You need to trust me, Kit dearest."

Kit blew a raspberry. "Hell will freeze over before I trust anyone!" She paused as Jerry's words returned to bite her. He'd said she didn't even trust herself, but she pushed off the sting from his perceptive character assessment.

Devilment filled her eyes and she reached for a mini packet of wipes stacked with its mates on the counter. "I'll just use these then," she announced. "I'm sure a good employment relations lawyer will back me if I can't pay for them on account of having no wages. Also, you're not allowed to make comments about my appearance. I think there are hefty fines for employers who refer to staff as animals."

Mr Rashid watched through the corner of his left eye as her fingers picked at the seal. His eye twitched, followed by the rest of his face. Then he exploded. "Upstairs this instant, naughty girl!" he shrieked. He snatched the unopened packet from her hand and took a swipe at her as Kit escaped beneath the counter flap without opening it. "Bloody staff!" he yelled after her retreating back.

Kit giggled and pressed the code into the apartment door and disappeared as the packet hit it with a thwack. In the upstairs bathroom, she used water and a tissue to clean up her eyes. A tired face stared back at her. Her phone rang and she fumbled the opportunity to inspect the number before ignoring the call. Her message box showed six more waiting; one from Gabby and five from other random Curlies now wanting her services. She'd called the number Raki used the night before and received no reply. Eleven times. Another attempt made it twelve. Nothing. She ended the call with the stab of her forefinger and accidentally answered the next one as it came through with a tired ring.

"Kit!" Her mother's voice sounded strained. She recognised the signs as Marian's pitch rose with her next sentence. "The beauty clinic said you didn't use your gift voucher," she squawked. "Why not? I gave it to you for Christmas. It's about to expire."

Kit cringed. The gift wasn't her favourite of the season. Unbeknown to her mother, she tried to donate the massage voucher to all three of her flatmates. Jerry had seemed rather keen, but Langdon had talked him out of it along the lines of behaviour unbecoming of a vicar. Fear of the bishop's wrath had won.

"I'll use it soon, Mum," Kit promised. Her eyes rolled in her head. Marian kept up a steady stream of complaint as Kit clumped down the stairs and joined her employer behind the counter. Marian spoke at such a volume that Mr Rashid's face broke into a grin. He took a roll of dollar coins and stacked them in a holder, which he placed into a money sack.

He shook his head as Kit ended the call and shoved the mobile phone back into her jeans pocket. "You are lying." The grin spread up his face to involve his ears. "I am ringing your mother."

Kit turned to face him and smiled. "Happy birthday, Mr Rashid. How would you like a full body massage?"

His head bobbled on his shoulders and he released an odd little giggle. "I am loving a full body massage," he simpered, "but I am wanting it from Mrs Rashid." His bushy eyebrows waggled and Kit made a sound in her throat like a retch.

"That's disgusting!" She flapped a hand in front of her face, trying to hide the flush which reached upward in a pink bloom. "What can I do with this voucher?"

Mr Rashid shrugged. "Use it. Your mother thinks you need loosening up a little. I agree with her." He chuckled at the thoughts in his own head and Kit frowned.

"I didn't think she'd follow up on whether the voucher got used." Kit drummed her fingers on the counter. "I don't have a choice. It looks as though I have to get this massage."

"What's so bad?" Mr Rashid hoisted the bag of coins onto the counter and turned his body to leave. He reached behind him and slammed the cash register drawer closed.

Kit gnawed on her lower lip. "I don't know. I've just never liked the idea of a stranger seeing me naked and rubbing oils into my body."

Mr Rashid's eyebrows formed an amusing Mexican wave as though he'd lost control of them. He waved his hand towards the door leading upstairs to the apartment. "I am being a while," he said. "I am discussing things with Mrs Rashid. Important things. Do not disturb." He shot behind Kit, almost trapping his fingers in his haste to lift the hatch.

"You dirty old man!" Kit called after his retreating footsteps. She gave a shudder and turned to load the cigarette cabinet with stock.

The buzzer over the front door signalled the entry of a customer. Kit clicked the cabinet closed and heard the lock engage before turning to locate the new customer on the security monitor. She saw a man browsing the confectionery aisle and frowned as she watched him pull a balaclava down over his face.

Kit's fingers fumbled to locate the alarm buzzer underneath the counter. Mr Rashid's warning about not wanting to be disturbed ran through her mind as she jabbed it hard. A faint buzzer sounded in the upstairs apartment. She hoped he hadn't got too far with his amorous intentions to be able to run downstairs and save her. Just in case, she dragged out her mobile phone and dialled the number for the emergency services.

The balaclava covered the man's face and he approached the counter at speed. Kit watched on the monitor as he lifted a machete from beneath his sweatshirt. She knew she should run towards the door leading upstairs and get to safety before the man reached the counter. Mr Rashid had taken everything but the float upstairs. Her feet refused to move. Having used up all her courage pressing the panic button, Kit waited to meet her fate.

"Hand it over!" He moved towards her, barefoot and wearing the balaclava. Floral shorts flapped around his ample thighs. A voice chirped from the mobile phone in Kit's hand, the operator asking her which service she required. "Give it to me!" the man screamed. He tried to haul his heavy body over the counter, waving the machete at Kit. She backed as far as the cigarette cabinet with nowhere left to run. The operator stopped speaking, drawing her own conclusions about which service Kit required.

Her fuddled brain fumbled over an inner conflict. Mr Rashid lived to make money. He would expect her to defend the few coins he'd left in the cash register. Mrs Rashid and his sons would expect her to abandon them and save herself. Kit pressed her spine against the cigarette cabinet, realising she'd left it too late to do either one. Her eyes gave a frantic scan of the shelving below the cash register, looking for a suitable weapon. The man heaved his huge stomach onto the counter and lifted a meaty thigh and hairy knee up next to it. His nearness coupled with the waving machete blade galvanised Kit.

Dipping forward, her fingers grappled in the box Mr Rashid kept for defective merchandise. They closed around a jumbo bar of Toblerone which arrived the day before with its packaging crushed. Kit lifted it like a baton and swiped at her attacker's head. Forgotten, her phone hit the rubber mat on the floor. The satisfying sound of solid milk chocolate pyramids hitting the man's skull emboldened her, and Kit hit him again. The Toblerone pyramids crumbled inside the packet with the third whack and left Kit weaponless. She added a few more slaps around the man's face with the floppy chocolate before dropping it to the floor.

The Toblerone had stopped him crossing the counter, distracting him in the effort of hoisting himself into Kit's narrow space. Seizing on her momentary advantage, Kit looked for other items she could use as a weapon. Her fingers snatched at the mug containing Mr Rashid's forgotten coffee. She seized it and sloshed the half cup of cold liquid into the man's eyes. He screamed and blinked as brown coffee trickled over his balaclava and seeped through the eye holes. Kit smashed the mug over his head, feeling the hard clunk and then the shattering of ceramic. The impact ricocheted up her arm.

Kit's temper flared, fed by her father's red headed genetics. Glancing sideways, she spotted the wooden cricket bat she should have picked up first. Her fingers closed around the rubber grips on the handle and she hoisted it over her head. The large attacker used his free hand to brush coffee and chocolate sprinkles from his eyes before looking up just as Kit finished a graceful downward arc with the bat.

"Oh, no you don't!" The deep male voice sounded capable and familiar. The robber disappeared backwards off the counter and hit the floor with a heavy thump and a groan. Kit heard his bones make contact with the hard tiles. Her arms pulled out of the downward action of the cricket bat too late and she hit the edge of the counter, splitting the bat along its longest side. She sank to her knees and shards of willow from the broken bat clattered to the tiles in front of her.

CHAPTER 12

Curly Saviour

"Just sit there for a moment, Miss Maguire." The police chief collected the shards of the cricket bat into a pile with his foot. He squatted down next to Kit and rested a hand on her shoulder. "Did he hurt you?"

Mr Rashid's face appeared over the counter. His fingers fumbled with the clasp to lift the hatch. "It's bent!" He rattled it a few times before admitting defeat. "Why didn't you press the panic button?" he demanded, jabbing a finger at Kit.

"I did!" she shouted. Mr Jim reared back at her vitriol as angry veins protruded from her neck. Kit's feet scrabbled against the tiles as she fought to stand. Mr Jim's hand on her shoulder kept her pinned in place. His severe expression suggested he expected more violence. "I pressed it hard enough to raise an army, but you obviously got your pants off quicker than I thought possible!" Kit snarled. "I'm sick of your kinky exploits." Her anger faded to misery as she observed the broken cricket bat. Cue the next trigger for Mr Rashid's rage.

"My bat!" he shrieked. "My Rahul Dravid bat!" Unable to lift the hatch, he stretched his stumpy leg up on the counter and attempted to clamber over it. The front of a sensible leather shoe appeared and then popped free, making him bounce up and down on the other side of the counter like an angry pixie. "He scored a century with that bat!" he wailed. "What have you done?"

Mr Jim removed his hand from Kit's shoulder and his head jerked back in surprise. He blinked and looked over the counter at Mr Rashid. "Steady on, sir. This young lady defended your livelihood." His indignant tone did nothing to cool Mr Rashid's ardour, and he resorted to crawling under the hatch. His brown fingers closed over the handle of his bat. As he lifted it high, a long shard separated itself and plunged to the floor where it landed with a clatter. Mr Rashid bent and retrieved the broken piece, pursing his lips and trying to fit it back into place.

Kit narrowed her eyes and spoke to the police chief. "He doesn't care about me," she growled. "He keeps me hostage behind this bloody counter. I'm not even allowed to go to the toilet." She ran a shaking hand over her face and then remembered the balaclava-wearing assailant. "Where's the man?" Her eyes widened in panic and she shot backwards. The glass on the cigarette cabinet gave an unhealthy clang.

"Don't break anything else!" Mr Rashid wailed. "I'll take it out of your wages." His head wobbled from side to side as he searched for a missing fragment of bat to complete his jigsaw puzzle.

Mr Jim stood up straight, his height imposing. He seemed to swell in importance and the narrow space behind the counter shrank. "Is he using slave labour?" His tone sounded serious and hinted at dire consequences.

Mr Rashid blustered, but his denial sounded fake. "No, no. She's a family friend. We abuse each other. It's all good."

"What?" Mr Jim's lips curled back into a snarl. His head turned to Kit so fast, he made himself a candidate for whiplash. "Is that true?"

Kit pushed her face into her hands. "Stop listening to him. Where's the man in the balaclava?"

"I just took him to the car." The familiar voice screamed of comfort and safety. Kit dropped to her knees and scrambled underneath the counter, throwing herself into the newcomer's arms.

"It was awful." She squashed her nose against his Kevlar vest and breathed in male deodorant and the institutional scent associated with uniforms. "I thought he wanted to kill me." She blinked up at Jackson. "He can't get out of the car, can he?"

"Na." Jackson slipped an arm around her shoulders and gave her a side hug. His vest dug into the softer parts of her body, reminding her of the other barriers between them. Kit wiped her nose on the back of her hand and took a step away. Jackson's smile reached his eyes and he clamped a large hand over her writhing fingers. "He's handcuffed." Jackson's eyes narrowed. "And also covered in flakes of chocolate. The boys sat him on a dustbin bag to stop him melting on the seats."

"First the bat and now product?" Mr Rashid looked appalled. He retrieved the ragged Toblerone wrapper from the floor and peered inside it. "I should take this from your wages too!" he snapped.

Mr Jim left the counter area via the space beneath the hatch. He managed to make the action look far more elegant than anyone else had so far. With a nod of acknowledgement to Jackson, he used a gentle hand to move Kit between the two policemen and provide her with a protective hedge from the angry man alternately waving a broken bat and a floppy chocolate wrapper. "What happened?" he demanded.

Kit began her story, starting with the man entering the store and pulling the balaclava over his face. Mr Jim shook his head. "I meant with your boss. What's the deal with him?"

"Oh." Kit sighed. "He got overexcited thinking about the full body massage I didn't want," she said. "He went upstairs like a cork out of a bottle."

Mr Jim shook his head and patted the air between them. "Does your employer harass you, Miss Maguire," he asked with perfect seriousness. His hazel eyes narrowed, and he glared at Mr Rashid. Kit's employer continued to rampage behind the counter. He counted the cigarettes in the cabinet and moved on to checking the cash in the register. The bat disappeared beneath the counter along with the wrapper in an admirable sleight of hand.

Kit closed her eyes and shook her head. "Someone else," she murmured. "I'm getting it from someone else."

"Someone else is harassing you?" Mr Jim concluded. His dark eyes radiated concern. "I can help you."

Kit released a groan filled with exhaustion. "Someone else is giving me the massage," she sighed. "No one is harassing me except the man who threatened me with the machete."

As if on cue, a ruckus sounded from near the front door. Mr Rashid shrieked at the sound of tins thunking to the ground as a departing police officer collided with Kit's stylish pyramid of expiring beans.

"You pay for any breakages!" Mr Rashid shouted as the man disappeared into the street.

Mr Jim bent his knees to achieve Kit's height and gave her a kind smile. "So, you're not hurt?"

Kit shook her head. "Just my pride," she concluded. "Will you arrest me for trying to beat a man to death with a bar of chocolate?"

Despite himself, Mr Jim laughed. "No, the least said about that, the better." He cocked an eyebrow at Jackson. "Senior Sergeant Delaney and I think a nice relaxing massage sounds like a jolly good idea."

Kit's face brightened. "Would you like it? As a reward for coming to my aid." She scowled at the top of Mr Rashid's head as he peered into the cash register. "Unlike some people who didn't bother."

Mr Jim gave her a wink. "You have it, Miss Maguire." He lifted two fingers to his temple in a salute and nodded to Jackson. He picked up his discarded carton of soymilk and strode from the shop.

Mr Rashid bounced up on the balls of his feet. "You didn't pay for that!" He waved his arms over his head.

Kit gasped in horror. "Are you serious?" she demanded. "He just forgot! You're actually intending to charge him even though he rescued me from a robber because you couldn't get your pants on fast enough?"

Mr Rashid chuntered until Jackson pulled a handful of coins from his pocket and dumped them on the counter. To his credit, he made no comment and didn't wait to collect his change. Steering Kit to the front door, he pulled her outside into the sunshine. "What exactly did the guy say?" he demanded. "Tell me again."

Kit sighed and her shoulders slumped. She'd repeated her story until she grew sick of hearing it. "He said, 'Hand it over,' and 'Give it to me,' I think." Her brows furrowed as she began to doubt her memory of the incident despite it having only just happened. "Why?"

Jackson frowned. "Give him what, Kit?"

Her head jerked back in surprise. "The money in the cash register." She crinkled her nose in confusion. "What else is there? Cigarettes or cash. Take your choice."

"But he didn't say the words, did he? He didn't ask you to open the till or give him the cigarettes?"

"No." Kit's ringlets bounced against her ears. "I just assumed." Her eyes widened. "Why? What do you suppose he wanted?" She felt the colour drain from her cheeks and a chill rip through her body. The sunshine burning through her tee shirt hardly touched her.

"Nothing." Jackson settled firm hands over her shoulders and forced her to face him. "We'll get to the bottom of it." He lifted his right hand and cupped her cheek. "Sorry, Kit. I'm just speculating. Don't worry about anything."

Kit swallowed and nodded, though a hard lump had settled in her gut. She turned at the sound of an engine starting and saw the face of her attacker peering from the rear window of a police car. He glared at her as he passed and narrowed his eyes. She released a held breath as the car scrunched off the car park and took a shower of gravel with it. Mr Rashid would probably be out to count the chunks next.

Glancing up, she felt Jackson withdraw his hand from her cheek, but his perceptive eyes bore into her soul. "Do you know him?" he asked, one eyebrow quirked.

Kit shook her head and her shoulders slumped. "Even without the balaclava, I've never seen that man in my life before," she admitted.

CHAPTER 13

An Unusual Kink

"Hi, how can I help you?" The girl behind the counter at the beauty clinic wore heavy makeup. She'd tied her ponytail so tight it gave her eyes an odd slant.

"I have an appointment with Kas." Kit tried not to appear as sulky as she felt. Her mother had called again to say she'd made the appointment and expected Kit to drive straight to the beauty clinic after work. Kit looked down at her dirty clothes and cringed. The knees of her jeans bore grey smudges from clambering under the counter, and stress had made her tee shirt stick to her armpits. Kit had argued for going home for a shower first, but Marian threatened to drive to the shop and take her to the appointment. Kit felt more partial to enduring a full-frontal lobotomy by a scalpel wielding Mr Rashid than subjecting her dirty, smelly body to a clinician's massaging hands. Marian's pitiful complaints had fritzed her brain and heaped on the offence. She'd reiterated at least thirty times how difficult it had been to book her very own masseuse at such short notice.

The girl behind the reception desk gave a wooden smile, which didn't reach her eyes. As Kit watched in amazement, no muscle in her face moved apart from the occasional twitch of her lips. Kit's discomfort grew and she focussed on a noticeboard to her left. A poster announced the arrival of Botox on the clinic's list of services. "Kas is just finishing up with another client," the girl announced. "He'll be with you shortly."

Kit's eyes bugged on stalks and she took a step backwards. "A man? My mother booked me a massage with a man!" Her head began an involuntary shaking motion and she continued backing towards the outer door.

"Katharine! You came!" A deep masculine voice made Kit jump and her gaze darted to an open door behind the reception desk. Her mother's masseuse looked like a Greek demigod. A short, middle-aged woman scooted out of the room behind him. The puce colour speckling her cheeks and the dazed look in her eyes suggested a high derived from more than just an average massage. Kit continued to back towards the door and became entangled with the departing woman.

"I can't take my clothes off in front of him!" Kit hissed.

"I did." The woman's pink cheeks showed no sign of calming. Extra chins wobbled from the collar of her blouse. She waggled her eyebrows in a curious slithery dance and jerked her head back towards the masseuse. "Best thing I've done all year! I can recommend it."

Kit performed the little pirouette required for the woman to swap places with her and then grip the door handle in a meaty fist. Kit shook her head in disbelief at her confession. "But it's only February!" she replied. "The year isn't over yet."

The woman grinned and her eyes sparkled. "Yes, but I've worked out I can afford one appointment per week until the end of the year." With a pointed wink at Kas, she hauled on the door handle and sashayed through the gap with all the poise of a supermodel. Kit turned to follow her, certain that subjecting her stinky body to the ministrations of a demigod would not make this the best thing she'd done all year. A large hand landed on her shoulder.

"I'm so excited to meet you." Before Kit could respond, the hand steered her towards Treatment Room One and the doorway of doom.

"I've changed my mind," she squeaked. "It's best if I come back another day after a shower. I came straight from work."

Kas gave a deep rumbling laugh, reminiscent of the trains which shunted over the level crossing in Hamilton East. He propelled her forward under the tight smile of the receptionist and the door closed behind them with an ominous click.

"Take off your clothes," Kas instructed. His tone made him sound like a prison guard. He jabbed a long index finger at the massage table. "I'll change the towels and then you can lie face down in your underwear."

Kit gave a tiny whimper and took refuge next to a floral-patterned armchair. She hugged her arms around herself in a protective action, as though Kas might strip her himself. His accent sounded exotic and his dark handsome features and regal, hooked nose backed up the Bollywood illusion. As Kit hovered by the armchair, he made short work of changing the coverings on the massage table. Deft fingers rolled towels and placed them at the head and foot of the bed. Glancing up, he appeared surprised to find Kit still fully dressed. His brow furrowed and his lips parted.

"Your mama booked for a one-hour massage," he said. He flapped a hand at the bed. "I want to give you a good experience. You must not waste the time."

"But I stink!" Kit exclaimed. "Mr Rashid dropped a whole bottle of raspberry fizzy drink and it exploded all over me." Kit shook her head and her curls bounced against her cheek. "Not to mention the rest of my day." She lifted a hand to her hair which had avoided the spraying liquid. A quick prayer went up alongside a hurried thanks for the miracle of not having to do an apple cider vinegar rinse later.

"No matter," Kas responded. He flapped an olive hand towards the neat bed. "I will make you smell of roses. I promised your mama I'd give you a good time." He frowned and cocked his head as though deliberating an internal dilemma. "I wanted to give you something a little special. Maybe next time." He swished from the room in his soft-soled shoes and the door closed behind him.

Kit wasted a precious whole minute galvanising herself into action. She wasted two more trying to work out how to lift the Venetian blinds and inspect the window as a possible escape route. She didn't want a good time. Not then, and definitely not with a stranger who seemed to give lots of women a dubious good time. The slats gave a sickening groan as she hauled them up using the flimsy string on one side. A ping sounded from inside the spring at the top. The blinds gave an unhealthy lurch as the left side crashed onto the windowsill. With a hiss of dismay, Kit tried to release the right-hand side, but the string had jammed in the mechanism. The blinds hung at a jaunty angle and nothing she did made any difference. In desperation, she yanked the curtains closed against her vandalism and discovered that their ornamental function meant they didn't meet in the middle. The wonky blinds accused her from between the gap.

"Why me?" Kit wailed, muting the sound under her breath. With no obvious choice left other than to attempt to sneak past the Botoxed receptionist, she stripped off her soiled clothes and buried herself beneath the second layer of towels on the massage table.

Less than a minute later, Kas gave a polite knock on the door. He didn't wait for a response, which was just as well, as Kit hadn't managed to formulate one before he entered the room. He clapped his hands together as though preparing for a bar fight instead of administering a relaxing massage. Kit cringed beneath the towels.

She hadn't quite managed to get the two horizontal towels to join in the middle. A draught told her they'd betrayed her and left her bottom sticking out. She closed her eyes against the abomination of her grey, over washed knickers which popped up as a haunting image in her inner vision.

Kas clattered around behind her, and Kit heard the sound of glass bottles chinking together. Soft piano music began piping from the speaker above the window. Kit opened one eye and the wonky blinds gave testament to her abuse of them. Pushing her nose through the hole at the face end of the table, she closed her eyes and wished the experience over.

The sound of Kas clearing his throat forced her to look up at him from an awkward angle. He dangled a glass bottle in front of her face and his other hand cupped a ceramic bowl. "I am mixing a special blend for you." His dark eyelashes fluttered over his nut-brown irises and his full lips lifted into a hundred-watt smile. "Essence of rose and ylang-ylang in an almond oil carrier." He tilted the ceramic bowl to display the clear liquid, rose petals floating on its surface. Kas' expression softened as though he'd personally picked the roses and crushed them for her satisfaction. Kit nodded and made a strangled noise, which Kas took as approval.

"Your mama thinks you can help me with my little problem." Kas moved his fingers over the balls of Kit's right foot, pressing sore spots she didn't know she had. His accent held an element of mystique. She groaned as the kneading fingers released a knot in the arch. "I'm pleased you agree," Kas continued. A muted warning sounded in Kit's brain, ignored as Kas moved on to her left foot and repeated the action.

By the time the experienced masseuse had worked his way over almost every inch of Kit's body, her muscles and her resolve had turned to jelly and she was putty in his hands.

CHAPTER 14

Threats and Warnings

"You tried to marry me to a stranger! What part of that seems okay to you, Mother?"

"Oh no, dear. I gave you the opportunity to marry a very nice young man. I left the decision up to you."

"Really? Is that how you see it? He kneaded my muscles into soup before mentioning the paperwork you apparently agreed I'd sign."

"That's not right." Marian sounded confused. "He said a marriage would help him stay in New Zealand. He's a science researcher and his four-year visa is due to expire. He needs another year to finish his study. The immigration department are being difficult. I mentioned I had an unmarried daughter and suggested he might like to meet you to discuss it. This happened before Christmas. He asked about it again in my appointment yesterday and I felt a little hurt you hadn't used the voucher. He's a miracle worker, Kit. The hands of a demigod. One stroke of his fingers and my arthritis is gone for days."

"Yeah?" Kit shivered at the thought of Kas' lithe fingers touching her mother's naked parts. "Well, he took your conversation as an agreement. I left him popping a champagne cork behind the reception desk and toasting his engagement. How could you set me up like that, Mother?"

"I thought you might like him." Marian sounded huffy. "I like him. The girls at the clinic like him. All the women from my crochet guild go to see him. I'm telling you, he has magic hands, Kit. What's wrong with me hoping you might enjoy a relationship with someone handsome?"

Kit snorted. "I can't believe you just used the women of Bitch and Stitch as a recommendation!" Her eyes narrowed. "Ugh! I think I met one of them on her way out. She was as high as a cloud on lust and peppermint oil. And for your information, I don't want or need a relationship to feel fulfilled. I've been there and it sucks. My life is perfect, thank you."

"Everyone needs someone. It's a lonely life with no one else in it." Marian paused, and Kit saw a mental snapshot of her mother's relationship with Kenny Rogers. It oozed desperation.

"It's illegal when you're only marrying so they can stay in the country," she growled. "I shouldn't need to tell you that. I can't believe my own mother wanted me to commit a crime." Her phone beeped and she registered the sound of an incoming text. Marian blustered a little more to cover her guilt. "I have to go," Kit said. "Please stop setting me up with strangers."

Marian sighed. "I just don't want you to be alone," she confessed. "Loneliness is the worst thing in the world."

Kit ended the call and waited until the traffic lights turned red to check for a text. The retrofitted Bluetooth on her dashboard flashed the message and Kit stabbed the screen to make it repeat the wording out loud. Despite the day's bright sunshine, a shiver ran down her spine. The lights turned green and she jammed her gear lever into drive to move away from the car behind. The driver exhibited his frustration at her delay with a loud honk of his horn. Kit pulled into a layby on the road out of town and found the number for Jerry's phone. She waited until he answered, her fingers tapping a nervous beat on the steering wheel. The school traffic surged past her as parents drove their offspring to sports' practice or home.

"Hey." Jerry sounded out of breath. "Kit's been worried about you."

"What?" She frowned and wrinkled her nose. "Jerry, this is Kit. I've got Raki's old phone, remember?"

"Oh, yeah. What's wrong, Kit? I'm in the middle of something."

Kit's eyes widened as she heard a male voice in the background. It sounded like Langdon's. "Hurry up, Jerry," he called. "I need you."

"What are you doing?" she demanded. "Where are you?"

"At work." Jerry sounded cagey, and Kit's eyes narrowed at the lie. She couldn't detect the usual background echo of the cavernous church. When she paused, she thought she heard the cuckoo clock at home chiming the hour. Kit pursed her lips.

"What do you want?" Jerry asked. He huffed as though he'd been out for a run. "Can it wait?"

"No!" Kit wailed. "We've got a problem. A really big one."

"What, now?" Jerry sounded frantic, and Kit paused at the sound of huffing and puffing in the background.

"Come on, Jerry," the voice repeated. "I'm sweating on the carpet!"

Kit swallowed. "Is that Langdon? What are you doing?"

"Nothing!" Jerry's reply sounded snippy. "It's someone in the church. They're cleaning the carpets. An industrial company. They're very noisy."

Kit heard him hissing in a loud whisper. The words sounded indistinct and the connection wavered. "You're breaking up now. But I'm on my way home. I'll meet you there," she said. "I'll probably get there first. See you soon."

Kit drove as fast as she dared, pushing the bug to its limits. She arrived home with her brain rattling in time to the clanking of various important pieces of the bug's chassis. She slammed the driver's door, wincing at the grinding creak of protest.

To her surprise, Jerry's car sat on the driveway. A dubious looking patch of black oil left spots beneath the chassis as though the car tried to paint its own shadow. Langdon had squeezed his station wagon next to it, so Kit knew they were home. Dropping her keys twice before jamming the right one into the lock, she turned it but nothing happened. "What now?" she wailed. She hammered on the wooden front door with the flat of her hand. "Open the door Jerry!" she demanded, furious when she realised someone had deadlocked it. "What are you doing in there?" she yelled. Her hand hurt, so she switched to using the other one. The door flew open without warning, and Kit's angry slap landed on Langdon's face.

She gasped in shock and her fingers tingled with the impact. Langdon rocked back on his heels with the force of the blow, and his eyes widened in indignation. "What was that for?" he demanded.

"Sorry!" Kit didn't sound sorry at all. "I just spoke to Jerry, so he knew I was on my way. How did you get home so fast? And why did you lock me out?" Kit pushed past him and stalked through the hallway and into the lounge. She spun on the spot and inspected her surroundings. "Where's Jerry?"

Langdon ran a hand through his damp hair. "He's in the shower." He looked away; his movements jerky as he avoided Kit's puzzled gaze. Raising a square hand, Langdon conducted a tentative examination of his red chin. The heated outline of Kit's fingers radiated from it.

Kit dumped her keys on the dining table and turned with her hands on her hips. "I need you both here," she said. Her tone held a note of hysteria as she worked hard to ignore the slap mark. "Get Jerry!"

Langdon left the room at a trot, offering no justification for his speedy trip home or his and Jerry's need for an impromptu shower. Kit frowned as his footsteps pounded up the stairs and onto the landing. She wondered why Jerry would shower upstairs instead of using the one in his sleep out. Her brow creased into deeper furrows, although Jerry's hygiene habits seemed the least of her problems when Raki's safety hung in the balance.

Langdon reappeared at the same time as Jerry, but neither offered any excuse for their odd behaviour. They slumped onto the sofa together like two naughty little boys waiting for their punishment.

Kit paced up and down in front of them. When she stopped, she took time to stare at them both. "I don't know what's going on here," she said, "and I don't really care. But I just had a worrying text and I don't know what to do." Kit dragged her phone from her back pocket and activated the screen. She called up the text and read it out loud to them. "Today was just a little taster of what you'll get if you don't hand it over. Give us the stuff or the girl gets hurt. This is your last warning." Kit looked up at the boys to find them mirroring her confusion. "What are they talking about? Who's the girl. And what did Raki do?"

Jerry shook his head and his expression hardened. "I think you're the girl, Kit? They mean you."

CHAPTER 15

Scientific Twists

Jerry took the phone and made a note of the number. He called an ex-colleague from his legal days, but the plan failed at the first hurdle. "It's a burner phone number," he said after thanking his friend and disconnecting. "They just buy a SIM card and throw it away after a couple of uses. That number isn't registered to anyone."

Kit frowned. "That's what Raki said when he phoned me." She gnawed on her lower lip. "He hasn't called again."

Langdon leaned forward and rested his elbows on his knees. His bulging arm muscles stretched the sleeves of his tee shirt. Kit watched as he flexed them one at a time and examined them. A look of pride crossed his face and she cleared her throat to refocus him. "So, the robber didn't want the money from the cash register," she concluded. "It was a warning and he wanted whatever Raki took."

"But we don't know what that is." Langdon ran a speculative hand down his left calf and gave a nod of approval at whatever he found there. "It could be a case of mistaken identity."

Jerry breathed out and his chest deflated. "Let's think about this logically. You've got Raki's old phone number, so they think they're talking to him. He's stolen something and gone on the run with it."

Kit shook her head. "No. Raki wouldn't do that. This is serious." She tapped her temple and her eyelashes blinked in rapid succession. "I spoke to my mother on my way home and I have this crazy plan." She looked from Langdon to Jerry and back again. "But you're not going to like it."

Despite their protests, Kit arrived at the pub with her hair still wet and her damp curls sticking to her neck. She tried not to interfere with them as she settled her ringlets over her collar. Squaring her shoulders, she took a deep breath and prepared herself to meet trouble head on as usual. The boys had set up an expected protest, but she saw no alternative than to forge ahead with her mission to find their missing flatmate. A throwaway comment of Marian's had given her the link she needed to Raki.

Kit pushed the door open and a wall of brewer's yeast and stale beer hit her full in the face. Like a comforting blanket, she allowed it to wrap itself around her shoulders as she passed over the threshold to meet her fate.

"I am very grateful you called to meet me." Kas rose and pulled a stool for Kit from beneath the high table. He held it until she sat. She laid her phone face down on the table before settling her hands in her lap.

"I'm waiting for a call from my mother," she said, jerking her head at the phone as though justifying its presence on the table. "We had a bit of a disagreement after my appointment."

"About me?" Kas frowned. "I'm sorry. She's a lovely lady and a good client. I sensed I would like her daughter."

Kit released her held breath and nodded. "Let's start at the basics. You know a lot about me, but I don't even have your full name."

"Kasouf Mohammed Kashif." He held out his fingers in an exaggerated flourish and Kit smiled and accepted the handshake.

"Which do you prefer? Kas or Kasouf?"

"Kasouf." He wrinkled his nose. "But the receptionist abbreviates everything." He waggled his eyebrows and Kit released a polite laugh.

"And where are you from, Kasouf?"

"Faisalabad in Pakistan." His irises darkened to match his pupils, creating a strange bottomless effect. "I miss my home, but I need to stay here for my research."

Kit nodded. "I'd love to hear about it." She jerked her head towards the bar. "Would you like a drink?"

"Oh. I'll get them." Kasouf stood and shook his head from side to side. He withdrew a wallet from his trouser pocket. "I have money."

"It's fine." Kit hoisted her handbag onto her wrist and slipped her phone into her left hand. Jerry's warnings about not accepting drinks from strange men resonated in her brain. He'd lent a twenty dollar note towards the cause. Kit walked to the bar and ordered a soft drink for herself and the lemonade Kasouf requested. She borrowed a tray to make carrying everything through the crowded bar less hazardous.

Kasouf offered a tight smile as he settled himself back on the other side of the table. "This was your mother's idea," he maintained, beginning his protest even before Kit had collected her thoughts. "She thought you might help me."

Kit's elegant left eyebrow rose into her hairline. She put her phone on the table and sent it spinning with an absentminded flick of her index finger. "I'm sure she had a little help thinking up the idea." Her expression oozed fake confidence. "I'm not some hard luck little spinster desperate enough for a husband to buy one," she said. "What you're proposing is illegal."

Kasouf ran slender fingers through his dark hair. His brow furrowed and Kit detected a healthy dose of disappointment mingled with regret. "You won't help me?"

Kit sighed. "Maybe you can help me first. Do you know a postgraduate student by the name of Raki Han?"

Kasouf's brows furrowed into a heavy crease and his eyes widened. "Where is he?" His voice rose and nearby customers turned their way.

"Missing." Kit watched the anger heighten and then fade in Kasouf's expression. "He's a friend. I'm worried."

Kasouf pushed his drink aside and laid his palms flat on the table. His eyes narrowed to slits. "You will marry me for information about Raki Han?"

Kit swallowed. She'd lost control of the conversation already. Panic began to tick in her chest. She lifted her phone and glanced at the screen. "Perhaps I should call my mother and put her on speaker-phone. I feel we should clarify exactly what she agreed."

"She agreed nothing." Kasouf struggled to subdue the rising temper which flashed behind his dark eyes. "She speaks of you often. She wishes you would marry and give her babies. It was a simple deduction."

Kit laid her phone back on the table and with the threat of calling Marian delayed, she saw Kasouf's shoulders relax a little. His fingers stroked a line of condensation trailing down his glass and he took a sip. Kit swallowed and blew out a breath. "Tell me about yourself," she said, trying to steer the conversation back to Raki without pressing the self-destruct button. "Tell me about your research."

She reached for her drink and Kasouf's fingers brushed hers in a movement which appeared unintentional. He cupped his glass with both hands as though nestling a baby bird in his palms. Lemonade sloshed against rocks of ice. "I'm a biochemist," he said. "And a qualified pharmacist. I came to New Zealand four years ago on a scholarship from my homeland. My post graduate study focused on finding ways to create suitable carriers for certain chemicals used to assist the medical profession. I achieved enough of a breakthrough to secure a research scholarship to further develop my findings over here. I've been living here since I finished my doctorate."

Kit jerked backwards in surprise. Fizzy drink slopped over her hand. Kasouf reached across the table and he removed a napkin from around a set of cutlery. He handed it to her without comment. "Gosh!" Kit couldn't keep the awe from her voice. "So, you're actually Dr Kasouf?"

Kasouf appeared bashful. He nodded his head in an awkward side-to-side rolling motion. His eyelashes fluttered and he reminded Kit of a deer she'd once seen on a hunting expedition with her father and his lawyer friends. The memory tasted like chalk in her mouth. She hadn't coped well with the killing or the carcass and she could still hear her father's voice laden with sadness as he apologised all the way home.

"This is true. I am a doctor." His long lashes swished against his cheek as he gave her a rueful smile. "But do not have a heart attack," he advised. "I'm not the right kind of doctor."

Kit smiled and lifted her drink to her lips. The carbonated liquid tickled her nose. "I'm not so sure," she admitted. "You did a pretty good job on my human anatomy earlier." Realising the comment sounded inappropriate, the smile faded from her lips.

Kasouf appeared oblivious. The clear liquid in his glass sloshed and the ice tinkled like bells as he lifted it to his lips. "It must seem ridiculous that I work as a masseuse," he said. His voice lowered. "But, I'm good at what I do. And I enjoy it."

Kit shrugged. "It's not weird," she lied. It was very weird. Kasouf sent a covert, darting glance around the crowded pub. "I don't have a work visa, so the owner won't advertise my services."

Kit pinched her lips together in a tight line. It seemed Kasouf trod the line between acceptable and illegal in every facet of his life. She sought to change the subject but found it difficult not to trespass on something contentious within his minefield of issues. It seemed unkind to drag his attention back to his research when it gave him such obvious distress at the thought of not finishing it.

Kit shook her head. "I appreciate how difficult it must be not to complete your work," she said, forcing a soothing lilt into her tone. "It's not that I won't help you, Kasouf. But what you're asking is illegal."

"But your mother said you would marry me, so I could finish my research." He clasped both hands over his left pectoral. "She said you had a kind heart."

Kit gave a dismissive wave of her hand. "I'm sure my mother said a lot of things, but most of them aren't worth listening to, trust me."

Kasouf released a sigh, and Kit acknowledged a rising sense of empathy for him. She let her shoulders relax and rested her elbows on the table. "Tell me about your interest in Raki Han."

Kasouf downed the dregs of his lemonade and rose. "I get more drink," he said. "I have plenty of money. It's time I'm lacking and a way of satisfying the immigration department."

Kit offered him a sympathetic smile but shook her head. "I'm fine," she said, clutching her glass closer. She quirked an eyebrow higher. "Raki?"

Kasouf thudded onto his stool, an attitude of sullenness turning his lips down and darkening his handsome features. "Yes, Raki!" he spat. The sugary remnants of his lemonade left a distorted line around the upper edge of his glass as he pushed it aside. "The postgraduates share the same office. It's easier to access their supervisors. I met Raki Han there last year." Kasouf's eyes narrowed and a light seemed to switch on behind his eyes. He sat up straighter and became more attentive. "Raki helped me with my design," he said. "My work is confidential. He knew that, but I fear he has sold the idea to a pharmaceutical company." Kasouf dropped his hand into his lap. The action seemed innocuous until Kit felt his fingers close around hers beneath the table. She held her breath as he pressed against the delicate joints. "Where is Raki?" he demanded. "You do not want my engagement ring, Katharine, so why are you here?"

CHAPTER 16

Curly Escapes

"I want to find my friend," Kit said. "I'm worried about him." Pain shot through her knuckles as she dragged her hand free of Kasouf's grip and pushed herself back from the table. "Raki is a good person. He wouldn't steal anything."

Kasouf's eyes flashed with a dangerous spark. "He took the data," he snarled. "All of it. I can't continue my research without it. He wiped the server and stole the backups. The university can't retrieve the other copies because of the way he deleted it. It was deliberate. He knew what he was doing. I need it."

Kit licked her lips and shoved her stool further back from the table. She bought herself a few extra feet away from Kasouf's grabbing fingers. Her mind flicked to Raki's skill with computers, and she made a mental decision to trust him. If he'd wiped it, he had a good reason. Kit rose and snatched up her phone from the table's sticky surface. "I can't help you, Kasouf," she said, setting her face into a stern expression. "I won't break the law by lying to the immigration officers."

Kasouf skirted the table and before she could move, gripped her chin in his fingers. He squeezed and Kit blanched. His kiss to her forehead seemed to burn through the skin. His body blocked Kit from the view of the other customers at the bar. "I hope you can keep this discussion to yourself," he whispered. "I'd hate anything to happen to you." He released her and the roughness of the action grazed her soft skin.

Kit's heart pounded as she watched Kasouf leave the pub. He paused to hold the door open for a couple entering and then left. As the sound of her blood thudding through her ears steadied, Kit became hyper aware of the other customers. She looked around her, clutching her phone to her chest and waiting for her fingers to stop shaking. A man at the bar caught her eye and looked quickly away. Kit's brow furrowed. She felt as though she'd seen him before somewhere. Embarrassment flushed the skin on her neck. She imagined what he might think of her argument with Kasouf and wondered if he'd understood the heat in it. Pursing her lips, she focused on the redness of the man's beard. It aged him and created an upside-down illusion against the starkness of his bald head. He appeared edgy and nervous, as though uncomfortable beneath her gaze. Kit gave herself a mental shake and lifted her handbag from the tabletop.

"Are you okay?" The voice sounded calm and reassuring. Kit swallowed and cleared her throat before attempting to answer.

"Officer Delaney." She tried to sound upbeat, but Jackson's frown told her she'd failed.

"What was that about?" He frowned at the closed pub door. His bulk towered above her and she gave an involuntary shiver.

"Nothing," she lied.

Jackson raised an eyebrow, which betrayed his disbelief. "I thought he might be your boyfriend, but your face at the end said otherwise." He glanced at the door again. "Did he hurt you, Kit? I can go after him." He frowned. "I should have come straight over when I saw how he behaved. Sorry for doubting what I saw. It took me by surprise, but I should be used to seeing stuff like that by now."

Kit swallowed and her voice croaked. "Don't go after him." She closed her eyes to avoid seeing the pity in Jackson's. After a shuddering breath, she managed, "It's not what you think."

Jackson waggled his eyebrows. "It never is." He lifted his hand and laid it on her shoulder with such tenderness that Kit fought the urge to cry. His sympathy gave her a squirmy sensation inside her chest. Jackson forced a smile onto his lips. "Can I get you a refill? What are you drinking?"

"Isn't that classed as bribery, Officer?" Kit replied with a watery smile.

Jackson shook his head. "Not when I'm paying and the recipient is a friend." He lowered his voice, his tone confidential. Kit experienced the familiar uptick of her heartbeat as he leaned closer and pushed her back towards her stool. "Take a seat. I'll swap the lemonade for something alcoholic."

"Thank you," Kit replied. Her knees knocked too much to remain standing and she glanced at the door, wanting to give Kasouf time to leave the car park before venturing outside again.

Jackson visited the bar and Kit used the time to decompress. She dumped her phone and bag back on the table. The man with the red beard slunk away and left without looking at her again. Kit turned her attention to a businessman who wore a pinstriped suit and smart shirt. He looked overheated in the warmth of the pub and kept pulling his shirt collar away from his neck. A navy tie hung like a noose as though he'd loosened it at the earliest opportunity. Kit pitied him, stuffed into his suit like a sausage. When he turned to search for an empty table she gave him a smile and he frowned and looked away. Kit shook her head and blew out through her nose. "Nice," she remarked to herself. "You're meant to return smiles, ass-hat."

Jackson returned with more drinks and caught the insult. He chose to ignore it. Kit frowned at the bubbles on the top of her white wine. "Is this where you lecture me about taking drinks from strange men?" she asked.

Jackson grinned. "I've been called a lot of things," he conceded. "Never strange. I guess there's a first time for everything."

Kit smiled. "You know what I mean," she replied, reaching for her glass. Her hand shook and she left it where it sat. Jackson settled on Kasouf's vacated stool and lifted his glass of beer.

"So, what trouble are you in now Miss Maguire?" he asked, his tone light. Kit grimaced, wishing she could tell him but aware of both Kasouf and Raki's warnings.

Kit stared down at the table unable to summon up a suitable reply.

"It's a shame your date had to leave." Jackson's eyebrows rose into his dark salt-and-pepper hair. He blinked and the ghost of a frown crossed his face. "He's not your usual."

Kit snorted. "What's my usual?" she demanded. Her colour rose as she remembered the confession of her indiscretion with Alec during her last brush with the law. Her gaze fixed on the glass and she managed to pick it up and swill it around in a mini cyclone.

"Hey." Jackson touched the back of her hand. "It was a joke. I meant nothing by it."

Kit nodded and tears pricked behind her eyelids. Loneliness seemed a constant spectre of late, replacing her usual camaraderie with the boys and isolating her. "I'm getting left behind," she confessed without looking up to meet Jackson's gaze. "Everyone's pairing off except me." She blinked as her mind drifted to the strangeness of Jerry and Langdon's behaviour. The conclusion felt like a slap to the face and she shook her head to dislodge it. No. Absolutely not.

Jackson removed his hand and clasped his drink. He took a sip. "You don't strike me as the sort to make bad decisions based on other people's behaviour."

"Bad decisions?" Kit's eyes flashed as she looked up at him. "What bad decisions?"

"Nothing. Forget I said anything." Jackson's gaze darted to the door and then back again.

Kit screwed her toes up in her plimsolls. Jackson couldn't know about Kasouf's proposal. Yet he watched her with interest as myriad guilty thoughts spread through her mind and fired her cheeks an attractive pink. "It's not what you think," she reiterated, cringing as the words made it worse. Not with Kasouf. But maybe if she slipped Jackson's rugged features into the vacant space, she might find herself open to persuasion. Glancing up, she found him pinning his lower lip between his teeth. The action did a poor job of masking his grin. "What?" she snapped.

Jackson shook his head. "You have no idea how many times a day I hear that phrase. People say it's not what I think, but it's usually worse than I could imagine. Life can be stranger than fiction."

Kit thudded her glass on the table. "So, what do you suppose it is then? If it's worse than you can imagine, then go for it."

Jackson cocked his head and studied her expression. His eyes narrowed at whatever he saw there. His fingers traced an invisible line along the rim of his beer glass. Then he rested his elbows on the table. "It's definitely something," he concluded. "Do you want to confess?"

Kit's cheeks flared crimson and she blustered. "No!" But she didn't sound convincing even to herself.

Jackson gave a little snuffle of mirth and his smile returned. "You'll keep, Miss Maguire," he said, sounding older and wiser than his years. He lifted a hand and ran it through the unruly curls gracing the top of his head. Without his police issue cap, they performed a riotous dance across his crown.

"Don't do that." Kit shook her head and frowned. "You'll make it frizzy."

Jackson quirked an eyebrow. "And I thought it made me look rugged." His shoulders drooped beneath Kit's scrutiny and his expression became guarded, the brilliance of his hazel eyes dulling in the shadows of the pub. Kit's fingers twitched against the tabletop, itching to take control of Jackson's hair and work it into Curly submission. She licked her lips, the impulse almost too great to resist. Every fibre of her being longed to fix it, to make him love it.

"You should stop using shampoo," she ordered, seeing his frown deepen at a perceived criticism of his appearance. Her expression softened. "If you gave me a week, I could help you make it look amazing."

"Na." Jackson lifted his right hand and then corrected himself, dropping it to cradle his beer glass. "It's due for the chop, anyway."

"Oh." Kit sensed he wanted the conversation over and hated the wave of disappointment which flooded her chest. He didn't want her help. He didn't want her fixing him.

She shrugged and snagged her keys from her jeans pocket. Her fingers reached for her phone and she slipped it into her handbag without drawing attention to the flashing red light indicating an open call. Her teeth gritted at the realisation she should have killed the connection before Jackson sat down with her. "Thanks for the drink. I should go home. I have an early start tomorrow."

Jackson half rose and a screen crashed down over his emotions. "You didn't ask about the dude who tried to rob your store."

Kit shrugged. "Let me guess. He got a slap on the wrist and will probably return tomorrow for another go?" She turned her face away and tried to appear bored. The text had been clear. The crazy man's visit was a warning.

Jackson's expression darkened. "No, actually. He went before the magistrate this afternoon and was remanded in custody. He had outstanding warrants with his name on them. He won't be bothering you again."

Kit paused in the process of slipping from the stool. "I don't believe he wanted money," she said. A nervous swallow split her sentence in half. "I think like it was about something else."

"What else?" Jackson's body stiffened and defined muscles stretched his tee shirt taut. "Something didn't add up and I wondered at the time. I put it down to him being high. Tell me why you've come to that conclusion."

Kit shook her head. She ached to tell him about the threatening text, but Raki had said no cops. It put her in a dilemma, and she tried to shut down the curiosity she saw building in Jackson's eyes. Besides, his rejection of her Curly help had driven a wedge between them, though she didn't yet understand why it mattered so much. He didn't want her help and she returned the favour by swatting aside his curiosity like an uninvited fly at a barbecue. "He looked crazy, like an addict. Anyway, I should go," she said, fixing a bright smile on her lips. She needed to get back to the car without Jackson noticing her passenger peering through the side window.

Outside in the car park, Kit turned her body enough to force Jackson to shift in response. It meant he had his back to her car. "Hopefully I won't see you around." She gulped at the unintentional slight and waved her hand. "I meant hopefully I won't need the cops for a while." She didn't wait for his answer, giving a feckless wave and running to her car. "Thank you, thank you," she breathed as the little yellow bug started first time and propelled her home, a haze of confusing emotions trailing her like a swarm of bees.

"Slow down!" Jerry complained. He shifted in the passenger seat as Kit lurched onto the main road. He turned to face her. "They were both very interesting conversations," he said, ending the call between his phone and Kit's. He waggled an eyebrow at her. "The first guy is desperate to stay in New Zealand and doesn't care how he achieves it. Not so sure about the policeman's motives though." His dark brows furrowed.

Kit glanced across at him as car lights scattered sparkles over his dark features. "Did you record the conversation with Kasouf?"

Jerry's eyes narrowed and his lips tightened into a firm line. "I recorded everything." He tapped the phone and slid it into his top pocket. "But it just seems to have muddied the waters in ways I didn't expect."

CHAPTER 17

Ear-holes and Eye-holes

Kit leaned on the counter and contemplated the twenty missed calls, which made her phone screen flash with an intermittent red light. Each caller had sent a text when the silent phone thwarted their desire to contact their potential new hairdresser. She sighed and looked up as Jerry plonked a carton of milk in front of her on the counter. "Just this," he said. A yawn spread his lips wide and he apologised and covered his mouth with his hand. "Sorry. Tired."

Nodding, Kit pressed buttons on the cash register and winced at its cheerful ping. The drawer released and hit her in the stomach. Jerry pressed coins into her palm and she dumped them in the relevant compartments without looking before slamming the drawer shut. "Tell me about it," she replied. "These early starts are killing me." Jerry's yawn infected her and Kit released her own. His phone rang, sending a loud trilling into the stillness of the shop. Jerry frowned as he inspected the screen.

"It's just Langdon." He pressed a button and Langdon's voice boomed from the speaker.

"Where are you? I thought we were going to do it in your room this time. We almost got caught yesterday."

Jerry's fingers fumbled over the screen and the colour faded from his cheeks. He almost dropped the phone in his haste to halt Langdon's revelation. "Kit's here!" He lifted the phone to his ear and shouted into it. "I took her to work before five o'clock. You weren't awake."

"Did she hear me?" Anxiety crossed the shop in rolling waves. Jerry thudded his index finger at the screen twice before muting Langdon's next comment. He jerked his head towards the front door and headed out to finish the conversation.

"Oh, my goodness!" Kit breathed. "Oh, my goodness!" As though an invisible hand had waved silent scissors over her life, the reality of Langdon's budding relationship with Jerry left Kit feeling out in the cold. She became the third wheel, the hairy green gooseberry or worse; the spinster landlady.

When Jerry returned, Kit's tone sounded frostier than she intended. "You don't have to drive me everywhere, Jerry. I'm capable of taking myself to work and home."

He ran a hand through his dark hair and left the fringe sticking bolt upright as though electrified. "It's no trouble. We agreed after that threatening text message that this would be best." He jerked his head at the phone in her left hand. "What's going on with your phone? Are you scared of getting another spiteful text?"

Kit rolled her eyes and pouted. She dropped her phone on the counter as another text alert vibrated it away from her. "A little, but I've got another, bigger problem right now. Gabby. I asked her not to tell the others I sorted her hair out for her. So, what did she do? She shoved a picture of her new cut on Instagram last night and tagged me as some kind of life saver." Kit's lips curled back in disgust. "Now they won't leave me alone. I have to keep my phone on vibrate."

Jerry shrugged. "So, cut their hair and charge them hard cash. Wouldn't that solve your money problems?"

"Not if it goes wrong. I've never trained as a hairdresser, Jerry. I probably don't even do it right. The first time it went wrong or someone didn't get what they thought they should, they'd sue my ass and bad mouth me from here to Stewart Island."

Jerry gave a slow nod and Kit watched the cogs of his ex-lawyer's brain turning. "You could ask for a koha," he suggested. "A donation. Let them pay what they think you deserve."

Kit snorted. "That would involve me trusting them to be honest. Who pays when they think they don't have to? I know someone who worked as a marriage celebrant and she tried operating by donation only. She wanted to give poorer couples an opportunity to get married and pay what they could afford. Do you know what she earned last year?" Kit didn't wait for Jerry's reply. She blasted on, tiredness adding pique to her tone. "A big fat nothing. People just used and abused her generosity. The donation was meant to cover her petrol expenses for driving to rehearsals and the actual wedding, but she ended up out of pocket. So, she just stopped doing any free ones at all. I don't want to end up feeling used. It sucks."

"Then what will you do?" Jerry cocked his head as the paperboys rampaged through the front door. They chittered like excited mice, and Kit winced at their early morning enthusiasm.

"Shut up!" she snapped, levelling an index finger at the group. "It's way too early for such happiness."

"Sorry, Miss." They chorused the words as a group and Jerry smiled and shook his head. The boys drifted towards the storeroom and resumed their noise as they hauled the heavy sacks of newspapers into the shop. "I've sorted them already," Kit called. "You're good to go." She gave Jerry a concessionary smile. "Sorry, we sorted them." Jerry touched his temple in a mock salute.

In a whirr of activity and an argument about a gaming character, the boys shouldered their sacks and left on their deliveries. Bicycle bells sounded outside in the semi darkness as they mounted up and went their separate ways. Jerry jerked his head towards the door. "I'll come back for you later," he promised. "What time do you finish?"

"Two." Kit cocked her head and felt the weight of her headscarf tilt. "Please will you drive me to the university campus instead?"

"Why?" Jerry's sharp tone indicated his reluctance. "You don't need to go near there." He paused mid-turn, his feet aimed for the exit, but his torso swivelled to face Kit. "I have a really bad instinct about that biochemist."

"I need to go back there." She infused a whine into her voice in the hope of persuading him. "Raki's disappearance is related to his research. I just know it in my knower." Kit patted her sternum and fixed a pleading look on her face. "Please? I'll be real quick and I promise to avoid Kasouf and the weird professor."

"No." Jerry frowned. "The more you poke around the worse things get. Ring the police again and let them investigate."

Kit's shoulders slumped and she released a groan of irritation. "They don't care, Jerry," she complained. "And you know Raki asked me not to involve them. Just drive me down to the university. I only need half an hour. That's all I'm asking."

Jerry shook his head and his face expression hardened. "No, Kit. You've sleuthed enough and it hasn't ended well. I'll pick you up at two o'clock but I'm taking you straight home."

Kit made a growl low in her throat and narrowed her eyes at Jerry's retreating spine. The isolation stretched its tendrils around her heart and spite bloomed where they touched. "What if the bishop finds out what you two are doing?" she called.

Jerry halted and his brows narrowed to a dark, sinister line. "She won't." He heightened his sense of certainty with a nonchalant shrug. "It's fine, anyway. As long as we don't get too involved in the spiritual angle, she won't care."

"Please, drive me to the university?" Kit pleaded. The veiled emotional blackmail had failed and she saw her goal slipping away. Besides, she didn't understand Jerry's answer.

"No." The door buzzer pinged twice in quick succession as Jerry left the shop and another customer entered. Kit turned away, irritated with his stubborn refusal to help her. "You're not the boss of me," she hissed.

"No, I don't suppose anyone is the boss of you." The gentle baritone made Kit jump as Jackson selected two packets of chewing gum from the rack on the counter and picked up a paper bag. He used a set of tongs to grab a pre-made sausage sandwich from the warmer. Digging in his trouser pocket for his wallet, his lips quirked upward at the edges. His gaze flicked to the headscarf covering Kit's curls, but he made no comment about the green fabric baking her damp hair into perfect ringlets. She squirmed beneath his scrutiny. Deflecting, she narrowed her eyes and scorned his poor choice of breakfast. Or a post night shift dinner. "I can't sell that to you," she said, adding a haughty air to her sentence. She jabbed an index finger at his food. "The gum is full of really bad chemicals and the sausage isn't real sausage."

Jackson frowned. "Then what is it?" He separated the edges of the paper bag to peer inside it. "It says it's a sausage sandwich on the wrapper."

Kit glanced around and lowered her voice. "There's no meat in them at all. It's all ear-holes, eye-holes and ass-holes." Her eyelashes fluttered. Despite her tiredness, she didn't miss the grin breaking out across Jackson's face.

"You're not kidding?" He waved his payment card at her. "Ah well, I spend my working life dealing with ass holes. Might as well eat one as arrest it."

With a shrug of feigned indifference, Kit rang up the amount and waited for him to swipe his card. Silence hung between them like an uninvited third guest on an intimate date.

"See you then." Awkwardness descended over Kit and Jackson frowned. Their easy camaraderie seemed to exit the shop ahead of him. Kit heard his traffic car start up outside and waves of regret rolled through her chest. Grabbing her phone, she sent a swift text to Raj and begged for a ride to the university.

"Sorry, I can't," he replied. "Stock taking my shop."

When Mr Rashid appeared in the shop an hour later, he wore the kind of grin that made Kit not want to ask what had delighted him. He counted the cash in the register twice while sighing. Kit's fingers worried at the scarf covering her hair as she pondered what might be happening beneath it. An unfortunate oversight meant she'd run out of flaxseed gel and needed to make more. It created an unusual deviation from her routine and filled her with anxiety left over from years of permanent bad hair days.

Mr Rashid lined up the gold one-dollar coins into a tower and slipped them into a holder. His dark eyelashes fluttered and he gave a little chuckle before releasing the coins back into the drawer. Kit fidgeted with the display of chewing gum packets, trying to line them up against the side of the container. Jackson's purchase of the spearmint flavour had left a gap which acted as a constant reminder of the inexplicable strangeness between them. Kit stripped them off the rack and replaced them from scratch. As she leaned across the counter, a curl sagged from beneath the headscarf and Kit watched as it unfurled in front of her left eye. She took a fortifying breath and turned to face Mr Rashid. "Please can I take my bathroom break now?" Her voice held a note of frenzied demand.

"Oh, yes." Mr Rashid closed his eyes and tilted his head backwards to expose a raised mark on his neck. It nestled between the end of his neat beard and the collar of his shirt. Kit gaped in horror at the love bite, temporarily struck dumb by a sudden understanding for his happy state. She swallowed the gagging sensation and shot beneath the counter hatch with exaggerated enthusiasm. For once, she suspected he wouldn't time her.

The upstairs bathroom mirror revealed a half decent job beneath the headscarf. Kit wrinkled her nose as the red curls tumbled free and hung in ringlets either side of her face. "Not bad," she said with a sigh. "I guess it'll do for today." She hung the scarf to dry over a towel rail and cracked open the window to allow in a breeze. The scarf usually dried enough by the end of her shift for her to take it home ready for the next morning. Kit gave her head a shake and resisted touching any of the damp curls. She'd overused the lube Raki made her and she did a mental calculation to work out how much she still had left in the freezer. "Heaps," she reassured herself.

Her phone vibrated in her back pocket and she pulled it free with a glance at the caller's identity. Debbie. Kit winced and didn't dare ignore her. She connected the call, her lips tightening as Debbie's voice grated loud in the bathroom. She didn't wait for Kit to give her customary greeting. "Another tube exploded!" she snapped. "And one yesterday. There's something wrong with them. You need to contact the company."

Kit exhaled. "Why can't you do it? You have the boxes and packing slips with the order numbers. It makes more sense for you to contact them." She ground her teeth in her jaw and stopped herself adding the biting comment that Debbie had made a profit out of the misfortune.

"Just do it!" Debbie growled. "I'll send you a photo on Facebook Messenger."

"A photo?" Kit frowned. "Of the order numbers?"

"Yes! A photo. Of Dawn's bathroom. The last one exploded and covered it. We're lucky it didn't blind her. I promised her a free haircut to calm her down and stop her suing us for damages. She's expecting you just after two o'clock."

"Wait, what?" Kit's chest tightened. "Then cancel it! I don't finish work until two and I don't have my car. All my hairdressing stuff is at home." But Kit's protests fell on deaf ears as Debbie killed the call. Kit's phone vibrated and an icon lit up on her screen. She opened Messenger to discover a photo of a burst tube of purple-willy-shaped lube and a bathroom covered in goop. Another vibration from Debbie's next message included Dawn's address. Kit groaned.

She used the shop's Wi-Fi to search through her emails and locate the order confirmation from the lube company in Australia. Her fingers dashed across her phone screen as she pasted the order number into a complaint form on the company's website. After a final inspection of her curls, she left the bathroom and strode back to the counter.

"Five minutes and thirty-three seconds." Mr Rashid raised an eyebrow. He'd moved a few steps to the left during Kit's absence, so he could read the headline of a newspaper laid on the counter. "You can make up the time at the end of your shift."

Kit's heart sank and she snatched up the pricing gun, brandishing it in her right hand like a weapon. "I needed a poo," she stated. "And I got my period."

Mr Rashid's ears flushed a darker shade and Kit pursed her lips and dug in for battle. "Getting my period always makes me a little runny in the bathroom department. Do you have a business policy relating to health conditions? Can I see it? I'm afraid it might discriminate between men and women. We need longer bathroom breaks because there's more going on." Kit pointed to the crotch of her jeans. "Down there."

"Shut up! Shut up! Shut up!" Mr Rashid waggled his arms in front of his face. "I don't care. Your lady parts are not my concern."

Kit gave a gasp of indignation. "That's terrible! How can you say you don't care about my lady parts? That's offensive! You wouldn't say that to a man. My flatmate is a lawyer."

Mr Rashid blew his cheeks out and blustered as embarrassment muddled his thoughts. The mention of a lawyer tipped him over the edge. "I do care about your lady parts!" he shrieked. "I care about them very much!"

The clearing of a male throat made them both jump and Kit held her breath. Mr Rashid's eyes bulged and his jaw hung loose. Mr Jim looked from him to Kit and focussed his attention on her. "Is everything okay, Miss Maguire?" he asked, his tone gravelled and serious. "Can I be of assistance?"

Kit suppressed her smirk and let her gaze slide to Mr Rashid. Sweat beaded on his forehead and his breathing appeared faster than usual. Afraid she might have driven him to another heart attack, Kit released the old man from his self-imposed pickle. "No, thanks," she said. Reaching out, she accepted the carton of soymilk from Mr Jim's hand and ducked under the counter. She sought to change the subject at the same time as edging Mr Rashid aside with her hip. "Aren't you working today?"

With a glare of suspicion at Mr Rashid, Mr Jim shook his head and reached into his wallet for his cash card. "I've taken today off because it's been a crazy few weeks."

Kit nodded and tried not to look at Mr Rashid blustering next to her. He bent to scrabble around on the shelves beneath the counter in a pretence of tidying. He didn't miss hearing Mr Jim's parting shot as the police chief leaned across the counter. "Call me if you need anything," he said with a stress on the last part of the sentence. "Harassment is not acceptable."

"Thank you." Kit pursed her lips and gave a contrite nod. "I'll remember that."

CHAPTER 18

Pineapple Lumps

Jerry appeared before the end of Kit's shift, leaning against the drinks' chiller while she gathered her belongings from the apartment upstairs. He looked refreshed, his hair combed into place and his smart vicar's uniform sitting on his broad shoulders. Kit envied him the nap he'd obviously grabbed after dropping her at work. She'd suspected she woke him up with her earlier phone call.

"What's the story with your boss?" he demanded, opening the passenger door and waiting for Kit to climb into the car. "You could cut the air with a knife."

Kit shrugged and pursed her lips. A smirk broke across her face, crinkling the mischievous laughter lines next to her eyes. "He got caught by the police chief saying something a little inappropriate." She stifled a snort. "Correct that. Mr Jim caught him shouting it."

"Oh." Jerry started the engine and frowned. "I thought you liked him."

"I do." Kit screwed her body round as she connected her seat belt and peered into the back seat. "Did you bring my hairdressing bag?"

"Yep." Jerry nodded. "I hope this woman is paying you."

Kit cringed and turned her body to face forward. "Not exactly. Debbie offered my services as compensation.

Another tube of the purple-willy-shaped lube exploded and covered her bathroom."

"That massive shipment you got from Australia?" Jerry waited for a truck to pass on the Gordonton Road before tucking his old Ford in behind it. "Is it a faulty batch?"

Kit shrugged. "I don't know. I emailed them. Debbie is holding me responsible. Again."

Jerry humphed and shook his head. He changed the subject with dizzying speed, perhaps sensing Kit's reticence in discussing her latest drama. "Did you eat my pineapple lumps?" he asked.

"Huh?" Kit turned to see if he was joking. His handsome profile showed no sign of mirth. "What pineapple lumps?"

Jerry breathed out through his nose in a snorting sound. "Well, that answers that then. Langdon didn't eat them either."

"Sorry." Kit peered down at her jeans, inspecting her stomach from beneath her lashes. A tiny bulge rose from the crease across her waist, but it would disappear when she got out of the car and straightened. Ten years ago, the fat would have piled over much larger sized pants. "Are we talking about a tin of actual pineapple chunks, or the chocolate wrapped sweet variety which serves as a Kiwi staple food item?"

"The chocolate variety." Jerry glanced sideways at her. "I bought them yesterday at the supermarket. Two packets. I put them in the salad drawer in the fridge to stop them melting in this heatwave. They're gone."

A line of concern divided Kit's eyebrows. She worried at her lower lip. "And you're certain Langdon didn't move them or have a clandestine midnight feast?" The alternative seemed too miserable to contemplate. It meant that someone uninvited had been in their home.

"Nope." Jerry shook his head and his brown curls moved in the breeze through the open driver's window. "Langdon is on a big health kick and anyway, he said he didn't know I'd bought them."

Kit nodded and faced forward. She flipped the visor down to shield her eyes from the bright afternoon sun. "And Langdon never lies," she admitted. "So, where could they have gone? Have you checked the cupboards in the kitchen?"

Jerry nodded. "Nothing else is missing. Just the Pineapple Lumps."

Kit groaned. "Did you call the cops?"

"Why?" Jerry shrugged his shoulders. "They're just chocolate and they went missing from a shared fridge. It's not a mystery the cops will put much effort into solving."

Kit humphed. "Did you think any more about taking me to the university after I've cut Dawn's hair?" She fluttered her eyelashes at Jerry and he inhaled.

"I gave it no thought whatsoever. You're not going back there."

Kit made a sound like a thwarted toddler and drummed her feet on the passenger floor. "Please, Jerry!"

"Nope." He shook his dark head from side to side and laid his wide palm over Kit's writhing fingers. "We need to leave this complete mess alone until the cops can search for Raki. Then we'll give them all the information and let them do their job."

Kit snorted. "When is that, Jerry?" she demanded, aggravation leaking from her voice. "When will they be interested? And what information do we have? A nasty text, a man with a machete and a biochemist who's up to his neck in this thing."

Jerry shook his head again. "It's irrelevant, Kit. Raki doesn't want the police involved. So, for now, we're stuck in the middle. But at some point, we need to decide that enough is enough and make them listen to us. Your friend Jackson might be an excellent place to start."

Jerry drove the rest of the journey in silence. Kit nibbled at a hang nail and worried about Raki. He'd disappeared just over a week ago. An entire week with only one strange communication. She pondered on the information they'd gleaned so far. It didn't amount to much, pointing at Raki as a thief who'd stolen someone else's work. Kit sighed. It wasn't the Raki she knew.

She wondered about the missing Pineapple Lumps, and her thoughts turned to Langdon and his subdued behaviour of late. "What's wrong with our resident vicar?" she asked as Jerry made the last turn into Dawn's street.

"He's grumpier than usual." She sighed. "I guess he's got a lot to process right now."

Jerry pursed his lips and gave Kit a pointed look as he pulled up in front of the address she'd given him. "Our resident curate doesn't gossip," he replied. "If I tell you Langdon's secrets, then I'll also tell him yours, won't I?"

Kit's features relaxed into a beatific smile. "But I have no secrets, Reverend Jerry." She fluttered her eyelashes and tasted victory.

Jerry leaned across the car and his warm, minty breath stirred Kit's fringe. "So, you don't mind him knowing you used his expensive cheese last week on your salad?"

Kit gulped. Langdon would hate knowing she did that, which was her justification for not telling him. "It was an emergency," she protested, her eyes widening. Jerry grinned, and Kit gripped his nose and gave it a light twist. "Oh, you're good, Vicar. You're very good." She shook her head and climbed out of the car. Jerry met her on the pavement and handed over her bag of hairdressing paraphernalia.

"Behave, Miss Maguire," he said with a smile. "And if you can't be good, be careful."

Kit wrinkled her nose and extracted her keys and phone from her handbag. She thrust the leather bag at his chest. "Please, can you take this with you? I don't need two bags. I'll shove everything in this one." She hoisted her frayed hairdressing bag in front of her.

Jerry gave her a look of mock annoyance, back lit by a smile. "What am I? Your husband?" He smirked and accepted the handbag strap Kit laid over his wrist. "I'll come back for you when I'm done." He got into his car and after laying the bag on the passenger seat, drove away with a wave.

Dawn met Kit on the porch of the cedar clad house, her eyes bugging and her neck craning for a better view of the retreating Jerry. "You should have brought him in for a cup of coffee," she said, an edge of longing in her voice.

"He's got a funeral," Kit replied. She kicked off her plimsolls and stepped over the threshold. Dawn scurried in behind her.

"Oh, that's sad. Is it someone close?"

"I doubt it. He's a vicar." Kit frowned and glanced at her watch. "I need to get on with cutting your hair, Dawn. There's somewhere I should be."

CHAPTER 19

Curly Sleuthing

Cutting Dawn's hair proved easier than Kit imagined. Performing a unicorn cut on someone else seemed infinitely easier than doing it on herself because she could see from every angle. After her fix-up-jobs on both Debbie and Gabby, cutting hair that hadn't been previously wrecked seemed like a luxury. She took off all the dead ends and finished with a Curl by Curl trim which ensured a neat, rounded bob.

Trapped in the bathroom with Dawn to avoid the curiosity of two toddlers and the grumpy teenage babysitter, Kit fought claustrophobia as the time seemed to move extra slow. Not content with just the cut as ample compensation for the exploding lube, Dawn complained as Kit gathered together her scissors and wide-toothed comb. "Debbie said you'd show me how to style it," she whined. A cough punctuated her sentence as water dripped into her eyes. With her head suspended over the bathroom sink, she lifted her face to glare at Kit's reflection in the mirror. "She promised."

Kit closed her eyes and released the groan of exasperation. "She had no right to bargain with my time," she replied. "I have another appointment and this was really brief notice. Sorry about your lube and I've complained to the company who shipped it here. I'll let you know what they say."

Dawn rose from the sink like Medusa, wet curls dangling in front of her eyes. "Please," she begged. "Just five more minutes."

It took ten. Kit instructed Dawn on how to comb her curls in an upside-down position, using the wide teeth to create clumps. Then she added conditioner, Dawn's lumpy flaxseed gel, and the remains of the purple-willy-shaped lube left in the bottom of the container. "Rake your fingers through the curls like this," she said, finishing with a flourishing shake. "It's called the Rake and Shake method. It's what I use."

Dawn copied the precise finger movements and paused to allow Kit to fix the ratty tee shirt over her head. "You probably shouldn't Plop with the tee shirt for more than half an hour," Kit advised. "And I'm guessing your hair needs a protein treatment but test it first. If you give hair more protein than it needs, it gets brittle and snaps."

It took another five minutes for Kit to Google the correct test for protein, and she managed to explain at speed. When she looked at her watch again, Dawn's brow furrowed. "I'm sorry," she admitted. "It was unfair of Debbie to volunteer you without permission and unkind of me to insist you did it today." She blinked and touched her unusual head covering. "Where's your appointment?"

Kit released a sigh. "Waikato University. My friend dropped me off, but I forgot to ask what time his funeral finishes."

"Can you get the bus?" Dawn pressed at the tee shirt and jumped as Kit swatted her hand.

"Leave it alone!" she insisted. "You'll get frizz. Whip it off in about half an hour and give your head a light shake. Don't touch it again." Kit shook her head at the transport suggestion. "The bus will take too long to get there after it's skirted the entire city." She didn't want to admit to the emptiness of her wallet and the distinct lack of bus fare.

Dawn stared at the closed bathroom door for a moment, eyes narrowed and her teeth gnawing at her lower lip. "I'll take you there," she said. Her face brightened. "To pay you back for cutting and styling my hair."

Kit blinked. "But what about your kids?"

Dawn's grin held a trace of wickedness. "The teenager also belongs to me, and my husband caught her texting a boy she's banned from seeing. He confiscated her phone which will hurt more than any other punishment we could concoct. I'll negotiate her getting it back a day early for the chance to escape for an hour." She gave her head a shake and pointed her finger at the Plop. "I should be able to take this off by the time I get to the uni, shouldn't I?"

"Yeah." Hope budded in Kit's heart. She pushed aside Jerry's warnings and concern. "I'll help you."

"Great!" Dawn escaped to her bedroom to switch her current attire of tee shirt and jeans for a dress which she slid on feet-first to avoid disturbing her headgear. Strappy sandals completed the fresh look. "Let's go," she said to Kit and headed for the stairs.

The teenager took little convincing. She sat on the sofa with a toddler either side of her and cartoons twittered through the surround sound. "Fine," she grumbled. "A day early for every hour you're away."

Dawn rolled her eyes and Kit pursed her lips at the inherited negotiating skills, which were the reason for her presence at the Curly's house at short notice. They climbed into Dawn's car and the other woman rang her husband to insist he left work early and met her at a local bar in town. She drove like a maniac, making Kit wish she'd flagged the whole idea and walked home.

"I love my hair." Dawn glanced in the rear-view mirror and smiled at herself as she cornered a roundabout at breakneck speed. The Plop hid her curls, but her irises sparkled as she contemplated the twirls forming beneath its folds. "The other girls will be so jealous."

"Please, don't tell them?" Kit begged. "I've ignored about twenty-five calls today so far."

"I know." Dawn grinned. "You ignored mine too."

Kit shook her head. "I'm not trained to cut hair. If it goes wrong, I'll find myself in big trouble."

Dawn's brow furrowed. "You could accept donations."

"Yeah, right?" Kit couldn't keep the sarcasm from her voice. "They won't pay."

"You'd be surprised." Dawn twisted her lips. "There's nobody local who knows how to cut curly hair without shampoos and damaging conditioners. We've all suffered humiliation in the hairdressing salon when we admit we use a sugar scrub instead of sulfate and silicon loaded shampoo. And have you ever met a hairdresser willing to do a dry cut so that your fringe doesn't end up as a receding hairline?"

"No," Kit admitted. "It just seems too difficult to contemplate changing my career to something so drastic." She groaned. "I can't be self-employed. I just bought my first house. The bank will go nuts."

Dawn nodded and narrowed her eyes. She drove through the gate of the university campus without indicating before the turn. A young man waiting to turn right gave her the middle finger sign. In a bid to upset every other driver on route, Dawn tussled with another vehicle for a parking spot. As the bigger SUV, she won and the other driver honked his horn. Kit kept her head lowered and tried not to get eye contact with Dawn's victims.

Dawn yanked on the handbrake with a sigh and contemplated the mirror again. "Will you help me?" she asked, turning to Kit with an expectant tilt to her eyebrows.

"Let's see how it looks." Kit waited for her to release the tee shirt covering her hair, and glossy curls tumbled around her face. "Excellent job." Kit's face creased into a smile of appreciation.

Dawn admired herself in the mirror. "Do I need to do anything else?" she asked.

"No." Kit reached up and twisted a curl in front of Dawn's eyes. She pulled it back and slotted it behind another. "I'd leave it alone now. Let the curls dry and then Scrunch Out the Crunch. I don't think it'll be dry enough to do that tonight, though. Mine takes a couple of hours to dry enough to touch it. Sleep on something silky and just spritz it in the morning to refresh it."

"You're amazing." Dawn twisted her neck to admire her hair from different angles. "I'm glad the lube burst all over the bathroom now." Her eyes twinkled.

Kit bit her lower lip and shoved aside yet another issue. But curiosity got the better of her. "How many tubes did you buy from Debbie?" she asked.

"Three." Dawn lowered her chin and tried to peer at the top of her own head in the mirror.

"Was anything different about the one that exploded?"

Dawn's eyes narrowed and she stared at the ceiling of the car. "Now you mention it, there was less in that one.

The others were full almost to the top, but the one that popped had only been filled about three quarters. Do you think that matters?"

"I don't know." Kit sighed. "Thanks for the ride." She released her seatbelt with a click and pushed open the door.

"Wait!" Dawn reached for her handbag on the back seat and pulled out her purse. "Let's call it fifty dollars," she said. The note looked huge in her fingers and Kit paused with her hand on the car door.

"It's fine," she said, discomfort making her squirm.

Dawn shook her head and flapped the note over the empty passenger seat as Kit tried to escape. "Take it," she said. "I'll put the word out that it's a minimum of a hundred-dollar donation for cutting and style advice." She flapped the note a few more times until Kit's reluctant fingers took it from her. "Just keep decent records for the tax department," Dawn advised. "See if you can save enough to do the next Curly course. That will count as personal development and stop them taking so much tax from your earnings. The trick is to break even. There are all kinds of benefits with running a business from home."

Kit squirmed and hunched her shoulders up to her ears in dismissal. "I can't retrain as a hairdresser now. It's too late."

"Don't be daft," Dawn scoffed. "I think Australia is the nearest location for the Curly courses, but I heard the Curl Queen was considering running one in New Zealand."

Kit stared down at the colourful note in her hand. She closed her fingers over it and nodded. Dawn winked at her as Kit closed the door. She pulled back out into the traffic to the tune of several angry honks.

Crumpling the fifty dollar note and shoving it into the front of her jeans, Kit sighed and mentally put it towards her next mortgage payment.

The car park looked much emptier than on her last visit. As the afternoon ticked on, most of the students had left for the day. Kit used the data on her phone to pull up a map of the university and found her way back to the science building. She avoided the narrow path she'd used before and headed straight to the wide front doors. To her great relief, they opened as she got to them. Two girls passed through, deep in conversation. Kit skipped through the closing gap and found herself inside a wide lobby. A breeze ruffled her curls and she detected the chill of air conditioning. Her arms prickled with goose bumps, exacerbated by fear.

The usefulness of the map ceased as it led her to the building but offered no further information. Without the name of Raki's laboratory or some distinguishing landmark, Kit realised she'd wasted her time and effort. She groaned and sank into a stained armchair pushed against the lobby wall, clutching her hairdressing bag to her chest. She let her head fall and her chin rest on the bag while she sought divine intervention.

"Are you okay?"

Kit looked up at the sound of the female voice and gave a wan smile devoid of hope. "Yes thanks," she replied with a sigh. "I'm just lost."

"Oh." The girl straightened. Younger than Kit by a decade, she wore her blonde hair in two straight braids. A dusting of light freckles speckled her nose. She carried a binder under her left arm and a white laboratory coat dangled over her elbow. "Where do you need to be?"

Kit blew out her cheeks and rose. Outclassed by the girl's comfortableness with the academia surrounding her, Kit wished she'd never come. "I'm not sure. My friend is a postgrad student here. Raki Han. He's missing. I just wondered if I could find a clue that might explain where he's gone."

"Raki." The girl said his name and then licked her lips. She released a tiny sigh. "He's my lecture crush."

"Your what?" Kit frowned. She didn't understand. "What's a lecture crush?"

The girl squared her shoulders and her lab coat slipped down to cover her forearm. "It's a lecturer who ticks all the boxes."

Kit tipped her head and looked at the girl from beneath her eyelashes. "You're in love with Raki?"

"No!" The girl took a step back, her eyes widening at the violence of her own reply. "I want to be like him. He's the perfect scientist. I want to be him."

"Right." Kit drew out the sound as she considered the complexity of the answer. "Well, he's missing. I don't know where else to look or who to speak with about it. I'm worried."

The girl nodded. "He hasn't taken a class all week. The professor covered a few of them, but she doesn't go nearly deep enough into the science like Raki does." She sighed and her eyes glazed. "He's the best."

Kit nodded and turned her feet towards the front doors. As if on cue, they opened to admit a man in his mid-twenties. He shuffled past in baggy jeans, which sagged around his backside. A hooded sweater covered his head and part of his face. But the fluffy red beard protruding from the gap between his hood and his chin looked familiar. Kit frowned and watched him cross the lobby and take the stairs two at a time to the next floor. "I think I know him," she breathed. "From the pub last night." Her eyes followed his scruffy trainers up the stairs as the balustrade covered the rest of him. The trainers turned left on the first landing.

The girl followed Kit's gaze and gave a definitive nod. "Well, let's start there then," she suggested. "We'll follow him."

At the first of the dogleg landings, she informed Kit her name was Bindy. "I graduated early," she said with a wide-eyed smirk. "Child genius and all that."

Kit gulped as words failed her. She looked down at her jeans and plimsolls, feeling out of her depth next to someone with such proven intelligence. "Nice to meet you," she mumbled. "I'm Kit."

"Are you a student here?" Bindy set off up the next set of stairs, but she kept her gaze on Kit.

"No." Kit sighed. "I work in a shop and cut hair for a hobby."

"Neat." Bindy blinked and nodded, unfazed by Kit's reply. "Your hair is beautiful. I have to keep mine tied up in the lab. Bunsen burners." She patted one of her plaits, seeming resigned to the sacrifice of her hair in the name of science. Kit's eyes widened at the frayed edges of the plait nearest her. It looked singed.

Bindy led Kit down a long corridor and stopped at an office doorway. "Did you see where that boy went?" she asked.

Kit shook her head and frowned. The bearded man had looked at least her age, if not older still. She sighed, remembering how she thought his beard had aged him.

Perhaps he was really nineteen and hiding beneath a man's facial curtaining.

Bindy touched the plate clinging to the office door. It showed four names. It had lost one of its screws and sticky tack splurged through the vacant hole, giving it a jaunty angle. Raki's full name stretched across the name plate, the Chinese Christian name looking elegant and complicated next to the shortened version which Raki used. Bindy tapped on the door and listened. No sound issued from inside and she wrinkled her nose as though surprised at the conclusion. "He's not here," she stated. "I'll take you to his lab."

Kit followed her as they backtracked to the stairs. Bindy seemed to have forgotten about the boy and fixated on Raki. Kit wondered how much of a genius she was if she'd just knocked on the office door of a man who was missing. Perhaps she was one of those child geniuses who could cure cancer but didn't know how to open an oven door.

She followed as Bindy hung a right towards a wall of glass. They passed a series of access-controlled doors before stopping at the last one. "Is this where he works?" Kit stepped closer to the glass and imagined Raki cooking up the vat of lube he'd presented her with just a month ago. He'd turned a terrible day into a wonderful one with his generous gift. Kit's fingers reached up to touch her glossy curls like a silent homage to Raki's kindness.

"Yeah." Bindy turned to her with pursed lips. "It's limited access. I can't let you in, but I could ask someone to come out to speak to you."

Kit nodded and waited as Bindy used an access card to release the door. She disappeared inside the laboratory and Kit lost sight of her beyond the frosted glass. When she returned, a confused expression covered her face. "I can't find him," she said. "Maybe he went somewhere else instead."

Kit shrugged. "Thanks for your time, anyway. Raki's missing, so I didn't expect him to be in the lab." She sighed. "Did you ask anyone about the man with the red beard?"

"Ooh, no. Hang on." Bindy disappeared again. When the door clicked open, Kit steeled herself for more disappointment. What she got was far worse.

"You!" The raised voice and sharp accent sent a bolt of tension up Kit's spine. She didn't need to look to identify the speaker. Kasouf strode from the laboratory and barrelled towards her, his face reddening in anger. "One minute you'll marry me, the next you won't. Is this another change of heart? Or are you stalking me?" His clipped tone oozed aggression. Kit took a step back as he advanced.

"What?" Bindy's eyes widened as she reappeared through the lab door. She looked from Kit to Kasouf. "Is that true?"

"No." Kit shook her head. But she understood as Bindy withdrew her head and shoulders back into the lab and abandoned her to her fate.

Kasouf appeared menacing as he reached Kit. She glanced behind her, but the corridor ended, leaving her no alternative but to face him. "I'm here for Raki," she asserted, injecting determination into her tone. "Something has happened to him. He's still missing."

"He stole my research!" Kasouf leaned closer and Kit smelled almond oil and peppermint. His pupils appeared dilated and a frenzied look occupied his narrow features. She gulped, recognising the outworking of a chemical high running through his veins. "You're an addict," she breathed. She tried to circumnavigate him, but he grabbed her arm above the elbow and hauled her around to face him.

"What do you know about anything?" Kasouf scoffed. "You work in a shop selling milk and cigarettes."

Kit swallowed. She'd never told him how she earned her money. It occurred to her that Marian might have given him a complete rundown on everything relating to her daughter in her eagerness to marry her off to him. Or that he'd known where to find her when he sent another addict to threaten her. Kit stood her ground and clutched her hairdressing bag closer. "I work in a shop frequented by junkies," she replied, her tone biting. "I know one when I see one."

Kasouf gave a nasty laugh and increased the pressure on her arm. "Whatever!" His thick accent mangled the word as anger stole his mastery of English. Dragging a mobile phone from his back pocket, he dialled a number and then spoke to the person who answered. "Hello, is that security? I've caught a woman trespassing in the science block." His lips curled backwards to reveal straight white teeth. "The postgraduate labs contain sensitive information. I believe that's what she wants."

Kit gasped and struggled to free her arm. Kasouf kept hold of her, his grip intensifying to affect the circulation to her elbow and wrist. The pulsing became a painful ache. "Let me go!" she grunted. Her bag fell to the floor and the magnetic clasp popped free. Hair clips and a wide-toothed comb skittered across the tiles along with a pair of sharp hairdressing scissors. Kasouf's lips quirked upwards into an expression of glee. "She has a weapon," he whined, adding a high-pitched squeak into his voice in a poor impression of a hapless victim. "You should call the cops."

Kit held her breath and looked up in dismay. A man cut across the end of the corridor and disappeared down the stairs. A man wearing a pinstriped suit and a buttoned shirt. He looked overheated and frantic to escape her notice.

CHAPTER 20

Curly Custody

Kasouf caused a scene bad enough to summon most of the science department, including Professor Kirke with an 'e'. His claims of a woman bearing a weapon put that part of the university campus into a full lock down for the afternoon. Kit wasn't surprised when the professor made things ten times worse by instructing the security officers to call the police. She watched the stringy ringlets bounce against the professor's cheeks as she postured in front of her. She bit her lip to stop herself suggesting the woman made more time to Scrunch Out the Crunch. She would have applauded any other new Curly, but this one ground her gears.

Bindy appeared at the laboratory window behind a group of other spectators and begged Kit with her eyes not to give her away. She peered over the frosted portion of the glass with wide-eyed terror. When she drew a line across her throat, Kit changed her story to a version that didn't involve the younger girl's guided tour.

Jackson held onto Kit's arm as he strode towards his police car. She sensed people stopping to watch her shameful progress. His hands were gentle but firm, the effect reducing Kit to the status of a naughty child. She sat in the front of Jackson's police car in silence, staring at the corner of her hairdressing bag as it shivered on the dashboard with the motion of the vehicle. He'd confiscated her scissors.

Jackson took furtive, sideways glances at her when he thought she wasn't looking. Kit pursed her lips and ignored him, turning her face away from his scrutiny. She'd hoped he might realise she presented no direct threat to the staff or students. But he'd made her feel like a terrorist, as though her ratty bag contained a bomb or a loaded gun instead of hair clips and shears.

A heavy shower came from nowhere and doused the rock-hard earth. It appeared the parched ground rejected it, sending it running across roads and shooting from drains in dirty fountains. As visibility grew difficult through the swishing windscreen wipers, Jackson pulled the police car over on the side of a rural road just north of the city. The wheels bumped over grit and the brakes squeaked as they splashed through puddles forming in potholes. Kit tensed as Jackson killed the engine. Then he turned in his seat. "What are you playing at?" he demanded. "Don't you understand how bad that could have got? You're lucky that alert got squashed before it became a full-blown crisis. Why did you even go to the university?"

"Because my friend is missing!" Kit slammed her fists into the seat either side of her. "And nobody cares except me. And maybe Jerry." The thought of Jerry took her mind to the missing Pineapple Lumps and she released a gasp of realisation. "Oh, my goodness!" She clapped her hands over her mouth.

"What?" Jackson's eyes widened in alarm and he twisted his body further. He caught Kit's flailing hand as she released her seat belt and pushed herself forward.

"I need to go," she said. A fire burned behind her eyes and her excitement added heightened spots of colour to her cheeks. "I have to check."

She lurched for her bag on the dashboard and Jackson prevented her. His forceful grip tightened around her wrist. "Check what?" he demanded.

A grin broke out across Kit's lips. "I just realised something." Her eyes danced. "Don't worry, it's something good."

Jackson released her wrist and a frown crossed his face. Kit felt the inexplicable urge to reassure him; a maternal instinct she didn't know she possessed. Without putting enough thought into it, she reached out to touch Jackson's shoulder. His reaction surprised her. As though her touch had put him under starters orders, Jackson cupped her cheek and pressed his forehead against hers. It began as a release of confused emotions and ended as a burning, hungry kiss. As soon as his lips touched Kit's and the connection flared between them, she knew it was a terrible mistake. But it seemed Jackson didn't agree. His hand snaked behind her neck and his fingers splayed under her curls. His lips intensified the kiss until he sensed her pulling back. Then only awkwardness remained between them. Kit shoved herself backwards against the door, her fingers grappling for the handle as heavy droplets of rain pelted the metal roof like a drum roll.

"Am I under arrest?" Her voice sounded subdued as she struggled to bury the heady rush of emotion.

Jackson snorted and rubbed his fingers over his eyes. "No." He ground out the word, frustration in the single syllable.

"But you treated me like a criminal." Kit swallowed. She needed to irritate him and get them both past the searing warmth of the kiss still burning on her lips.

"Then stop behaving like one." Jackson blew out a breath and removed his police cap. His flattened curls sprang upwards in disobedient glee, still not butchered by the buzzing razor of a barber. He turned his head and stared through the windscreen, his gaze growing misty as though his mind wandered elsewhere. Kit watched his profile, fascinated by the salt and pepper grey infiltrating his sideburns and ignoring mental images of how his curls might look with a cast of flaxseed gel and lube. She itched to reach out and touch a wayward twist which rebelled against the rest. It stuck out like an alfalfa sprout over his left eye.

Jackson shook his head and clamped his hat back into place. The curl disappeared and Kit frowned. It represented her; unfettered and free until Jackson squashed it. She gritted her teeth, not wanting to tow his line and end up just like the poor curl.

"If I'm not under arrest, can I go now?" she asked. She dragged the bag to her chest. "Can I have my scissors, please?".

Jackson's eyes narrowed and he reached for the bag, his fingers splaying across the patterned surface and his thumb brushing over the magnetic button. "I'm confiscating the scissors. And next time you go poking around somewhere you shouldn't, make sure you don't carry sharps." He made it sound like serious advice, but Kit peered at his blank expression, looking for humour. She saw none. A speck of blood betrayed an earlier accident with his shaver, and the faint scars beneath his throat looked reddened. The sight infused Kit with sadness. His link to her father had made him an automatic ally, but his behaviour had trashed that notion and left it like the remnants of a pub brawl. "I'm trying to take care of you," he said, his tone softer. He released his hold on the bag and dropped his hand into his lap.

"Thanks for your advice," Kit replied. She didn't feel as confident as she sounded, but it wasn't the time to display her overwhelming sense of defeat. "I can walk from here."

Jackson blew out a breath through his nose. It sounded like the snort of an angry horse. "Don't be ridiculous!" he snapped, turning back to the steering wheel. "I'll drop you at home." His fingers flexed over the leather, the knuckles showing white through his skin. Kit refastened her seat belt and sat in silence, her spine ramrod straight and her fingers worrying at a hair clip poking through the thin fabric of the bag. The rain eased, leaving rivers cascading across the rural roads and flooding the gullies either side.

"Here's fine." Kit snapped off her belt and a warning sound toned from the dashboard. Jackson pressed on the brakes at the end of her road and let the car roll to a stop. A stream of dirty, gushing water blocked the road as it made its way from the overflowing gully on one side to the river in the distance. It danced across the road and spread out in the nearest paddock, resembling a gargantuan spill on the landscape.

Kit tried the door handle, panicking as it refused to budge.

"Just hang on," Jackson said. He opened his door and walked around the vehicle. With a swift pull on her handle, he opened it from the outside. His gaze fixed on her face as he held out his other hand to assist her. "I work alone. I don't want the criminals jumping out at traffic lights, do I?" he asked. His fingers felt warm beneath Kit's as she accepted his help. "Stay away from the university, Kit. And stay away from that Kasouf guy. You'll end up with a trespass order against you. And that bloke gives me a really bad feeling."

"Is that an official warning?" Kit knew as she spoke the words she pushed her luck beyond what was sensible.

Jackson bridled and his lips tightened. "No, Kit! It's me caring for your welfare. Stay away."

Kit clutched her bag to her chest like a shield. "No, it's you blocking my goals," she muttered under her breath. A flicker of anger darted through her chest. Jackson watched her with a shuttered expression. He kept hold of her hand and led her around a sizeable puddle. Kit's lips quirked upwards in a smile that didn't reach her eyes as she stepped onto solid ground. "Thanks for the ride. I hope I don't see you again for a while."

Jackson grinned and the expression looked genuine. The familiar joke eased the awkwardness. "Not in uniform anyway," he replied. Shaking his head, he settled himself into the driver's seat of the powerful police car and gave her a wink just as the radio burst to life on the dashboard. "I give it five minutes until you're in trouble again, Kit Maguire," he said before closing his car door.

"Whatever!" Kit frowned and began her walk home along the sloshing mud of the verge. A kind neighbour had placed a sign next to the stream gushing across the lane. It indicated that foot traffic could use his front garden to skirt the rushing water. His driveway ran behind the gully, protected by a huge concrete pipe which funnelled the water away from his house. Kit looked down at her ruined plimsolls with a deep sigh. The former white fabric had become a dingy grey with specks of brown water promising permanent blemishes. She eyed the stream and decided it wasn't the sort of wash her footwear needed. Instead, she tramped across her neighbour's lawn, giving him a wave as he sat in his armchair by the front window. He waved back and she sacrificed her plimsolls to the cause of walking home, taking with her bits of cut grass and a bevy of green stains.

CHAPTER 21

Bouffant

Jackson had dropped her at the end of her road, but it still took Kit ten minutes to walk to her house in the last of the rain shower. The detour across Mr Pattinson's front garden involved mud up to her ankles and a tussle with a rosebush. She cursed her misguided pride and wished she'd stayed in the police car and forced Jackson to drive the long way home and drop her at the door.

A truck blocked her driveway, dwarfing her tiny Volkswagen Beetle. Kit saw it from a distance and pushed herself to hurry. Sweat ran down her face and turned her curls into a fuzzy haze as the humidity returned. Her ruined plimsolls rubbed up a blister on the back of her heel from the sodden, heavy fabric.

"Can I help you?" she called as she reached her house. She strode towards the driver, a man in a Jackaroo cowboy hat who greeted her with a nod.

"Na, Miss. I'm good," he replied as she stepped up behind him. He slammed the rear door of the truck and secured the latch. "I just said my goodbyes."

"What? You did what?" Kit followed him to the driver's door, jogging to keep up with his long stride. Standing water splashed up and soaked as far as her thighs.

The man lifted his hat and wiped his wrist across his sweating brow. Wrinkles like tree lines set his age around sixty. "He's such a wily bugger." He gave Kit a wavering smile. "But I've said goodbye to Bouff now. Thanks for taking care of him. We appreciate it."

"Bouff? Who's Bouff?" Kit swallowed, her gaze taking in the truck's size and its very specific design. A sickening sensation of dread started at her toes and stretched its grip over her eyes. "What's a Bouff exactly?"

"My daughter called him Bouffant on account of his hair. He's an American Bashkir Curly."

Kit swallowed. "Who is?"

"The horse." Deep creases showed at the corners of the man's mouth. His hand shook as he sat his hat back on his crown. "He's in your paddock out the back of the property. Your husband is with him now."

"My what? My husband?" Kit closed her eyes and shook her head. The action invited dizziness and she rocked on her feet. "I don't own a paddock and I definitely don't have a husband." She opened her eyes to the click of the truck's door. "No, please, it's a terrible mistake. You can't leave a horse here!"

The engine roared next to her and the driver ground the gear stick into reverse. An inky cloud of burning oil filled Kit's nostrils. She banged the flat of her palm on the driver's door and he ignored her, easing the truck off her driveway and almost hitting her yellow Beetle on the lawn as he swung wide. Kit shouted and waved her arms to no avail. Having dumped his unwanted cargo, he seemed keen to leave before Kit forced him to abandon his quest for freedom.

"I'm calling the cops!" Kit yanked her mobile phone from her jeans pocket, growling in frustration as the back fell off and the battery clattered into the mud. She found herself torn between trying to retrieve the scattered parts of her borrowed phone and memorising the registration number of the truck as it picked up speed towards the junction. "L28 40V," she muttered, picking up the battery and wiping it on her jeans. "L28 40V or is that a W?" She shielded her eyes against the sun and stamped her foot as the truck powered along the main road. She heard the gears grinding as it tore away without its cargo.

It took a long moment for her to fit the pieces of the phone back together. She gave it a shake for good measure and then dialled the emergency number. A horrible dryness stuck her tongue to the roof of her mouth as the operator answered. "Emergency, which service do you require?"

"Cops please," Kit croaked. "A guy in a truck just dumped a horse I don't want in a paddock I don't own. Can I give you the registration number first? It's starting to fall out of my brain."

"One moment please." The operator tapped on a keyboard, sounding competent and unruffled. "What's the address you're calling from?"

Kit provided all the information the male operator demanded, using his typing pauses to repeat the registration number to herself. "Oh, no!" she cried after a solid minute. "I've lost the last three digits now!"

"Lost them, Miss?" the operator repeated. A greater sense of urgency entered his tone. "What did you lose? Is someone in danger?" Tap, tap, tap went his keys. "I've dispatched an ambulance. Someone should be with you very soon. Stay on the line and keep talking."

"The last three letters and numbers!" Kit wailed. "It could've been 6CW. I wish you'd written that part first."

"Keep as calm as you can, Miss," the voice replied. "Help is on the way."

"It's an American one," Kit added, keen not to lose any other information in the delay. "He said the name, but it sounded odd and ended in Curly." Her index finger strayed to her hair and she tweaked a ringlet. Its frizzled state offered sympathy for a shared day of misery. It looked like she felt. But the horror wasn't over yet. Her lips formed a little 'o' as she thought. "ABC. American something Curly. I'm sure that's what he said before he did a runner."

"ABC? As in ABC transporters? Did you take a drug?" The operator's tone held incredulity. "What did you take, Miss? Can you remember the name of the drug?"

"There's a horse!" Kit raised her voice. "A horse I don't want. And it's American."

"Keep calm, Miss. Find a place to sit and pop your head between your knees. Keep talking to me. Tell me about the horse. What colour is it?"

Kit slumped to the soaked grass verge and put her head between her knees in obedience. Damp seeped through the bottom of her jeans. She rested an elbow on her thigh so she could keep the phone pressed against her ear. "I haven't seen it yet," she sighed. "But I know it's here."

"Okay, Miss. I'm sure it's a very nice horse. Keep calm and still. You'll hear the sirens soon. Is there any nausea or vomiting?"

"I hope not!" Kit's head shot up and her lips parted in disgust. "Do you think that's why he dumped it? Because it's sick. This is so unfair! My life is too complicated. I can't do this anymore."

"Don't make any rash decisions. Listen to me, Katharine. Can I call you Katharine? Are you listening? Help is coming. You need to keep hold of the pills, so the paramedics know what you've taken. They can help you."

"Pills?" Kit looked around her in the dirt. Then she looked up into the sky as though fearful the operator could see another hazard unknown to her. Loneliness and vulnerability conspired to reduce her to the thing she most hated, a weak and pathetic woman. "Don't call me Katharine," she whined. "My dad called me Katharine and he's dead."

Sirens sounded in the distance, accompanied by a high and shrill whinny. Kit gasped. "I heard it. It's calling," she said. Excitement ticked behind all the misery and she scrambled to her feet. "I want to see it."

The operator called a warning, which made little sense and involved something about a hallucinogenic. Kit killed the call with a hurried, "Thanks," and stuffed her phone into her jeans pocket. She shook her head. "That operator must be on drugs," she muttered to herself. "He made no sense." As a nasal snort and a shout hit the airwaves, she sloshed across the front garden and traversed the side of the house.

CHAPTER 22

Curly Flatmates

K it skidded to a halt next to Jerry's sleep-out. The rickety garden fence gave way to an extensive section of land spanning the width of the property. It led towards a ridge in the distance and a wide gully lay beyond that. At the tallest part of the landscape, sat a rusty shed constructed from mismatched pieces of corrugated iron like a boil on a lumpy bottom. A gate from the main road wore a sign declaring, "Trespassers will be persecuted." In the years she'd rented the house from the land agent, Kit hadn't explored the paddock. Lack of time and an even bigger lack of interest deterred the treacherous climb over the fence. Besides, she wasn't sure what sort of persecution might result from getting caught trespassing.

As vicars, Jerry and Langdon seemed immune to persecution. Kit reasoned they perhaps welcomed it, because both stood in the forbidden paddock wearing gumboots and waving their arms despite the written threat. "Oh, my stars!" she breathed.

"Talk to me! What happened?" Strong fingers seized Kit's shoulders and spun her around so fast she almost fell. The action made her gasp as she stared into Jackson's concerned eyes. "This strange call came over the radio, saying you'd taken drugs and felt suicidal." Jackson's brow furrowed as he looked her up and down as though trying to assess the damage. "What did you take?" he demanded.

"The ambulance is on its way. How the hell did you manage that in the fifteen minutes since I dropped you? Geez Maguire!"

Kit gaped and shook her head. She lacked the words to explain the catastrophe which had culminated in something extremely curly and very traumatised storming around the paddock behind her house with Jerry and Langdon in hot pursuit. Kit turned her head to observe the spectacle unfolding in front of her as Jerry gave a loud shout and fell over backwards. His legs went up in the air and one of his gumboots shot off in a different direction. Langdon continued his quest to capture the odd-looking horse galloping around him in wide arcs. It tightened its circle until he spun in the same spot for too long and then joined Jerry in the mud.

Jackson followed Kit's gaze and stared at the two men rolling around on the ground. His lips parted in surprise at the sight of the chestnut horse as it gave a happy buck and made a dash for the broken fence bordering the gully. "What the hell is that?" Jackson gasped.

Kit swallowed. "I'm not sure," she admitted. "When I got home, a strange man had blocked the driveway with his truck. He seemed upset. I tried to stop him leaving, but he ignored me and drove away." She pursed her lips and her gaze sunk to register Jackson's Kevlar vest. "I shouldn't have called the emergency number," she said with a gulp. "I'm sorry I've wasted your time."

Jackson's jaw worked against his cheek, creating a hard line. He stared at her, lost for words. His fingers flexed over her shoulders before letting go, and he took a step back as though afraid of contamination. "The operator said you sounded confused and mentioned drugs." His tone became hard. "We thought you'd taken something and got into difficulty."

Kit pressed a hand to her chest. "I would never do that!" She sounded shocked that he thought her capable of such foolishness. Her brow furrowed and antagonism tapped a beat in her chest. It shouldn't have annoyed her as much as it did. "You must think very little of me," she concluded. "As you can see, I'm fine. I needed help because someone dumped their horse in this paddock and it can't stay here." She sighed as Jerry tried to reach his fallen gumboot. He hopped on one leg across the grass. There was no sign of Langdon. He'd disappeared over the brow of the hill and into the gully.

Jackson rubbed a hand across his eyes and took another step back, putting a decent distance between him and Kit. He pulled his notebook from behind his vest. "Wasting police time is a serious offence," he said, his tone harsh. "You've stopped me attending another emergency."

Kit's eyes flashed. "It was an emergency to me!" she maintained. "I wanted you to intercept the man and make him come back for the horse. I took the registration number of his truck, but the operator wouldn't listen to me. It's not my fault he misunderstood everything I said." Her eyes became gimlet hard as Jackson turned to greet the two paramedics stumping across Jerry's veggie patch.

"It's a waste of bloody time!" Jackson growled. He intercepted the paramedics and steered them towards the side of the house.

"I'm sorry!" Kit called after their retreating backs, but Jackson didn't stop to listen. His single act of ignoring Kit hurt her more than she expected. Her shoulders slumped as the group disappeared around the side of the house. He'd predicted more catastrophe linked to her, and she hated that she'd proved him right.

With a sigh, she turned to watch the comedy unfolding in the paddock. The horse reappeared, its mane and tail streaming behind its muscular body like the coiled dreadlocks of a Rastafarian. A sheen of sweat dappled its curly body, collecting in patches of white foam across its chest and along its magnificent back. Its behaviour held an element of mischief as it gave a determined buck and lifted its back hooves into the air. "Bouffant," Kit murmured to herself. "Of course, you are."

CHAPTER 23

Purchasing Power

Langdon and Jerry ran out of energy long before Bouffant. The horse seemed happy to just keep galloping in ever decreasing circles. The sole fell off Jerry's boot and left him with a muddy sock. Despite Langdon's superior physique and stamina, the horse out manoeuvred him for the next hour.

Jackson didn't return, and Kit felt both grateful and disappointed. It meant he didn't issue her with an infringement notice, but it also robbed her of the opportunity to apologise.

"Please come and help us?" Jerry begged, hopping up to the fence with his ruined boot in his hand. "We can't work out how to catch this thing."

Kit sighed and kept her chin resting on her hands. The fence panel felt worn and smooth beneath her fingers. "Not until you explain what's happening," she demanded. "I'm in so much trouble. I called the cops about the man with the horse truck and now Jackson is mad at me."

Jerry hopped on the spot and fixed muddy fingers over the fence post. He wrinkled his nose at the state of his boot. "I'm sorry," he said with a wince. "It all happened so fast. Langdon came out of church after the funeral and saw the horse truck broken down outside on the street. A few of the deacons helped us give it a bump start. We got talking to the driver and he said he was on his way to the slaughterhouse.

Before I could stop Langdon, he'd said he'd take the horse and given the man our address. We almost didn't make it home in time. He'd started unloading by the time we got here." Jerry frowned. "Did the delivery guy look shifty to you? I'm afraid the horse is stolen. What do you think?"

"No," Kit sighed. "He looked upset, like he didn't want to get rid of the horse but had no choice."

Jerry frowned. "That's what I thought," he said. "But it's all looking a little dodgy now."

Kit shielded her eyes from the glare of the sun and watched Langdon pick himself up and attempt another valiant battle to recapture the horse. "What is he doing?" she demanded. "Does he know anything about horses?"

"No," Jerry grumbled, "and here lies the problem."

"What was he thinking?" Kit mused. "I didn't even realise he liked horses."

Jerry winced. "He's having a crisis," he confided. "That's what I didn't want to tell you earlier."

"What kind of crisis?" Kit eyed him with suspicion. She hadn't broached the issue of their budding relationship. It was such a personal thing, and she hadn't decided how she should handle it. It seemed the moment of truth had come.

"I think it's a midlife crisis," Jerry said, sounding serious.

Kit's eyes widened and she battled her irritation as Jerry settled on another excuse. "Really? That's what you're going for?" she snapped. "He can't have a midlife crisis! If he's having one, then I need to have one too because we're the same age. And I can't have one yet because I don't have the time."

"Well, I hope he gets over it soon because otherwise I'll be joining him and having my own," Jerry grumbled.

Kit gave his muddy shoulder a reassuring pat and then grimaced. She wiped her palm on the only clean part of his jacket. "It must be hard admitting you're gay," she commiserated. "I'm sure it'll be okay." She held her hand out for the lead rope dangling around Jerry's neck. "I'll help you catch the horse just this once," she said. "But he can't stay here. I don't know who owns this paddock, but I don't imagine them feeling overjoyed to discover a horse frolicking around in it. Langdon will have to call the SPCA to come and get it."

Jerry's eyebrows shot up into his dark fringe and confusion reflected across his handsome features. He seemed a little lost for words. "Gay?" he spluttered, his expression a picture of innocence.

Kit shook her head and offered him a benevolent smile. "Langdon," she said. A flicker of guilt stabbed at the deflection as she dodged the issue in front of her and placed it all on Langdon's broad shoulders.

"Langdon's gay." Jerry closed his eyes and a strange mix of unreadable emotions shunted across his face. "God."

"God is the least of your problems right now," Kit replied. "We need to get this horse out of here before the owner comes back. See if you can call the SPCA. They might still be open for emergencies."

Jerry stamped his foot in a fit of uncharacteristic frustration. His sock disappeared in the mud up to the ankle. "You're the owner, Kit!" he exclaimed. "Didn't you know?"

Kit hefted the lead rope and her eyes widened. "It's not my horse!" She gave a definitive shake of her head. "I've never seen it before in my life!"

Jerry groaned and rubbed orange streaks of clay across his forehead. "The paddock, Kit! The paddock is yours! How did you manage to buy a house without checking the deeds?"

CHAPTER 24

Best Laid Plans

It took Kit five minutes to catch the mischievous horse and tie his head collar to the fence. Five minutes in which she displayed her childhood prowess in Pony Club and earned her flatmates' admiration. She dispatched Jerry to fetch one of her old hairbrushes and tried to de-tangle the snagged mane enough to reveal a pair of wise brown eyes beneath the wiry bush. Her heart sank as she realised she didn't have the heart to send the horse to slaughter or to the SPCA.

Langdon's car tore off the driveway as he headed into Hamilton and raced to the nearest horse shop before it closed. Kit had given him a list of supplies and hoped the stream crossing the lane had abated enough for him to get through it. The hours until darkness became focussed on fixing the broken fence leading to the gully and settling Bouffant into his new paddock. Kit threw her fated plimsolls in the rubbish bin.

Then she showered and drove back to the local pub where she'd met Kasouf. And Jackson.

"Hey." Jackson gave Kit a sideways smile and lifted a glass of wine from the bar as she arrived. "Is Merlot okay?"

Kit nodded. She accepted the drink and turned to look for a spare table. Jackson carried his beer and followed Kit to a booth in the corner. Condensation covered the glass as he laid it on the table between them and slipped into the seat opposite her. "What's up?" he asked. His brown eyes held a glint of humour. "I'm guessing this isn't a date."

Kit swallowed and stared at the deep red liquid in her glass. A speck of the cork floated near the top like a trick of the light. Her mind ventured into dangerous territory, exploring what a date with Jackson Delaney might entail. Kit shut the thoughts down before they blossomed, reiterating her life's mantra about not needing a man to survive. A terrible thread of consciousness snaked free. She might not need one, but what if she wanted one?

"Kit?" Jackson reached across the table and his hand pressed over hers. Kit's twitching fingers stilled beneath the warmth of his palm. "Joke. I wasn't serious. I know this isn't a date."

Kit glanced up in time to see his forehead furrow into lines. Their eyes met and something passed between them, an understanding of sorts. He got her. She liked him. Leave it at that.

She swallowed and resisted the urge to tap the table beneath the cage of his warm hand. The fingers of her other hand jerked against the stem of the wine glass and almost sent it pitching over sideways. Wine slopped like thin blood onto the table. Jackson released her hand and waited while she found a tissue in her pocket and mopped it up with frantic movements. "Sorry," she managed, her voice wavering. "For wasting your time earlier and baiting you in the car. You didn't deserve it."

"Talk to me." Jackson took a sip of his beer and set it back on the table. The action gave Kit time to collect her thoughts and stop fussing.

"Someone is watching me," she whispered. "And following me. I think he's waiting for me to lead him to my missing flatmate." She pursed her lips and leaned closer. "Raki made me promise not to involve the cops." She winced. "But I called the watch house because I thought I knew best. Now everything has gone wrong." She reached up and covered her eyes, afraid she might embarrass herself by crying.

Jackson's body stiffened and Kit dropped her hand and clamped it over his wrist to prevent him swivelling to scan the room. "Who's watching you? Are they here?" He checked himself and leaned forward as though to catch each of her words instead. "Tell me everything." He lowered his voice before pushing his glass across the table. Then he rose and switched to Kit's side of the booth. Their thighs touched on the narrow red bench seat and Jackson pressed closer. "Come on, Maguire. Spill."

Kit told him what she knew but missed out some of her own conclusions. She realised her surmising sounded ridiculous when she said it out loud. It also meant that her information boiled down to a series of disjointed coincidences with a heady dollop of guesswork. Jackson listened to her with careful intention despite her bumbling account. He hung on her every word.

Kit pushed herself back against the leatherette seat and sighed. "I sound like a lunatic, don't I?" she said with a sigh. "There's no evidence of a crime. At the watch house in Hamilton last week, the desk officer took Raki's details. She said there's nothing the police can do until he's been missing for a decent amount of time." Kit gnawed on her lower lip and shifted on the seat. Curling her left leg beneath her, she frowned as her knee pressed against Jackson's thigh. Awkwardness settled over her like a shroud and she tensed her muscles, ready to move herself backwards.

"I saw how upset you were earlier." Jackson's fingers tensed around his glass and he leaned closer. "I listened to what you said. When I got back to the station, I checked out the report you made. It's not actioned yet." He pursed his lips and appeared conflicted. "I know your friend hasn't been absent for long enough yet, but I don't want you to worry anymore. Someone is looking into it."

"Really?" Kit's head jerked and she turned to look at him. Relief and terror filled her chest in equal parts. "I'm so grateful." She gnawed on her lower lip. "I'm just conflicted because it's the opposite of what Raki wants." Her head dipped low as the battle raged within her. It didn't seem possible to protect Raki's interests without breaking her promise.

"It's okay, I understand." Jackson's other hand caught her chin and lifted her head. Kit gasped as his lips dipped close enough to graze hers, but didn't. He pulled back without following through on the kiss, though she saw his lips twitch to take it. Kit's brow creased in confusion, but she said nothing.

Jackson blew out a breath and cleared his throat. She sensed him looking for an excuse and turmoil budded in his eyes, creating a glittering effect beneath the dim lights of the pub. "Sorry." Jackson's lips pursed into thin lines. "I lose my head around you."

Kit smiled. "Then glue it back on because I need you for your mind."

"Charming." Jackson sighed. "Look, you mustn't repeat this, but one of the guys in here is an undercover police officer."

"Oh." Kit's eyes widened and she swallowed. She tried to dodge around Jackson to look at the gathered crowd. "Which one?"

"Not subtle!" Jackson rebuked. "I don't know any details, Kit, but I recognised him from a job he ran with uniformed officers a while ago. I had to be careful checking out your friend. Our computer system leaves a trace when we log in. I need to justify every search I make, or I open myself up to disciplinary action. I found your friend's name by searching for your report. You seemed so upset, I figured you'd made one. The undercover cop had been looking at it. I recognised his initials and then saw him follow you into the pub."

Kit swallowed and lifted her fingers to stroke his cheek. A dusting of light stubble felt rough beneath her hand. "You did that for me?"

Jackson nodded and his eyelashes fluttered against her skin. "Kind of. But I'm not an idiot. I used the fracas at the university and your reason for being there as a cover. Your friend's name is flagged." The sudden sense of camaraderie hung between them like a silent paralysis. Kit's lips parted, but she found no more sensible conversation in the annals of her mind. She dropped her hand as a weightless sensation began in her stomach; like she'd ridden too high on a swing. Jackson's fingers brushed over her wrist and she did nothing to discourage him. She closed her eyes and forgot about Raki, about the man at the bar and the reason she'd rung Jackson in the first place. The world stopped and the bustling bar silenced in her mind.

Regret blossomed in her heart as he withdrew his hand and sat up straight. Clearing his throat again broke the spell and Kit started as Jackson shifted in his seat, his expression a mask of discomfort.

"Sorry." He licked his lips and his expression mirrored that of a small boy who'd got caught with his hand in the cookie jar. "Again." His cheeks pinked beneath the shadow of his stubble.

Kit pursed her lips and a giggle bubbled up from deep in her chest. Jackson Delaney challenged her inner resolve, minimising her reasons for swearing off men for ever. Her valid excuses seemed feeble in the face of their budding attraction. She sighed and wiped the smile from her lips. Her father warned her never to get involved with lawyers or policemen. The trouble was, he hadn't said why. "It's fine." She swallowed and let him off the hook. His proximity meant nothing, just a cover for their meeting. She told herself that and forced her addled mind to accept it as the truth.

Kit straightened her blouse to hide the flush prickling along her collarbone and into her cheeks. Jackson returned to his beer. His head hung low as though he regretted the simple action which had detonated another unexpected bomb. They sat in silence and Kit turned her attention to the men at the bar. She tried to spot the police officer and studied each of the males.

An overweight man with bushy white hair and a matching beard kept his gaze on the pint glass in his hand. His eyes appeared glazed, as though his mind strayed to another realm. A man in an expensive suit perched sideways on a bar stool. He held his tumbler in one hand and peered at the phone in his other. Scrolling with his thumb, he didn't look up or engage with Kit's curious stare. Her lips creased into a smile. The favoured pinstriped fabric gave him away. Slightly less creased than last time she saw him, the man wore it with ease. He'd chosen a material with a darker base grey. Light blue stripes left highlights over the pants. A blue shirt collar poked from the top of the matching jacket. No tie this time. Kit heaved a sigh of relief. She'd solved the mystery of the businessman, at least.

Two young men in their early twenties leaned against the bar next to him, pints in hands and the soles of their left trainers resting on the metal rail at their feet. They mirrored one another's stance like twins, jeans hanging low enough to display their underwear.

Jackson leaned sideways and his shoulder bumped hers. "Stop being obvious and tell me about this horse at your place?" he said.

Kit rolled her eyes. "He's an American Bashkir Curly apparently. Langdon acquired him in a kind of happy accident. I have no idea what he plans to do with him." She frowned. "Jerry thinks he's having a mid-life crisis, but I'm fairly sure it's something else."

Jackson winced. "This is why I live alone. It's less troublesome."

Kit laughed. "Na, I don't know how I'd cope without my crazy vicars." Her expression sobered. "And Raki." She licked her lips and returned to the original topic, voicing a worrying thought. "Why would your undercover cop follow me?" she asked. Her complexion paled and she clapped a hand over her mouth. "Oh, no! I didn't want to believe that Raki did something bad." She leaned around Jackson to check out the man at the bar. He kept his gaze fixed on his phone.

"Stop!" Jackson soothed. "The most important thing is that you're not in any danger. If he's keeping an eye on you, that's a good thing."

"Maybe." Kit frowned. "I hadn't considered I might be in danger. I was more worried about Raki."

Jackson twisted his lips. "Yeah, I figured. Promise you'll stay away from the university and that guy?"

"Absolutely." Kit blinked. She squeaked as Jackson dragged her hand from beneath the table.

"You're lying!" He inspected her crossed fingers. "Maguire! You're a pain!"

Kit pulled her hand free with a coy smile. "The barman is watching. He's about to come over and ask you to leave." She peeked over Jackson's shoulder and caught the man's eye. He winked at her and Kit swallowed. Jackson followed her gaze and released a sigh.

"Perhaps he likes you." His eyes sparkled. "You must get that a lot."

Kit snorted through her nose. "You saw my driving licence, Officer Delaney. Fat, frumpy and frizzy until a few years ago. That's how I see myself. If someone's staring at me, I assume it's for a bad reason."

"You're an enigma, Katharine Maguire," Jackson sighed. "And you don't know how to take a compliment."

"That was a compliment?" Kit shoved at his shoulder. "You need practice."

"I do." Jackson glanced at his watch and winced. "I also need to leave soon."

Kit nodded and avoided looking at the barman. She sensed his gaze burning into her cheek. "Is that so you can go to your other job as a male stripper?"

Crow's feet appeared at the corners of Jackson's eyes as he smiled. "Something like that."

"I rang you because I needed to apologise for earlier," Kit said. Her teeth gnawed on her lower lip. "But also, to ask your advice. I bought some product from a company in Australia and some of it's faulty. I sold it to other people and now, it's exploding. What should I do?"

Jackson sighed and huffed out a breath. He licked his lips and leaned closer to Kit, struggling to keep the intensity from his expression. "What kind of explosions, Kit? Is it the kind of thing which might gain the interest of an undercover cop?"

Kit jerked back in shock. She inhaled at the same time as sipping her Merlot and choked. Jackson pressed her face against his shoulder and lowered his mouth to her ear. "You're fine," he soothed. His hand performed brief pats against her spine as she hacked against his sleeve. "But if you're part of a terrorist cell, then it's an excellent idea to tell me now."

Kit nodded, more through an inability to do anything else. When Jackson gripped her arm above the elbow, she panicked. "Not those kinds of explosions," she rasped, her throat sore. "Lube. Exploding lube."

"Wow." He gave an involuntary shudder and released her arm. "I did not see that coming."

Kit reached for his beer and took a fortifying slurp. It calmed the frog occupying her throat. Jackson frowned and amusement tilted the corners of his lips. He waited for her to put his glass back on its mat, his keen gaze studying her movements. Kit made a few attempts at clearing her throat. Her voice still squeaked. "You might not have noticed, but there's a lube shortage. I managed to get some from Australia, but everything went a little wrong during the ordering process and I ended up with a thousand tubes instead of ten." She sighed and waved her hand in dismissal. "Remember the riot at my place a few weeks ago? Well, that was over a lack of lube. Now, I have an abundance in a friend's garage, but the stuff keeps exploding."

"Have you emailed your supplier?" Jackson blinked. "I can't believe we're having this conversation." His lips quirked upwards and he reached for his glass and took a drag of his beer.

"Yes. They haven't got back to me." Kit frowned. "I wondered if you could check them out and see if they're a legitimate company? Jerry gave me some lawyer advice about my liability, but I need the supplier to get back to me before I end up broke. Debbie is refusing to give anyone their money back, but Jerry thinks we should."

Jackson inhaled and leaned an elbow on the table. Firm abdominal muscles pulled his tee shirt tight across his midriff as he turned his body towards Kit. "I could probably check for a job relating to the company if I knew their name, but it's a civil matter. Only a large-scale fraud would involve the police. You'd need to make a complaint to give me the freedom to search."

Kit's nose twitched. "You think it's too much of a long shot?"

"I do. Sorry." Jackson pursed his lips. "Lube. Really?"

Kit nodded and grinned. "It's great for forming a cast in curly hair." Her gaze roamed to the unruly waves gracing the top of his head, and he jerked backwards and held his hands in front of his face.

"Oh, no you don't!" he protested. "I just need time between shifts to go to the barber."

"Pity." Kit sighed. "Your hair and my lube. They could be good together." Then she frowned. "If Raki was here, I'd ask him to test samples. He'd know straight away if something was wrong with this batch."

Jackson's face lost its humour and he frowned. "But you'll stop looking for him?"

Kit reached for her Merlot and twisted her lips to avoid lying to him. Perhaps he was an unsuitable ally in the hunt for Raki. He'd made it clear she should stop looking. Only she couldn't.

Jackson shook his head and his eyes narrowed. "Don't make me lock you up, Maguire. Because I will if it means keeping you safe." He jerked his head towards the door and rose. He offered her his hand to help her extract herself from the booth. "I'll walk you to your car. And do what I tell you for once, please? It's important."

Kit followed him from the booth. Turning to make sure she'd gathered up her purse and keys, she caught the eye of the man in the suit and froze. His gaze bored into her as though unpacking her soul. Her body stilled like a rabbit caught in the headlights of an oncoming truck, and then she did the only thing she could think of doing. She lifted her hand in a feckless little wave of solidarity. She felt better now she knew he was a cop. The man's lips parted and his brow narrowed into a thick line of surprise. He looked away as Jackson turned back to see what kept her, leaving Kit in the awkward position of being unacknowledged.

"Do I need the handcuffs?" Jackson said, his expression serious. "I'm not leaving you in a pub alone."

Kit shook her head and followed him through the front door, glancing back once more. The businessman had turned his attention back to his phone. As she watched, he lifted it to his ear and spoke to someone. Kit relaxed her shoulders and let go of the door. A hand caught it and she jumped back, guilt pinking her cheeks at having let it go in someone's face. "I'm so sorry," she began. Jackson paused and turned back to assess her delay, his brow puckering and a cute dimple appearing high on his left cheek.

The man with the red beard slid out next to her. He made no sign of recognition and Kit held her breath. Frayed jeans hung over his trainers and rips at the knees revealed hairy legs. He bumped her slightly as he passed, and Kit swallowed.

"Watch out!" Jackson's rebuke received a sneer in reply. A shiver ran through Kit and she sighed. The man ignored them and kept walking. Thin fingers shot out to flick his hood up and over his head, before both hands plunged into the pockets of his jeans. He sloped away, cutting across the car park to the main road.

"Nice!" Kit growled under her breath. She froze, not wanting Jackson to notice the frisson of fear which crawled across her expression. To him, she said, "I should go."

"Yep." Jackson rested a hand on her shoulder and looked down at her. His fingers closed around hers and he frowned at the tremor which began without warning. "It'll be okay, Kit. Trust me."

"I do," Kit lied. She let him open her creaky driver's door and then slumped into the worn seat. Her muscles relaxed with the familiarity of her little car. Jackson leaned over her, resting his forearms on the yellow roof. Night nipped at the edges of daylight, warning of the coming autumn and its promised chill. The scent of his aftershave cocooned her in a safe haze of masculinity, and she pushed away the growing yearning for more of his company. He didn't want her searching for Raki, and the fact made her doubt him. Fear prickled along her spine.

"You okay?" he asked, his voice soft but commanding. His long eyelashes flickered and she sensed he'd seen her waver. He studied her as though trying to tune into her thoughts.

"Great," she replied, the lie burning her tongue. "Thanks again."

Jackson squatted down next to her, his perceptive eyes reading her like an open book. "You're assuming I won't help you, and I didn't say that. Just trust me for a while, Kit. Sit tight. No more meddling, hey?"

Kit recognised her own loneliness mirrored in his eyes and a dart of pain shot through her heart. His left third finger showed a thinning where it met his hand, evidence of a discarded wedding ring. Her resolve stiffened and she nodded her thanks. He'd failed at love, just like her. They were both flotsam on a river of failure. A terrible match. "Thanks for the drink," she said, inserting steel into her voice. "And the free advice."

"You're welcome." Jackson rose and Kit reached out her hand as a thought popped into the forefront of her mind. "What happened about the man who appeared court?" she asked, her tone hopeful."

"Sorry?" Jackson cocked his head. "What court?"

Kit tapped an impatient beat on her thigh. "The man who tried to rob the shop. He went before the magistrates and you said they remanded him in custody. I forgot to ask what that meant. Did he tell you who put him up to the shop robbery?"

Jackson groaned and shook his head. "No, sorry. I mean, no, he didn't say who put him up to it, but the magistrates remanded him in custody pending a crown court trial. We had a warrant outstanding for a long list of offences he'd committed. He's an addict, Kit. He wanted money for drugs."

Kit shook her head. "That's not right," she said. "That's not right."

"But it's what happened." Jackson frowned. "I shouldn't have given the impression it was anything else. The guy couldn't walk in a straight line. He wanted cash for drugs. Take care, Kit." He closed her car door. His lips twisted into a police officer's sternness as Kit started the engine and the little yellow car released a cloud of grey smoke and a backfire to wake the dead.

She gave a feckless wave and drove away before he could magic an infringement notice out of thin air.

CHAPTER 25

Curly Detective Duo

Kit climbed into bed with her mind running through the day's events. Even an hour of yoga didn't seem able to switch it off enough to sleep. Sighing, she rolled onto her stomach and wrapped her arms around the pillow. Jackson's attentiveness had awoken something in her soul and she wished it hadn't. With a groan of annoyance, she shifted position again but found no hidden comfort in her usual safe place. "Bloody Jackson Delaney," she grumbled. "As much as I want to trust you, I can't." Silence from Raki's room next door offered no reply. She wished she'd told Jackson about the Pineapple Lumps. Keeping things from him didn't bode well for their friendship.

Kit lay still and listened. She should have heard Raki moving around, stomping from the desk to the bed as his laptop died and he searched for the charger. The soft beat of his beloved K-pop should have lulled her to sleep. "Where are you, Raki?" Kit whispered. "I need to talk to you."

Raki would have understood her explanation of how Jackson's kisses affected her. Squatting on his haunches in his favoured thinking pose, he'd have listened and commiserated over her decision to remain single. He'd taken a similar path, injecting his energy into studying complicated chemical formulae and dedicating every waking moment to the pursuit of science. His PhD represented his first love. Anyone sharing his affections would get sloppy seconds and he'd reconciled himself with his aloneness.

Kit pushed herself up the bed and leaned against the headboard. She missed Raki's honesty with a physical ache. Despite herself, she pressed an index finger over her mouth. The shadow of stubble gracing Jackson's chin had prickled the soft skin of her lips and awoken a dangerous craving for more intimate contact. It acted as an unwelcome dousing of freezing water. She'd chosen a life that didn't balance on the tightrope of another's expectations and emotions. She paddled her own canoe and liked not having to answer to someone else. Her mind flicked to an image of Piper's sad face at the last Curly meeting. Kit frowned, knowing she hadn't listened properly to her friend. Piper hadn't wanted to return to full time work after having her daughter, but her husband had insisted. Kit sighed. "See, this is why I'm alone," she said to herself. She listened to the crickets chirping beyond her open window. "I'm never running my life to someone else's timetable again."

When her phone vibrated on the nightstand, Kit leaned across and grabbed it. An unknown number flashed across the screen and she tried to recognise it. "Please don't be a Curly having a bad hair day," she groaned. She fumbled with the icon to answer the call. "Hello?" She infused her tone with enough hostility to make it clear she wouldn't tolerate midnight demands from another hysterical woman hiding in a bathroom.

"Miss Maguire, I presume." The male voice sounded clipped but calm.

"Who is this?" Kit gritted her teeth, guessing the late-night call wasn't a social one. "What do you want?"

He ignored her question and she recognised the dangerous edge in his voice. "You don't know where he is, do you?" A flat tone entered his words. "But you've heard from him." A statement, not a question.

Kit held her breath while she formulated a suitable answer. She released it by degrees, listening to the sounds at the man's end of the call. Outside noises; crickets and a morepork hunting a non-vegan dinner for its chicks. She cleared her throat. "If you're talking about Raki, then this is his old phone. We're worried sick. Do you know where he is? Why are you looking for him?"

The click of a hang-up greeted her and her torso slumped as the fake bravado stopped holding her upright against the headboard. Kit switched on the bedside light and swung to press her feet against the floorboards, trying to reclaim something of solidity in her shaking world. Her knees knocked together. The water pump whirred, sending a vibration through the house as Langdon used the upstairs shower. A low whistle accompanied the sounds of water slapping against the glass cubicle, and Kit frowned as she recognised the baritone. Jerry.

She groaned. "Please don't be in there together," she whispered. "It's already awkward enough." Kit stood and urged her legs to carry her to the hallway. She kept her phone in her hand in case the mystery caller restarted the conversation. Light pooled through the gap beneath the bathroom door. Darkness engulfed Langdon's room, the door standing wide and his curtains blowing in the thrall of a soft breeze from the open window. Turning right to face Raki's bedroom, Kit forced her fingers to close around the handle. The door creaked as it opened.

She'd searched the room before, a cursory glance when he first disappeared. It revealed nothing, but more perhaps because she didn't know what to look for. She still didn't but trying to sleep seemed futile. Light bloomed from the central pendant as Kit flicked the switch. It blinded her for a moment and she blinked until her pupils adjusted. The room looked like it always did with the bed made and papers stacked in neat piles on the desk. Raki's personality lent itself to a sense of chaos, but his habits showed otherwise. Clean and fastidious, he often performed everyone else's household chores, ignoring the rota and doing what appealed to him at that moment. He'd vacuum and polish as a diversion while his mind worked through some complicated problem with chemical components. Once the solution came, he'd rush back to his work. Kit often arrived home to find the vacuum cleaner sitting alone in the middle of the lounge, or the polish and duster halfway up the stairs. The flatmates flexed around him, not minding as they navigated their own busy schedules. But they felt his absence. The kitchen had begun to lose the subtle scent of rice and bean sprouts, and the lounge no longer echoed with Raki's easy laughter.

Kit swallowed as a ball of sadness lodged in her chest. "Where are you, Raki?" she whispered to herself. She pressed into the room and pushed the door partially closed, surveying the space with pursed lips. Everything looked normal, as though Raki had just nipped back to the university to explore his latest light bulb moment further. Kit shook her head, refusing to succumb to apathy. He was in trouble and he'd called her. Not Langdon. Not Jerry. Her.

"Raki? Mate! Where have you been?" Jerry's baritone cut through the silence as he pushed the door open with force. Kit jumped and shrieked. Disappointment clouded Jerry's eyes as he saw her standing in the centre of the room in an oversized tee shirt. "Sorry," he said, his tone hushed. "I thought he came home."

Kit nodded and forced a smile. "A man just phoned Raki's old number. He hung up on me when he realised I didn't know where Raki went."

"Oh. Sorry." Jerry's features tightened. He took a step into the room, a bath towel hanging low on his hips. Dark hair spread across his chest and the pectoral muscles flexed and released with his movement.

Kit sighed. "Where's Langdon? Is he in the bathroom?"

Jerry shook his head. "No, that was me. Langdon went outside to persuade the horse to come away from the shed. Then he had a baptismal evening class at church."

"Get the horse away from the shed?"

"Yeah. He's grazing in a circle around it. Langdon's scared he'll knock it over and hurt himself on the rusty metal." He jerked his head back towards the door. "I should have checked with you about using the family bathroom. Sorry. I plumbed the shower in the sleep out, but the pressure isn't right. I think I need a different pump. Langdon said I could use his and Raki's shower."

"It's fine." Kit waved away his protest. "It's not important." She gnawed on her lip and stared around Raki's bedroom. "I thought I might look in here for clues. Jackson told me to stay away from the university. He says they'll get a trespass order if I go back again."

Jerry sighed and shook his head. "You went there without me!"

Kit shrugged. "Dawn dropped me there." Her eyes brightened. "She gave me fifty dollars for cutting her curls."

Jerry ran his hands through his hair. "Anyone can walk around the campus, Kit. They don't end up with trespass orders against them."

She pursed her lips and her head bowed in defeat. "I followed a man I recognised. He didn't want me to find him, and I ended up at Raki's lab. Kasouf was there." Kit's cheeks flushed a heart attack inducing red. "It got nasty. The security officer called the police and Jackson searched my bag. He confiscated my hairdressing scissors." She wrinkled her nose. "Good job they weren't my best ones."

Jerry's brawny arm snaked around Kit's shoulders and tilted her body into his side. Her feet edged her closer and she pressed her cheek against the bunched muscle of his biceps. He smelled clean and she closed her eyes and allowed the scent of male soap and deodorant to wash over her. "What a mess." Jerry's voice sounded soothing and calm, echoing through his chest wall and vibrating the sinews beneath her cheek. Kit squeezed her eyes closed and remained still, not wanting to move and lose the sense of comfort and safety. Jerry exhaled through his nose and gave Kit's right shoulder a squeeze beneath his massive hand. "I'll pull clean clothes on," he breathed. "Then we'll take this room apart." The kiss he deposited on the top of her head felt rough, her curls snagging against his stubble. When he dropped his arm and turned towards the door, a cold draught and a sense of foreboding rushed to back-fill the space.

CHAPTER 26

Straight Search

"There's nothing different or out of place." Kit sank onto the soft mattress with a sigh. "His clothes are here, his computer, even his favourite shirt. When he left this room, he expected to return."

"What about his wallet?" Jerry asked. His head bobbed up and down as he searched under the bed. His long arms reached out of sight and his fingers hauled out a stray sock, which he deposited next to Kit's bare toes.

She shrugged and poked her index finger through a ringlet dangling near her left eye. "His car is at the university. I guess he took his wallet and keys and just nipped out like he said." Kit unwound the ringlet and watched it recoil as she let go. "I remember getting home from work and heard his radio. He didn't answer when I knocked. Later, I popped my head around the door and realised he'd left."

"Did you move anything in here?" Jerry rested one forearm on the mattress and his elbow brushed Kit's leg. "Who turned off the radio?"

Kit sighed. "Me. I got up in the night and heard it still playing. The lights were off and I assumed he'd just had some crazy thought about his research and rushed off to the university to play with chemicals."

Jerry inhaled and nodded. A smile played at the corners of his lips. "He did that a lot, didn't he?"

Kit wrinkled her nose. "I hoped Kasouf might tell me something. I overplayed that hand and got nothing apart from sore fingers." She rubbed her palm over her other hand and gave a sigh of regret. "Jackson said last night that someone was looking into Raki's disappearance."

Jerry raised a dark eyebrow and squinted at Kit. "You should have called for help when Kasouf got nasty in the pub. I've listened to the recording and you're lucky that didn't turn out worse. There's not much point me sitting outside if you don't ask for help when you need it."

Kit shrugged her shoulders as though the action might dispel the sense of panic she experienced when Kasouf squeezed her hand in his painful grip. "I didn't believe I was in any danger."

"Do you think Jackson knows more than he's saying?" Jerry asked.

Kit shook her head. "He wouldn't tell if he did. But he risked his job to help me. What do you think about Kasouf being the reason Raki left?"

Jerry sighed. He ran a hand across his chin before scratching his head. His hair stuck up at the front like a cockatoo's plume. "Kasouf might be the reason, but he didn't do anything to Raki. He has too much to lose with Raki's disappearance. It's clear he wants his data back and he needs Raki for that." Jerry blinked. "And I imagine Sergeant Delaney can cover his own ass quite well. I wouldn't worry about him." He ran his fingers through his fringe and left it flopped over his eyes.

Kit nodded. "Okay. I don't have the energy to worry about everyone." She checked the clock radio balanced on a cardboard box next to Raki's headboard and frowned.

"We should check Raki's drawers and wardrobe before I go back to bed." Jerry turned to her, a wince spoiling his handsome face. "It feels wrong though, like an imposition. Will you stay here while I do it?"

Kit pursed her lips. "Okay, but I can't stay up much longer. These early starts are killing me, and I'm becoming paranoid about not getting enough sleep. I go to bed early and worry about how many hours I have available to recharge my batteries. Then it stops me sleeping, so I wake up tired. I can't seem to adjust my body clock to cope."

"So, why do you get up an hour before you leave?" Jerry rose and pulled open Raki's wardrobe door. "Why not leave it until the last possible moment?"

Kit's fingers tracked straight up to her hair and lingered there before falling into her lap. "I need time to wake up," she lied. A glance at Jerry's profile showed his lips uplifting in a smirk. He didn't believe her.

The wardrobe revealed nothing but an overflowing washing basket and a stack of binders dating back to graduate study. Jerry found Raki's passport bundled together with a printout of his bank account transactions for the last month. He handed them to Kit and continued his fingertip search.

"Wow!" Kit flapped the paper against her leg. "No wonder he printed this off," she said. "I'd want a record of that for posterity too."

"What?" Jerry leaned across and snagged the paper from her hand. He gave a low whistle after reading the printed figure. "I wonder why he never mentioned this." His brow furrowed as confusion vied with disappointment. "I thought we were friends."

"Ninety thousand dollars." Kit's lips formed the words, having difficulty conjuring the reality of such a vast amount of money in her brain. "Maybe he felt embarrassed," she suggested. "Or guilty. Ever since I bought this house, I've done nothing but complain about how much it cost me and how I'm not coping with the debt. Raki's so kind. He'd hate to think he'd rubbed my nose in his good fortune." Kit's shoulders slumped as she recognised the recent horrible trait in herself. The burden of responsibility had made her vent the misery of her poverty on everyone else. "I need to stop doing that," she resolved. "It was my choice to buy the house."

Jerry slumped down next to her on the bed. His weight caused a dent and Kit rolled against him. "You're all right," he soothed. He slipped an arm around her shoulders and pressed his lips against her temple. "What next?"

"I don't know." Kit's brow furrowed into worry lines. "Professor Kirke with an 'e' wasn't much help." She sighed and rested her chin on her fist.

"We should contact his parents." Jerry ran his right hand through his damp fringe again and left it sticking out to the left in a series of dark antennae. His arm shifted against Kit's shoulder.

"No!" Kit protested. "He asked me not to do that. No parents and no police. His mum and dad are travelling, anyway."

Jerry shrugged. "You involved the police. Why not the parents?"

Kit sighed. "I went to the police before Raki phoned me. He expressly said no, which means I can't go to them again." Jackson's handsome features drifted past her inner vision and she pursed her lips. She blinked and the image dissipated.

Jerry shifted position and settled, so his spine rested against the pillows. He stretched his long legs out in front of him, his angular toes peeking from the ends of his jeans. He stared at Raki's desk as though it held the answer. Then he gave a low whistle. "That's what's wrong!" he hissed. A long finger lifted and pointed at the desk. "He didn't leave his computer."

"Yeah, he did." Kit frowned and peered at the double screens crowding the narrow desk. The black computer mouse sat on a mat, showing an image of Christchurch as it looked before the earthquake. The keyboard rested between the screens and completed the circuit.

Kit jumped as Jerry dipped forward and crawled off the bed. He kept going towards the desk. Reaching up, he shifted the office chair sideways on its casters. "Look," he said again, pointing to the gap beneath the desk. His tee shirt rode up to reveal a narrow waist and firm back muscles. He half turned and beckoned Kit over with a frantic hand movement, wanting her to peer into the space with him. Kit gave a groan of exasperation and dropped to her knees. One hand clamped her nightshirt down over her knickers as she knee-walked across the carpet.

"There's nothing there!" she exclaimed. "We already looked."

"Exactly!" Jerry popped up on his knees and mirrored Kit's stance, minus the clutching motion her fingers made. He held his left hand out, palm facing upwards. "Where's his PC?"

Kit frowned. "On the desk?"

Jerry shook his head. "No. He kept the base unit on the floor. Those are just his screens, mouse and keyboard. Where have the actual guts of it gone? Look, the wires are hanging down behind his desk."

Kit bobbed her head and the light from the overhead bulb cast a shadow on the wall behind the desk. Cables hung like spilled spaghetti. She held her breath. "What's going on here, Jerry?" she whispered, her tone tight. "What's happening?"

CHAPTER 27

A Brace of Clerics

"Did someone take it?" Langdon ran a shaking hand through his blond hair. He'd come when Jerry called, leaving one of his deacons to manage the baptismal class. Kit focused on the lines and shadows created by the black fabric of his shirt. The whiteness of his dog collar created a stark contrast.

"We should check the rest of the house." Jerry's tone sounded serious.

"And call the cops," Langdon added.

Kit shook her head. "No, I promised. Let's see what else is missing and go from there."

A thorough search of the entire property found nothing missing or out of place. The navy blue of the sky had deepened to indigo as the rest of the city shuffled to bed. They met back in the lounge like explorers reuniting after an expedition. Each had drawn the same conclusion.

"Nothing else looks disturbed." Langdon yawned and covered his mouth. Jerry copied.

"So, we're assuming Raki took the computer with him or hid it?" Kit sighed and pulled her legs into the armchair. She folded them beneath her and covered them with her nightshirt. "I'm not sure it would do us any good to find it," she admitted. "He probably put a complicated scientific password on it. There's no way any of us would guess something like that."

"Speak for yourself." Jerry sounded offended.

"Fine then!" Tiredness made Kit irritated. As the clock ticked on the wall of the kitchen, she watched the hands move past midnight and became acutely aware of how little time for sleep remained. She rose to her feet and the tail of the nightdress swished around her thighs. "You two work it out between you. I need to get to bed. I have three hours and fifty-nine minutes left for sleeping if I don't bother cleaning my teeth." She stalked from the room, the day's events catching her up with horrible intensity. Unable to cope with the thought of a furry tongue, Kit cleaned her teeth anyway and settled into her bed.

But she didn't sleep. Night noises and the sounds of the boys moving around downstairs left her turning from side to side, finding lumps and divots in her mattress. In desperation, she rose from her bed and did the thing she promised she wouldn't. She called the number Raki had used to contact her last.

Kit sank onto her bed and put the phone on speaker so she could lay it on the pillow next to her. The action brought her comfort as though by not touching it, she could pretend the phone acted under its own initiative. The number rang without a response and she listened to its melodious tones being ignored in another household.

She killed the call after a time and sat with her hands in her lap. Hope burgeoned as the phone trilled on the pillow. Her fingers fluttered as she answered. A different caller this time, she recognised the number too late and sighed. He didn't give her time to speak. "He stole our research; you know that don't you?" The clipped accent cut through the silence like a knife. "You're in more trouble than you can imagine." A sigh followed an interminable pause. "I need my share of the money, Katharine. I'm having unanticipated difficulties and I'm desperate. You must know where your friend is. What happened at the university earlier is just a taster. These people aren't messing around and you're lucky the cops let you go this time. Tell me where Raki Han is. He's up to his neck in this."

Kit pressed the button to disconnect the call. She'd heard enough. As her fingers writhed in her lap, the phone trilled its protest as Raki's co-conspirator tried to make contact. Kit lifted the phone, careful not to answer the call.

She carried it in her palm with it still ringing as she went in search of the boys.

Kit padded downstairs in the darkness. Her phone lit the way in the empty house, sending up an eerie blue glow as Raki's partner in crime became more frantic. She discovered the front and back doors locked, but saw a light showing through the windows of Jerry's sleepout. As the phone lit up in her hand again, she felt a wave of gratitude at the boys' attention to detail. Believing her vulnerable and asleep, they'd locked her inside the house.

Kit located the spare key to the back door hidden in the cutlery drawer. Not content with calling the number, Raki's partner started text bombing it.

Jerry's door flew open as Kit stepped out onto the porch. She glanced up, locking the door behind her one-handed while her phone rocked like a banshee in her palm.

"What happened?" Jerry demanded. He strode from the sleepout, his jeans riding low over his hips. His bare feet covered the short distance onto the porch without his face registering the myriad fine stones or pieces of gravel in their path. Reaching out, he took the key from Kit's fumbling fingers and checked the door before slipping a hand beneath her elbow. "Come on," he said, jerking his head towards the sleepout. He didn't take the phone, but supported Kit's arm as she picked her way across the garden.

Langdon met them at the door, a mug of coffee in his hand. He looked tired, his blond hair standing upright on his head like the plume of a cockatoo and shadows beginning under his sockets. Kit detected the merest flicker of disappointment in his eyes at the sight of her.

Oblivious, Jerry helped her up the single step and into the little annex he'd spent the last few weeks renovating. Kit gasped as she stepped over the threshold. Fairy lights flickered overhead, beginning at a central point and splaying out across the ceiling. The navy painted walls provided an effortless sense of cosiness and he'd maximised the space to its full advantage. The door to a tiny closet stood open, revealing a wet room containing a toilet, sink and shower. A bookcase and desk occupied one end of the larger room, and Jerry had somehow squeezed a king-size bed opposite them. The space appeared tidy to the point of immaculacy, books lining their shelves in regimental height order.

Langdon thudded back down onto the dent he'd already made at the end of the bed, and Kit saw a nerve twitch beneath Jerry's left eye.

"Wow!" she breathed. "It looks better than the rest of the house. I can't believe you've made that dingy little room on the back of the garage into this." Her phone gave another pitiful hiccough and the screen lit up with another text.

"What's going on?" Langdon demanded. "Why don't you answer the phone, Kit?"

Jerry edged her towards the bed and sat her down next to Langdon. He squatted on his haunches in front of her, giving her his unconditional attention. "Tell me what happened?" he asked. His tone sounded soothing. It explained why the more delicate members of Langdon's congregation had shifted their allegiance to Jerry.

Kit's brow furrowed as the phone trilled again. She held it up in front of Jerry's face like an offering, the desperation in her eyes begging him to take it away from her. "I did a stupid thing," she admitted. "I phoned the number Raki used before when he rang me. Do you think it's a coincidence that Kasouf phoned me straight after and started threatening me? He wants money and he's implicating Raki in whatever crime he's committed."

Kit exhaled and her chest deflated as Jerry lifted the phone from her palm. He rested his forearms on her knees for balance as he inspected it. His fingers worked over the keypad in between calls as he read the various texts. His brown eyes narrowed to slits as he looked up at Langdon. "She's right. He says here that Raki knew what he was doing. He says if Kit goes to the cops, someone else will make sure she regrets it."

Kit nodded. "The man who rang earlier sounded menacing. Perhaps he's putting pressure on Kasouf."

"What man?" Jerry frowned. "You need to tell us about this stuff, Kit."

"Okay, but what now?" Langdon asked. "If the texts are getting more desperate, should we try talking to him?"

Kit blanched. "No. Too risky." She waved her hand. "This is all my mother's fault. She just can't stand the fact I don't want a relationship. Now, she's got me involved with someone who wants me to commit a crime."

Langdon made a sound of disbelief with his lips, shaking his head at the same time. "Why do people insist on paring off singles?" he demanded, fixing on the wrong issue as a response to a familiar trigger. Jerry's lips lifted into a slight smile and he shot Kit a look which told her he'd heard it many times already.

Deciding alone, Jerry reached for the main button between Kasouf's irritating instances of speed dialling and turned off the phone. The hissing silence which remained made Kit realise how tense her muscles had become. Jerry dropped into a cross-legged pose in front of her and laid the phone on the floor next to him. "Right then," he said, looking at his flatmates with an air of expectancy "What now?"

Langdon ran a hand through his hair and flopped backwards on the bed. The tight muscles over his stomach tensed as he released a dramatic yawn. "I've prayed about it and got nothing. It's impossible to know what to do right now. I'm inclined to leave things until tomorrow. It might appear clearer." He sat up and rubbed his eyes. "What does anyone else think?"

Kit glanced at the curtain covering the glass in the door. A narrow gap reflected their tired faces overlaid by the darkness outside the sleepout. She gave an involuntary shiver and tried to blink away her growing sense of fear. Jerry patted her knee. "You need to be at work in less than three hours. You should sleep." Kit pressed her toes against the floorboards and her tension hiked. The thought of returning to her bedroom alone chased sleep even further away from her reality. She shook her head.

"I won't sleep," she concluded. Her fingers just covered the impromptu yawn in time as it made a liar of her. Her shoulders slumped in defeat. "As soon as my head touches the pillow, my brain will start whirring with ideas and possibilities. I can't get rid of the fear that Raki's in danger."

"Snuggle down in my bed for an hour," Jerry suggested. "I'll keep watch. Tomorrow is a late start for me, so I can catch up on my sleep while the rest of you are at work."

Langdon's eyes widened like saucers and his head started shaking before Jerry could finish his sentence. "That can't happen," he demanded. "It's improper. What would people say?"

"It's an emergency!" Jerry insisted. His eyes narrowed in an uncharacteristic display of irritation. "We spend far too much time worrying about what the congregation thinks of us. We're human, Langdon. Right now, this crazy dude's blowing up Kit's phone because of something Raki may or may not have done. I vote we stick together for tonight."

Langdon shot to his feet. "I'll take the floor. I can't sleep in the same bed as a girl." Kit's brow furrowed as Langdon discussed her as an object for passing around or avoiding. Tiredness robbed her of the ability to offer a ready retort. Jerry rose and snagged a yoga mat from the corner of the room. He unfurled it on the floor and provided an extra pillow and a blanket for Langdon. His jerky mannerisms suggested Langdon could take it or leave it.

Kit scrambled towards the headboard and settled in the furthest corner of the bed. She snuggled down in Jerry's sheets and closed her eyes as his subtle haze of aftershave and masculinity shrouded her in a familiar comfort.

Kit didn't expect to sleep and laid awake listening to Langdon trying to settle. He moved around on his yoga mat until his body stilled and his breathing followed a steady pattern. Her mind ran over and over the clues without finding the one she needed. Lulled by the sound of Langdon's rhythmic inhalations, Kit relaxed and her eyelids fluttered closed.

CHAPTER 28

A Night Visitor

Kit stirred, over warm in the comfy bed. She pushed at the heavy weight laying across her shoulders, stilling as it gave a sigh and lifted. "Jerry?" Her voice sounded loud and afraid in the darkness. A long body pressed against her back and her cheek rested on something warm and fleshy. It moved as she panicked and disappeared from under her head.

A gentle finger pressed against her lips. "It's okay. You're okay." Jerry's soothing cadence provided immediate reassurance. As the adrenaline fled Kit's bloodstream, it left behind a tingling sensation in her extremities. Her breathing sounded rushed in the silence. Langdon's steady snores completed the illusion of surety, and Kit struggled to regain her composure.

She remembered settling down in Jerry's vast bed and drifting off to sleep just after Langdon. But she didn't recall Jerry slipping into the bed next to her or how their bodies became so entangled.

"Sorry," Kit whispered. She lifted her head to allow Jerry to properly retrieve his arm. The fluffy pillow made a poor replacement beneath her head. "I have a tendency to seek warmth when I'm asleep." She pursed her lips in embarrassment and unsnagged her right leg from Jerry's.

"It's fine." He sounded matter-of-fact, his tone just the same as always. Kit felt a surge of guilt when she remembered Langdon's earlier protest. She swallowed and resolved not to let him know that Jerry had spent the night spooning her sleeping body right under his nose. It seemed even more of a crime in the context of Langdon's own budding relationship with Jerry.

An inappropriate, embarrassed giggle bubbled from between her lips, and Jerry's fingers covered her mouth. "Naughty girl," he rebuked. "I know what you're thinking." She heard the laughter in his whisper. "And no, I won't tell him if you don't."

"What's the time?" Kit changed the subject.

Jerry shifted in the bed, his shoulder moving against Kit's. He wriggled around until a small light appeared in front of his face as an eerie glow. Kit watched him activate his phone screen. "Three thirty," he replied. The effort of whispering in his powerful baritone created crackles in his voice. "You shouldn't go back to sleep now, or it will make it harder to get up in half an hour."

"I know." Kit covered her mouth with her hand as a yawn convulsed her body. She fought the urge to groan out loud as she straightened her legs from their curled position. It seemed a crime to leave the warmth of Jerry's bed and the safety of his armpit. In an act of momentary rebellion, Kit turned on her side and snuggled closer to him until her knees touched the coarse fabric of his jeans. She lifted her head and placed it against his shoulder, trapping his muscular arm along the line of her body. A subdued voice in her mind warned her not to get used to it, but gratitude flooded her senses as his fingers clasped hers beneath the covers. They lay there in companionable silence as time marched onward. Work and responsibility tugged at Kit's sense of duty. But not hard enough.

Kit jerked as her body tipped her back over the edge into slumber. Jerry squeezed her fingers. "Up you get," he whispered. His knuckles nudged her leg. "I'll walk you back to the house. Don't step on Langdon unless you want to meet the incarnation of Satan."

The cold predawn air swirled around Kit's bare legs as she stepped out into the garden. As Jerry turned to pull the door closed behind them, Kit felt an odd sense of danger, like cold fingers fluttering across her spine. A shadow moved in her peripheral vision. Only the hand she clapped over her mouth prevented the scream escaping, but a high-pitched squeak still sounded the alarm.

"What?" Jerry spun and a protective arm slipped around Kit's shoulders in a reflex action. He pulled her close and scanned the garden. His gaze settled on Kit's frightened face, not doubting for a second that she'd seen something. "What happened?" He dragged Kit's hand away from her mouth, his strong fingers clasping her wrist.

Wide eyed and burbling, Kit pointed towards the back door with a shaking index finger. "Someone was standing on the porch," she squeaked. "Thin and dressed in black." Jerry followed her direction, peering through the darkness to where a soft glow lit the porch.

He frowned. "Where's that light coming from?"

Kit's head gave a jerky shake and her finger drifted higher until it pointed at the bright light glaring from an upstairs window. Raki's window. Jerry gaped, the frown lines on his forehead carved deeper by shadows. "Oh, crap!" he breathed.

Making sure he'd locked the sleep-out behind them, Jerry took Kit's hand and they picked their way across the garden and onto the porch of the main house. Bouffant neighed and they froze and peered through the darkness. "I see nothing," Kit whispered. "Do you think the intruder went across the paddock?"

"Maybe," Jerry breathed. "It's too dark to see now. Let's check the house."

The back door opened at his twist of the handle and Kit held her breath. "But you locked it." She released the air in a whoosh of fear.

"I know. Stay here!" Jerry commanded.

Kit tugged on the belt loop of his jeans as he crossed the threshold. "What if they're inside the house?" she stage whispered. "What will you do?"

Jerry widened his eyes and shrugged, the action failing to fill Kit with any confidence. She groaned as he progressed further into the kitchen. His limbs worked in spiky movements as he readied himself, body and mind for a confrontation. Kit stood on the scratchy coconut doormat. Her knees banged together and fear ran rampant in its creation of terrible scenarios in her mind.

Then it occurred to her with a sudden stab of irritation that she'd allowed herself to fall into the role of a helpless woman without so much as a protest. It seemed such an easy and desirable place to stay, but she battled the stereotype despite herself and stepped across the threshold in Jerry's brave stead. Clattering a bread knife from the block, Kit held the weapon in front of her as she crept through the house. Light from the upstairs bedroom cast a glow over the stairs, creating shadows in pockets of the downstairs rooms. Kit jumped several times and made wild stabs with the knife. She realised she must look ridiculous.

Nothing appeared disturbed. The cushion she left on the floor the night before still sat like an island on the rug. Her latest read lay over the arm of her chair. Kit skirted the lounge and into the hallway. She'd made it as far as the bottom step when Jerry appeared on the landing. He looked calm and unhurried, all sense of alarm dissipated in the few moments since she'd last seen him.

"There's nobody up here," he said, jumping down the stairs two at a time. He winced at the sight of the serrated bread knife lifted in Kit's right hand. His fingers took it from her bunched fist with gentle wariness. "What did you think you'd do? Slice him like a loaf of bread?"

Kit frowned and shook her head. Her reply conveyed her irritation that he'd mocked her efforts. "What's happening, Jerry?" she hissed.

He released a sigh and gave her a one-armed hug, keeping the bread knife out of range. Kit's cheek pressed against the warm tee shirt covering his chest and she listened to the elevated thud of his heart making a liar of his calm. She both cherished and resented the comfort his presence offered, the conflict raging in her heart like a never-ending dialogue.

"There's nothing out of place," Jerry said. He pressed a kiss on the top of her head. "You can get ready for work. I'll grab my gear from the sleep-out and wait downstairs."

Kit drew back from his embrace, confusion on her face. Her head began shaking even before she spoke. "But we found the back door unlocked, Raki's bedroom light on and I saw a figure as we stepped onto your deck." Her eyes flashed, daring him to doubt her when he hadn't before that moment.

Jerry carried the challenge well. To his credit, he didn't betray her trust in denials. He fixed a smile on his lips and nodded. "I believe you, Kit. I've checked all the rooms upstairs and there's no one there now. They either didn't get what they came for, or we disturbed them on their way inside. I'll put the kettle on to boil and wait down here for you." He glanced at the watch on his hairy wrist. "You need to hurry, or you'll be late."

Kit nodded. "Okay. But I definitely saw someone there. Lock me inside the house and check on Langdon. Just in case."

Jerry gave a nod of agreement and set off back through the kitchen. His footsteps padded from the floorboards to the tiles. He detoured just once to lift the kettle, his long arm testing its weight to check for adequate water. Satisfied, he flicked the switch to make it boil before disappearing through the back door.

Kit waited in the hallway, watching his movements through the narrow aperture and listening for the rattle of his key in the door. Safe in the knowledge he'd secured her inside, she backed up enough to check the front door. The handle turned beneath her fingers, but the door remained shut. Peering through the leaded windows either side, she saw the outline of their three vehicles still sitting where they left them.

Only then did she skip upstairs and shower, irritated when she realised she'd still not boiled up any more flax seed gel. She pushed extra lube through her curls, for once distracted. The floral scent Raki had added to his mixture swirled around Kit's head as a continual reminder of his absence.

Running from her ensuite to her bedroom in a towel, Kit dressed with urgency. A strange sense prevailed, as though an uninvited guest had visited and stayed beyond their allotted time. It unnerved Kit, causing her fingers to fumble and her feet to trip. Mrs Rashid's green headscarf refused to do her bidding despite the expertise of her fingers. She cursed as it slipped from the bed for the third time and she grappled for it, her head down and curls dripping into her eyes. A damp patch began on the rug, growing as she leaned sideways to snatch up the scarf from its resting place. Her fingers closed around the slippery silk and she lifted it, irritated to find the end of her laptop charger wrapped in the cloth. With a groan, she separated the two and made a final attempt to wrap her wet curls in the scarf. Only when she had secured it with a knot at the back and wiped the sticky wetness from her eyes, could she contemplate the cable at her feet.

"Darn thing!" she commented, bending to retrieve it. She groped for her laptop beneath the bed to plug it back in, annoyed when her grasping fingers couldn't locate it. Dropping to her knees, she lifted the valance to perform a visual search. Then she sat back on her heels with a look of confusion, twirling the laptop end of the cable between her fingers.

Jerry gave a light knock on her bedroom door before poking his head through the gap. "I'll drop you at work this morning," he stated, his tone offering no discussion.

Kit turned to him with panic widening her eyes. "Look," she whispered. "Whoever got into the house stole my laptop."

CHAPTER 29

A Change of Religion

They turned Kit's room inside out before concluding the laptop had gone for good. Kit sat on the bed and worried at her thumbnail as Jerry finished searching underneath it. His brow furrowed as he exited backwards and clambered onto the mattress next to her. "We should call the cops," he suggested. His arm slipped around Kit's shoulders.

She sighed and shook her head. "I don't know for sure when it went missing."

"When did you last see it?" Jerry gave her a comforting squeeze. "What did you use it for? That might jog your memory."

Kit squirmed and released a groan of frustration. "I can't remember, Jerry." She closed her eyes and stared at a blurry spot drifting across the inside of her left eyelid. The floating shape looked like a wiggly snake. "I used it for a while after the cops returned mine broken. But then Raki gave me his old phone and I've been using that." She tapped a beat with her fingers on her thigh. "The laptop was more of a long-term loan than a gift, and now I've lost it."

Jerry tutted and pressed his lips against her temple. "Don't fret," he advised, employing his calming, vicar's tone. "We'll work this out."

"I need to get to the shop." Kit blinked as the digital display on her clock radio showed how late she'd left it to leave. "Damn! I hate these early starts."

"I'm driving." Jerry muffled a yawn by covering his mouth with a large hand. "I might as well, seeing as we're both awake."

Kit rolled her eyes. "I'm sorry. It's been a horrid few days." She rose and stifled her own wide yawn. "Is Langdon still sleeping?"

"Yeah." Jerry nodded. His fingers reached for her hand. "Maybe don't tell him we slept together."

Kit cocked her head and didn't hide her sarcasm. "Even though we actually slept?"

"He just wouldn't like it." Jerry stretched his long arms above his head and arched his back. The pads of his fingers touched the ceiling. His hastily donned shirt rode up to reveal his defined abdominal muscles and a belly button dusted with dark hair. He drew his arms back down as though deflated and gave a sigh. "Come on, Miss Maguire." His tone sounded affectionate. "Let's get you behind that counter."

Jerry waited in the car park as Kit unlocked the front door of the shop and turned on the lights. Darkness shrouded the rest of the building, creating an eeriness Kit hadn't noticed before then. She gave him a wave and he wound down his window and called to her in a whisper. "I'm helping with a tour of the cathedral after lunch, so I might be a little late collecting you. Stay inside and don't go anywhere!" He raised an eyebrow and jabbed a finger at her to emphasise his command, and Kit wrinkled her nose. She didn't like being told what to do, and it irked her he'd taken control of her safety. But she thanked him with a wave and forced a smile of gratitude onto her lips. He meant well.

Kit dragged the newspaper delivery from outside the front door and deposited it in the back room. It took four agonising trips and the string dug into her fingers despite the cloth she wrapped around them. She left the list of recipients on top of the nearest stack and lifted the paperboys' bags off their respective hooks. The dinging of the cash register made her jump with alarm, and she ran to the front of the shop.

Mr Rashid stood behind the counter in a pair of lurid pyjamas. Silhouettes of the Taj Mahal covered the orange fabric as though a child had gone crazy with an ink stamp. His hair stuck up in a series of crests and he blinked as Kit shot around the corner. "I forgot to leave a float," he said. His fingers struggled to replace the drawer Kit hadn't noticed missing in the belly of the cash register.

"You scared the crap out of me," she admitted. "I've been getting things ready for the boys." She leaned on the counter and narrowed her eyes, waiting for him to comment on her lateness of five minutes. He said nothing, tipping coins into the drawers with frowned concentration. Kit twisted her lips in thought. "It hadn't occurred to me before now. But what if I'm in the back room and someone comes through the front door and helps themselves to products or money? What did you do when you were here alone?"

"I didn't worry about it." Mr Rashid's head bobbled on his neck. "You'll hear the front door alert and come straight to the counter. That's why the front door is heavy, so it takes longer than average to escape through it." He blinked up at her. "And anyone who wants to get into the cash register needs you and your access key."

An icy hand snaked around Kit's heart and gave her an added sense of vulnerability. She swallowed. "I didn't think of that," she admitted. She considered the special code she held in her head, which activated the register's functions if she left the counter for an extended period. An involuntary shiver ricocheted through her body. It made her feel anxious; bearing the key to everything. "Please can you hang around for another ten minutes while I load up the bags for the boys?" she asked. Her accompanying wince pleaded with him for clemency.

As usual, missing all the cues, Mr Rashid declined with a shake of his glossy head. "Mrs Rashid is waiting," he replied. He gave several blinks in quick succession and Kit pursed her lips in revulsion.

"Too much information," she growled, twisting her pretty features into an ugly mask. She flapped her hand to emphasise her point. But as Mr Rashid's bare feet padded back to the apartment upstairs, Kit hauled the last newspaper stack out onto the shop floor to continue loading the bags. It put her within sight of the front door and gave her an added sense of security. Someone had been inside her home, and the notion filled her with a combination of fear and indignation. That they'd left no evidence of their entry bothered her even more. It meant they could return.

Kit ran through security measures in her mind, but none of them seemed effective against an unknown but ballsy intruder who'd left Raki's bedroom light on and stolen her laptop. "Booby traps," she breathed, stuffing rolled newspapers into a sack bound for the new housing estate. Kit rose and shook her head. "Not a good idea. Not if Jerry needs to use the upstairs shower." She imagined the handsome vicar falling over unexpected trip wires and plunging down the stairs in his towel. Her cheeks gained an unhealthy flush at the thought of his towel parting company with his muscular body on the way down, and she flapped her hand in front of her face.

Kit finished filling the last bag in record time and carried the remaining newspapers to the stand near the counter. A loud honk from a vehicle outside made her jump as she straightened the uppermost paper. Kit screamed in fright as a man burst through the front door.

"Sorry!" he called over his shoulder. "I'm on a mission!" He grabbed several bottles of an energy drink from the chiller and an armful of chocolate bars. Then he unloaded everything onto the counter. Kit stared at the woollen socks of his characteristic tradesman's uniform. His dirty boots sat on the mat outside the front door, back lit by a brilliant sunrise. She galvanised herself into action. Ducking beneath the counter hatch, Kit stepped behind the cash register. A sharp sense of vulnerability made her fingers shake as she tapped in her code and the register lit up like a Christmas tree.

"Hurry up!" the man urged as a horn honked from outside the shop. "You're holding up the entire gang. We need to get on the building site and we're late." He dug in the pocket of his paint-stained shorts and yanked out a handful of notes and change. Coins rolled across the counter in his haste. "I think that's right," he said, gathering the products against his chest. "Keep the change." He left, navigating his way through the front door using one unoccupied finger and his right foot. Kit heard him chasing his dirty boots around under the awning.

"Get it together, Kit," she urged herself. She closed her eyes and pictured the items the man had bought and tapped their price into the register. It lit up with a total, but she'd already calculated it in her head. The change on the counter amounted to three dollars too much, and she sealed it into a plastic wallet in the register and labelled it as an overpay.

She jumped again as the buzzer on the front door sounded. By the time Mr Jim approached the counter with his carton of soymilk, Kit stood clutching her chest in the faint hope of calming her frantic heartbeat.

"Everything okay?" Mr Jim asked. "You look rattled this morning." The fluorescent lighting added highlights to his hazel irises, and the kindness in his expression made Kit want to cry. She gave a wavering, unconvincing nod and tapped the soymilk's price into the register. Mr Jim's voice sounded soft. "I have time to talk."

Kit swallowed and handed him the machine so he could swipe his cash card. "My flatmate bought a horse yesterday," she said. Her voice sounded hollow. "Apparently I own a paddock." She pursed her lips. "And a rusty shed. I shouldn't forget the rusty shed."

Mr Jim's eyes narrowed. "But that's not what's upsetting you, is it?"

Kit closed her eyes and released a sigh. "No. My friend is missing and bad things keep happening."

"What bad things?"

Kit squirmed. "Remember the man who climbed over the counter?" She continued without Mr Jim's acknowledgement. "I don't think he wanted money. He was a warning to me. I'm not the only person looking for Raki."

Mr Jim cocked his head. "You suspect your friend is in trouble? Or dead?" His tone sounded serious.

"No." Kit released a snort which contained relief. "He's not dead." She opened her mouth to speak and a horrible metallic clang sounded from outside the shop. Mr Jim froze and his brows knitted.

"What on earth was that?"

Kit shook her head and Mr Jim abandoned his soymilk on the counter. Kit followed him to the door and watched as he approached two utes embroiled in a fender bender at the junction with Gordonton Road. She smacked her lips and released a sigh. "Just as well," she breathed. "I was in grave danger of telling you everything, Mr Jim."

But the moment had acted as a catalyst, and the puzzle pieces began to line up and fall into place. Kit let the process complete itself. She gave herself a physical shake, as though an ethereal being had alighted on her back. "Of course," she breathed. "Of course."

Mr Jim returned ten minutes later, his hair ruffled by the brisk morning breeze and his brow furrowed. "Is it always like this?" he demanded, hauling his tie from over his left shoulder.

"What? Crazy?" Kit smiled. "Yeah. I guess I'm just used to it." She pushed his soymilk across the counter towards him. "Mr Rashid would have put that back on the shelf and made you buy it again." She grinned. "You're lucky it's me and not him."

Mr Jim cocked an eyebrow and twisted his lips into a grimace. "You'd tell me if something was very wrong, wouldn't you?" he asked. He cocked his head to one side like a quizzical owl, and Kit nodded.

"I'm fine," she replied.

"You were talking about your friend." Mr Jim leaned his elbows on the counter, settling in for the long haul. Kit winced and waved his attention away as though their previous conversation hadn't happened.

"It's okay. He'll turn up again." She fixed a beatific smile on her face and touched the scarf covering her head. "You should come in one afternoon," she urged, changing the subject with dizzying speed. "I'm only a Muslim in the mornings."

Mr Jim's dancing eyebrows expressed his confusion. The creases around his mouth grew more prominent as he gave a definitive nod. "I might just do that," he said. His smile looked as false as Kit's. "Have a nice day, Miss Maguire." He strode towards the door and paused, his hand on the handle. "I'd like to talk about your friend's disappearance. Perhaps when you have more time." A policeman's hunger for a good mystery shrouded him like a tangible mist. The door closed behind him and Kit let out the tension in her spine. She slouched against the counter with her head resting on her forearms.

"I'm only a Muslim in the mornings," she repeated. "And just plain crazy at all other times."

CHAPTER 30

Piper's Dilemma

Mr Rashid arrived behind the counter after the paperboys left. He'd combed his hair in an amusing centre parting which appealed to the older ladies. Mrs Miller chuckled as she paid for her haemorrhoid cream. Her crabbed fingers reached up to the counter and she sat forward in her wheelchair. "Ooh, you look just like an Indian Humphrey Bogart," she crooned. Her change slipped into her purse and she held Mr Rashid's fingers a little too long as he passed her the box of cream. "No, Omar Sharif," she gushed. "That's who you are. Ooh, I just loved him in Lawrence of Arabia."

Mr Rashid's head bobbled on his neck and he beamed. Kit watched in amusement as he preened himself beneath the glare of an octogenarian's misplaced and short-sighted adoration. "I am also liking Omar Sharif," he agreed with enthusiasm. "Omar Sharif was a very good Muslim."

"I'll call you that from now on, Omar." Mrs Miller attempted a coquettish smile and her bottom set of false teeth slid out onto her lower lip. Mr Rashid's eyeballs bugged and he swallowed.

"I'm taking my break now," Kit interjected. She didn't wait around for him to respond, pounding up the stairs to the bathroom in the apartment before he could start counting.

Her phone vibrated with a message from Piper as Kit peeled the green scarf from her ringlets. It just said, '*We need to talk.*' She gave her head a shake and admired the rigid cast created by Raki's lube. Then, instead of texting back, she dialled the number for her friend.

"I'll bring the lube to yours one night this week." Kit tweaked a curl and let it bounce back into place. "There isn't any flaxseed gel in the freezer. I'm trying to make the lube do everything today and it's looking pretty good."

"I need to talk to you now." Piper lowered her voice and Kit recognised the familiar sounds of the office she worked in until a few weeks ago. It felt like a window into a whole other life. "And not about lube."

"Okay. Just talk. I have exactly four minutes and twenty-eight seconds." Kit frowned at her watch. "What's wrong?"

She heard Piper swallow and stilled as her friend paused. Piper reduced her voice to a hoarse whisper. "Something terrible happened and I don't know what to do."

Kit frowned. Dread washed over her like ice sliding down her spine and she cursed herself for her inattention. "I suspected something was wrong at that disastrous Curly meeting. Sorry, Piper. I should have pursued it."

"Alec kissed me." Piper's words emerged in a rush and Kit heard her friend gulp. "I've dreaded telling you. My husband deserves to know, but I can't bring myself to say the words."

Kit leaned against the bathroom door and took special notice of her breaths. They seemed a little more laboured than usual, as though the tide had gone out before a tsunami. She waited for the ringing numbness to strike, surprised when it didn't. Piper's distressed, heavy breathing puffed through the phone and into her ear. Kit sighed. "I don't care about Alec," she replied, knowing in that moment that she didn't. "I care about you and what you do next."

"Oh, Kit!" Piper's voice lifted to a wail. "I need to leave here. Today."

Kit stared at the ceiling and sighed. "Look, I think it's a pattern with Alec. He has a knack for sensing vulnerability. Less than a week ago he came in here declaring his love for me. I suspect he's left a string of office girls broken and bleeding in his wake. It's up to you what you tell your husband, Piper, but I suggest the truth. I'm guessing he didn't force himself on you, did he? It's not his style."

"No." Piper gave a ragged sniff and Kit imagined her puffy eyes and down-turned lips. "He started it and I didn't stop him straight away."

Kit's heart ached for her friend. The scene sounded achingly familiar and she softened her tone. "Go home, Piper. Sort it out. Call me if you need me."

A gentle tap on the bathroom door made her jump and she shoved her phone into her pocket as Piper ended the call. "Coming!" Kit called.

"Mr Rashid wants you back in the shop," a female voice chimed. "Sorry dear."

"It's fine." Kit glanced at the time. She still had thirty seconds left of her break and she shook her head and unlocked the bathroom door.

CHAPTER 31

A Secret Curly for Raj

"I need to go to the Cash and Carry." Mr Rashid slammed the cash register drawer closed. "Raj is coming to cover the afternoon shift. He'll get here before you leave."

Mrs Rashid straightened her purple hijab and gave Kit a wink. "We'll check out wedding venues," she said, her face expression serious.

Kit's head jerked back in surprise. "Who's getting married?"

"My Raj." Mrs Rashid waggled her eyebrows and Mr Rashid's lips settled into a smug smile.

Kit's face lit up in happiness. "Oh, wow! Congratulations! He didn't mention it when I last saw him."

"That's because he hasn't asked you yet." Mrs Rashid's head bobbled on her neck in an exact imitation of her husband's. Mr Rashid ducked under the counter hatch and they bobbled out of the shop together. Kit stood on the mat in front of the counter and shook her head.

"They're deluded," she breathed. "And more than a little insane."

Kit tidied the shelving and labelled the out-of-date stock for a quick sale. When her phone rang in her back pocket, she expected to hear Piper's voice on the other end. She dragged it free and answered the call. "Are you at home?" she demanded.

"No." The male voice sounded surprised. Kit glanced over her shoulder and lowered her voice, stalking to the back of the shop.

"Where have you been?" she demanded. "We were worried sick!"

"I wanted to say sorry for scaring you." Raki's voice sounded strained and he snuffed through his nose. "For frightening you this morning. I didn't mean for that to happen."

"That was you?" Kit's voice rose. "Why didn't you stay and talk to us?"

"I thought you were doing the walk of shame. I guessed Jerry liked you, but I didn't realise you two were an item. You didn't need me pointing it out, did you?"

"We're not an item!" Kit hissed. "And Langdon was in the sleep-out too."

"Oh. Ohhhh." Raki drew out the word as though undergoing a slow realisation. "Gee, I've missed a heap."

"Why did you break into the house?" Kit demanded. "Why not come to the front door during daylight?"

"You know why!" Raki's tone changed. "And I didn't break into the house. I used my key. I've taken all the tech. Just in case."

"In case what?" Hysteria bubbled beneath the surface of Kit's psyche. She struggled to stop it overflowing as curses and foot stamping.

"In case I left any data on it. Kasouf can't have it, Kit. It's important. I found out he was using the carrier to administer drugs to old people."

"What?" Kit shook her head and blinked. The door chimed as a customer entered the shop. "How?"

"Massages." Raki swallowed and became quiet for a moment. Kit moved around the shop, realising she'd missed the identity of the new customer. She saw a flash of blue fabric as a pair of man's legs walked along the toilet roll aisle. Her voice lowered to a whisper.

"Massages?" She gasped as the information clarified in her mind. "He's been drugging people through massages. Oh my goodness! My mother and her Bitch and Stitch group go to him. Kasouf's been getting my mother high!" Kit's hands balled into fists as her brain became stuck on that one fact. "She said he had dreamy hands."

Raki made a sound like a humph. "I bet. Look, I've destroyed all the data. I'll go to the cops soon. Sorry for bringing this mess to your door, but please believe me, I'm not a bad person. I've done none of what they're saying."

"It's okay," Kit gushed. "I know you haven't. But I spoke to Jackson. He said someone was looking into it."

"Jackson the cop? No, Kit! No!" Raki's voice rose, sounding tinny through the phone's speaker. "You won't know who to trust!" Distracted, Kit walked to the end of the toiletry aisle and around the corner. She shook her head in confusion, finding no one there. Walking to the other end of the aisle, she back tracked and stalked along the wall nearest the back of the shop. Raki's protests dulled in her ear and she frowned as she heard the distinct click of him ending the call.

"Damn!" she whispered. "I forgot to ask if he ate the Pineapple Lumps." Shoving her phone into her pocket, she walked towards the front of the shop. She didn't like someone being in the store without her knowing what they were doing. Raki's situation made her twitchy, and the high shelving offered far too many blind spots.

Kit reached the counter and slipped beneath the hatch. She peered at the security monitor next to the cash register and clicked a few buttons to zoom in on the cameras dotted around the shop. She checked the camera covering the counter and saw a black-and-white image of herself bent towards the screen. The flash of movement came too late to prepare her.

Kit squeaked as the man appeared in her eye line. "Oh, it's you." She grabbed her chest and gave a peculiar, high laugh. "You scared me," she admitted. "Where were you hiding?"

The dark-haired man quirked an eyebrow but didn't answer. He placed nothing on the counter to give Kit's shaking fingers something to key into the cash register. A heightened awareness of his silence sent Kit's brain out of sync with her mouth and her lips parted before she could stop them. "I guess you're good at hiding," she gushed. "You know, with your job."

The man's eyes gave the slightest flicker of a hidden emotion before he straightened the smart suit jacket covering a pristine white shirt. His lips curved into a smile.

"We should talk," he said. "Now." A clipped English accent made his command sound official.

Kit shook her head and waved a hand at the cash register. "I can't leave the shop." She fixed a smile on her lips. "I don't finish until two o'clock. You could come back then?" The door buzzer jangled, but the man cleared his throat as she raised herself on tiptoes to glance towards the door.

He fixed a lean hand around his necktie and gave it a tug. His fingers slipped behind his collar and popped open the top button. "Okay," he said, seeming to consider her suggestion with seriousness. He flicked his hand over and inspected an expensive gold watch. "I'll wait for you outside at two o'clock." Blue irises sparkled from behind long, dark lashes and Kit held her breath as he gasped and jumped backwards.

"I forgot my bunion plasters." Mrs Miller wheeled her mobility scooter across the cop's foot and he hissed in pain. Kit winced in sympathy and mouthed an apology to him. Mrs Miller peered up at him through glasses like old bottles and waved her hand. "I forgot all about it on account of meeting Omar Sharif," she said. Her aged voice crackled. "I put my best undies on specially. Where is he?"

"He nipped out." Kit pursed her lips and hovered behind the counter. "Do you want me to fetch the plasters for you?"

"Na." Mrs Miller's face crumpled into a series of creases as the disappointment took hold. Her shoulders slumped. "Is he in tomorrow? I'll come back for the plasters, but I can't promise my best undies will still be clean."

"He'll start work around nine o'clock." Kit bestowed a fond smile on the old lady and stirred the pot of mischief with a wooden spoon. "He always says how much he loves seeing you."

"He does?" Mrs Miller brightened. "That's nice. Mrs Truman said he likes her better. She said he came at her with a handful of kinky lube the other day. That's not fair!" She raised a gnarled fist and shook it. "He only gives me special permission to ride my scooter in here, but she said she rode right around the shop with him chasing her."

Kit shook her head. "That's not the exact truth," she admitted. "You come back for your bunion plasters tomorrow and see Mr Rashid."

"Sharif!" Mrs Millar swung her scooter in a wide arc and knocked a packet of crumpets off the shelf. "Omar Sharif."

"Okay." Kit watched her mow her way over another three customers before exiting the shop. She lifted the counter hatch and retrieved the fallen crumpets. Then she realised the undercover cop had left.

The time seemed to pass extra slow as Kit waited for two o'clock and the cop's return. She selected a box of chocolates from the top shelf of the confectionery aisle to thank him for looking out for her even before she knew of his existence. She wrote a note for Mr Rashid and popped it in the cash register, asking him to take the amount out of her wages. Mrs Miller returned twice more for her bunion plasters, having forgotten the other visits but remembering she had a date with Omar Sharif. Kit dealt with the shop's familiar operation in between constant checks of her phone for a message from Piper. She fired off a couple of texts when the waiting got too difficult. The first went to Jerry, informing him she didn't need a ride home. The second went to Piper expressing her support. Neither one received an answer.

When her phone rang before two o'clock, she answered it with caution. Raki had sounded apoplectic about her confessing his situation to Jackson and she wasn't keen on a repeat performance. She squared her shoulders and lifted the phone to her ear without speaking. Appropriate sentences formed on her tongue, ready to tell Raki exactly how his disappearing act and fake burglary antics had affected her and the boys.

"Hey, Maguire." Jackson's voice sounded cheerful and Kit relaxed.

"Hey," she replied. "What's up? Are you still holding my scissors hostage, or can I have them back now?"

Jackson sighed on the other end of the call and made a pretence of dragging out his answer. "Yeah," he said eventually. "I can drop them off, as long as you promise not to stick them in my forehead."

"I promise." Kit smiled. "But don't drop them off today. I'm about to leave."

"Oh." A trace of disappointment sounded in his less jovial tone. "Okay. I'll swing by tomorrow for another ear-hole, eye-hole and ass-hole sandwich."

Kit snorted. "Don't tell Mr Rashid I call them that, will you? He'll go nuts."

"What's it worth?" Jackson's tone reverted to flirtatious and a warm feeling spread outward from the pit of Kit's stomach.

"I'm not sure," she replied. "Oh, I met your friend." She checked the clock on the wall and sighed. The shorter hand hovered over the number two, but the long hand had fallen off weeks ago. Mr Rashid refused to replace it. He said he could still tell the time using it. Kit jiggled the phone, so she could read the small digital time at the top of the screen. Jackson spoke, sounding faraway and she pushed it back over her ear as a customer approached the counter. "Raj is late," she grumbled.

"My friend?" Jackson sounded confused. "I don't have a friend called Raj."

"Oh, never mind." Kit fixed a fake smile on her lips and shifted the phone into her other hand. She reached across the counter to check the price of a packet of soup. "They're a dollar each."

"How much?" The woman's lips formed into a disgusted 'o'. "That's expensive."

Kit frowned and pointed to the price tag situated below the manufacturer's logo. "Sorry. That's what it says," she countered. The woman slapped another six on the counter and they slid sideways. Each of them wore a clear price tag. "One second," Kit said to the customer. She needed both hands to collect the soup into a pile. To Jackson, she said, "I need to go, but he's coming back soon and I'll know more when I've seen him."

"No, Kit, don't hang up on me. What friend? Don't hang up!"

Kit hung up. She dealt with the grumpy customer and her soup fetish and smiled through the next four sales. Busyness forced her to ignore the vibrations shaking her left buttock as the phone danced in her pocket. Raj blasted through the front door and she frowned at him. "Your parents are supposedly at the Cash and Carry," she told him. "But your mother is secretly checking out wedding venues for your upcoming nuptials. And you're late!"

Raj groaned and lifted the hatch. His tee shirt flexed across his pectorals and he walked with a limp. "Thing is," he began, "I've hurt my ankle and I need to get it checked. The first available appointment is this afternoon. I tried to ring you, but I got your voicemail."

Kit's jaw hung slack and she jabbed a finger at the telephone fixed to the wall behind him. "I was speaking to Jackson; that's why. Duh! Why didn't you call that one?"

Raj shrugged. "I didn't think about it. But my doctor's appointment is in twenty minutes. Why isn't Dad here?" He paused and cocked his head. "I'm not meant to be working here this afternoon. And what nuptials?"

Kit waved her hand and puffed out a breath of frustration. "I can't stay, Raj! Shut the shop."

"Shut the shop?" Raj's jaw hung as though the hinge had broken. "Shut the shop?" he repeated.

"I'm meeting someone." Kit smiled at the last customer as the man collected his wallet, keys and a bottle of shower gel off the counter. "Thank you," she called after him. She turned to Raj and her smile descended into a glare. "It's after two o'clock. You're meant to cover the afternoon shift. I need to leave."

"Please, don't leave!" Raj wailed. He lifted his left leg and dangled his foot as though it might persuade Kit to change her mind. "It hurts!"

"How did you do it?" Kit narrowed her eyes and stared at Raj's foot. He'd wedged it into a flip-flop and the skin bulged around the straps like a banana straining at the skin. She wrinkled her nose. "It looks sore."

"It is sore." Raj clasped his hands in front of him in a prayer-like action. "Please, help me. Let me go to my doctor's appointment. I'll come straight back."

"How did you do it?" Kit repeated. Her lips quirked upwards and her eyes crinkled at the sides. "Your reluctance to tell me is making me suspicious."

Raj groaned and covered his face with both hands. "I've been seeing this girl. We drove back to her place for the first time and I asked to use the bathroom. I swear the lube just exploded in my face. It covered the bathroom! I slipped on the tiles and accidentally put a hole through her bathroom door with my foot. She threw me out."

"Lube?" Kit's head jerked back, but her feet edged closer. "You're saying it just exploded?"

"Yes!" Raj dragged his hands away and his features drooped into a sad expression. "I was washing my hands and noticed it sitting on the side of the sink. She said she used it for her hair."

"And you picked it up to look at it? Gross." Kit frowned.

Raj squirmed. His words emerged as a whisper. "Yeah. And it blew."

"Okay." Kit swallowed. "Does your girlfriend have curly hair?"

Raj shook his head and then changed it to a nod. "She's not my girlfriend. Not likely to be now, either. Apparently, there's a shortage and yes, she has curly hair. She went nuts and threw me out."

"Sorry." Kit's mind processed the information and her sense of empathy took a back seat. "Did you notice anything unusual about the tube before it exploded? How much did it contain?"

"I don't know!" Raj bit. "She said it was new and she paid too much for it because the woman who sold it to her is a real shark. Can I go to my doctor's appointment or not?"

Kit let her head fall back against her shoulders and she groaned. "Fine! Go! But I want to talk more about the lube when you get back. I think your new girlfriend is one of our Curlies and she got the lube from Debbie."

Raj didn't wait for further discussion. He limped from behind the counter and used every surface available to haul himself towards the front door like a baby trying out its first steps. Kit sighed and stared at a stain on the ceiling above her. The cop would guess she'd stood him up by now, but at least he knew where to find her.

CHAPTER 32

A Curly Crisis

"I'm sorry, I'm sorry." Kit winced as the dark-haired cop's appearance in the doorway triggered the buzzer. Her phone vibrated in her back pocket, sending a wave of tingling sensations over her left buttock. "Something happened to Raj. He's gone to the doctor's, so he can't cover the afternoon shift. Mr Rashid never answers his phone in the Cash and Carry while he's searching for bargains."

The man shrugged. "Shut the shop." He glanced around him with a look of dismissal creeping into his expression. Lifting his wrist, he checked his watch and his lips curved downward into a pout. His other hand snaked through his hair. "We need to talk."

"I know." Kit looked at the security monitor and her gaze flicked over the view from the cameras. Their unique perspectives of the shop showed that for once, no customers browsed the shelves or tried to secrete product about their person without her noticing. "We can talk here," she suggested. "We have a few minutes until another customer arrives."

He released a grunt of exasperation and stepped up to the counter. His gaze seemed to drink in everything at once as his eyes flicked to Kit and then the goods stacked in cabinets behind her. His full lips pursed in irritation. "We should go somewhere else," he insisted. "Not here." Dark eyelashes fluttered as he assessed the camera above Kit's head, which monitored the cash register and her movements.

"It's fine." Kit shook her head as she followed his gaze. "There's no audio. Buy something and it'll look like we're just passing the time." She frowned. "Anyway, I'm working overtime, so Mr Rashid can't tell me off for chatting. He won't pay me for this."

The cop sighed and shook his head. "I want nothing. You said you'd come with me."

Irritation burgeoned in Kit's chest and she bridled at the man's sense of superiority. Her phone started its jig in her pocket again and she dragged it out and looked at the screen. Jackson's number strobed with every silent ring. "What?" Kit pressed the button to activate the call, giving Jackson the full force of her aggravation. The undercover cop's dark eyes widened.

"Kit, I need to talk to you." Jackson's tone held urgency and she heard an echoing sound as though he'd called from his car. She sighed and shook her head.

"Join the queue," she snapped. "Everyone wants to talk to me today and I don't have time."

"What did you mean when you said you met my friend?" The crackle of radio static cut across the line and Kit frowned.

Awkwardness descended as she stared at the man tapping his fingers on top of the newspaper headline. With a bright flash of inspiration, she remembered the chocolates and reached beneath the counter for the box. "Your friend," she said to Jackson. "The one you told me about the other night." She fixed a demented smile onto her lips and pushed the gift across the counter towards the cop. More static mangled Jackson's reply, and Kit killed the call and shoved her phone into her back pocket. "These are for you," she said, edging the chocolates nearer the cop's tapping fingers. "To say thank you."

He cocked his head and frowned. "For what?"

"Looking out for me." She watched as his fingers touched the cellophane covering the pretty box. When he looked up at her, a pleasant smile spread across his lips.

"Thank you," he said and his body language relaxed by visible degrees. "You're welcome. I'm looking out for you when I tell you it's important we talk now. Please."

"Okay." Kit frowned and tutted. "I can't leave the money in the register. I need to lock it away before I leave." Her foot tapped against the tiles as she ran scenarios through her head. Mr Rashid or one of his sons always dealt with the cash register. She patted her jeans pockets and contemplated taking the notes with her, but dismissed the thought straight away. Too risky. A hole in the toe of her trainer distracted her as she missed her comfy plimsolls. She sighed. "It's been a hell of a week."

"Tell me about it." The cop's English accent sounded clipped against the strain in his voice. Impatience bristled like invisible hedgehog spines over his body. Kit's mind produced a stunning brain wave and she grinned.

"I know what I'll do," she said. She contemplated the camera behind her head and made a plan. "Just stand near the door," she instructed. "This will take me two minutes and then we'll leave."

The cop gritted his teeth and took a halting step away from the counter. He didn't go far, as though not trusting Kit to honour her word. Lifting a magazine from the stand, he browsed without interest.

Kit ignored him, grabbing a thick, black pen from under the counter and flipping over a flyer to write on its reverse. "I CAN'T STAY," she wrote in her neat, slanted hand. "I'M PUTTING THE CASH DRAWER IN THE DODGY TOILET." Then in a moment of sheer genius, she held her note up in front of the camera.

Tearing up the note and shoving it into the rubbish bin, Kit grabbed the cash drawer and killed the power to the register. She lifted the counter hatch and slid through the gap. "I'm just putting this away," she said, holding up the drawer. "I won't be a second."

A frown furrowed the cop's forehead into deep lines as Kit blasted past him. She jogged to the back of the shop and ran past the sacks dangling from their pegs. The toilet door opened with ease, its new architrave still waiting for a coat of paint. Kit shoved the cash drawer into the vanity unit and groaned as it wouldn't fit far enough back for her to close the door. "What now?" she complained.

Getting down on her knees, she pulled the drawer back out and looked behind it. Three tubes of purple-willy-shaped lube stood at the back of the cupboard like little soldiers. Kit frowned. "Why are they there?" she hissed. The one in the centre of the three looked emptier than the others, but only by a slight amount. Kit let the drawer rest across her thighs as she reached in and grabbed it. Her eyes narrowed into angry slits. "So, you thought you'd get your money back from me for more than you lost," she mused, considering the thought patterns of her wily employer. He'd claimed that two had exploded and he'd got rid of the rest. "You rotten liar!" Kit breathed. "You kept a stash for yourself!"

"What's the delay?" The cop sounded aggrieved, and Kit jumped at the sound of his voice. His footsteps echoed as he walked through the storeroom and past the newspaper sacks.

"Sorry!" Kit moved the lubes aside with the back of her hand and shoved the cash drawer into the space. It fitted enough for her to close the door. The cop's footsteps reached the bathroom and Kit's eyes widened as she noticed the last tube of purple-willy-shaped lube still in her hand. Her cheeks flushed with embarrassment and a deft sleight of hand sent it into the sleeve of her sweatshirt. It nestled above the cuff and she bunched the end of her sleeve into her fingers to stop it falling out again. "I'm done!" she gushed, her tone extra light. She depressed the button in the centre of the door handle and held her breath as it popped straight out again. "The miserable old cheap skate!" she cursed. "He repaired the door frame but left the old lock." Closer inspection revealed a line of grease trickling down the back of the door. Mr Rashid had put oil in the mechanism instead of replacing it. A grin spread across Kit's lips as the cop's smart business suit filled the doorway. "Good luck to him ever getting his money back out," she said in a sing-song voice. She depressed the button once more and the lock held. Then she closed the door behind her.

CHAPTER 33

No Way Out

The undercover police officer waited as Kit locked up the shop and poked the key into her pocket. The tube of lube bulged in her sleeve and pulled the fabric taut, but the cop didn't notice. He seemed impatient to get her into the expensive silver car parked at right angles to the front door. Deactivating the central locking with a decisive jab of his key, he hauled open the passenger door and tapped an impatient beat on the handle.

Kit turned with a smile which drooped as her phone vibrated in her pocket again. She pulled it free and winced as Jerry's phone number scrolled across the screen. She fumbled the button one-handed and watched as his call went to voicemail. Kit winced. "I should apologise," she mused. "He wanted to fetch me from work."

"Just get in the car!" The cop rolled his eyes in frustration and a vein began a warning tick in his jaw. Something about his demeanour made Kit stop and take stock of her situation. She needed peace to think and as though to intensify her confusion, her phone began its familiar vibration in her hand.

Kit swallowed. "I didn't catch your name," she said. The soles of her trainers scratched against the grit underfoot.

"I'll explain everything. Get in the car." The man jerked his head at the passenger seat and Kit's heart gave a frightened lurch in her chest.

"Explain here," she said, her voice wavering. "I don't want to get into the car. I don't know you."

"Get. In. The. Car."

Kit backed until her spine touched the glass of the wide shop window. "No." She gulped. "You're not a police officer, are you?" She blinked and looked at him as though for the first time. Nothing fitted. The car looked too expensive, the range of pinstriped suits too extensive, and then the obvious issue of the man's name. He hadn't given it to her and so she asked him again. "Tell me your name," she demanded.

He paused with his hand on the top of the open door. Then he tilted his head back to face the sun and closed his eyes. It looked like he had started counting to ten. "Get in the car." He spoke through gritted teeth and Kit slid sideways along the window, keeping the man in her peripheral vision as she headed back towards the shop door.

He gave a sigh and slammed the passenger side door. Placing his hands on his narrow hips, he glared at Kit. "You'd rather I dressed like a drug dealer?" he demanded. "Come with me or don't come with me. I don't care. I have information about your friend, but it's clear I misjudged your interest." He gave a shrug of his broad shoulders, skirted the rear of the vehicle and climbed into the driver's seat.

With the pressure in her chest lessened by his sudden lack of urgency, Kit reassessed her situation through a different lens. She regretted her haste and convinced herself he'd proved his point. His disinterest made her fearful for Raki and curious for the promised news of him. A kidnapper would have shoved her into the car when he had the opportunity. But he didn't.

As if to solidify her decision, another car pulled up across the road. The beaten up, dirty brown Toyota had seen better days. A nasty rattle emanated from its exhaust, accompanied by a belch of black smoke. Kit's eyes widened at the sight of the driver as he leaned across and fiddled with something in his glove box. The red beard gave him a rugged, dangerous appearance. Without the hoodie pulled high over his head, she noticed shaved, blond hair. A pair of dark sunglasses perched above his eyebrows. As Kit watched, he flipped them down over his eyes with a deft movement and turned in her direction.

The man in the smart suit started his engine. A gentle purr rumbled from beneath the hood. Kit burst into action. She pushed herself away from the shop window and stumbled in the grit as she jogged towards the car. "Wait!" she cried. With her phone in one hand and the lube wedged in her other sleeve, she fumbled to open the car door.

The driver leaned across to give it a helpful shove and Kit clambered inside at the same moment the red bearded man exited his vehicle. Glancing down, she realised her terrible error of judgement too late. A yellow university parking pass protruded from the cup holder and Kit jabbed her phone at it. "Why do you have one of those?" she demanded. The blush of exertion faded from her cheeks. "Cops don't have parking passes for the university. They can park anywhere. Who are you?"

The man gave a low chuckle and as her door clicked shut behind her, he activated the central locking. "We're going for drive and then you'll tell me where my data is," he snarled.

"But what about Raki?" Kit's voice emerged as a squeak. She dropped her phone into her lap and yanked on the door lock, but he'd already pressed a switch beneath the driver's window and turned on the kiddie locks. Her door remained fast against her struggling, only openable from the outside of the car. "I know nothing about your data. Where's Raki?"

The man snorted and looked over his shoulder at the road behind them. An SUV drove past, followed by a smaller vehicle, and he waited for a space. "Whatever! I didn't come all this way for nothing! Phoning you didn't work, so I thought a personal visit might jog your memory. Start talking girly. I'd rather not hurt you. The stupid kid said he was onto something, but it turns out he needed help."

"Raki needed help?" Kit hated the pitiful tone in her question.

The fake cop rolled his eyes. "No! The other one. Mr Doctoral-Science-Expert. He just wanted a free pass to a new life. He doesn't get to stay here until he delivers the goods." The man cast a roving eye over Kit's curls and his irises sparkled. "Clever idea, trying to marry a citizen."

"I wasn't gonna do it. Please, let me out!" Kit held her breath as he spied a gap in the traffic. "Oh no. You phoned me last night and threatened me? You sent the man with the machete?" She blinked and stopped riving on the door handle.

He stamped his foot on the accelerator and the car shot backwards. She lurched forward and her phone flew from her lap. It began vibrating as it arced through the air but stopped when it hit the windscreen. Desperate to save herself without a seat belt, Kit reached out to slam her right hand on the dashboard. The purple-willy-shaped lube sailed from her sleeve and got there first.

A sigh and a splat followed a muted pop. The tube cracked on impact and disgorged its contents over both occupants of the vehicle. Tyres screeched as the driver gave a strangled yell of shock and pressed down on the accelerator. He released the steering wheel to cover both eyes with his hands. His fingers clawed at the sticky mess stinging his eyeballs and the expensive vehicle careened backwards. It reversed across the road at speed and clipped the front of the beat-up Toyota parked behind it. The sound of screeching metal filled the airwaves as the Toyota's bumper peeled clean off and the bonnet shot open like a yawning mouth.

Kit held her breath as the car continued its backward trajectory, an airbag filling her view. "No, no, no!" she wailed as her fingers scrabbled for purchase on the taut fabric and her legs slid beneath it in the foot well. Clear, greasy lube covered her face, but her closed eyes had spared her the same blindness as the driver. Over the airbag, she noticed the shop growing smaller in the distance before disappearing completely. The vehicle's shiny bonnet seemed to rise like the crescendo of a dance in front of her and Kit watched the brilliant blueness of the summer sky replace it. An unhealthy grinding sound occupied her mind as she became airborne and hit the ceiling with her face. The distended airbag drove her backwards into the seat like an out-of-control boxing glove.

Silence filled the aftermath, punctuated by metallic groans and the sound of her own breathing. Kit tried to push herself up, confused by the reclined angle of the seat. She lay on her back and her limbs seemed reluctant to obey her instructions, leaden and heavier than usual. Her phone had landed on the seat next to her hand and as she touched its broken screen, she dislodged it and watched it shoot backwards past her. It landed with a clunk somewhere behind her seat. The brilliant blue sky looked like an azure canvas and she lifted a heavy hand to wipe lube from her lashes. Greasy blood coated her fingers and left a trail across the deflating airbag.

Kit gasped as the passenger window shattered in her peripheral vision before hanging like a curtain next to her face. A hand punched through it, followed by an elbow which used its sleeve to clear the shards from around the frame. Disembodied fingers reached for the button to unlock the door and then disappeared. A male voice shouted, "It's stuck! I can't open it. The gully's filling. They must have opened the dam after all the rain the other day!"

Kit glanced to her left and a sliver of sunburned grass appeared between the door and the chassis. The earth tilted at an odd angle and a pair of scuffed trainers scrabbled for grip on the slanted ground. The sky above her face and the strange sloping of the earth laid out a code which she struggled to decipher. Then it hit her like a second impact. "I'm upside down in here!" she wailed.

Panic sent adrenaline through Kit's bloodstream as she forced her stomach to lift her to a more upright position. Her elbows braced her against the seat and the windscreen offered a different view. The car had reversed into the gully across the road from the shop, and Kit craned her neck to look through the rear window. The boot of the expensive saloon obliterated the view, bent up like a duck's tail and shoved clean through the glass.

"Help!" she squeaked. "Help!" The sound of trickling water electrified her senses and activated her primal need for survival. A fear of drowning obscured all other threats.

The driver remained silent next to her and his seat belt and airbag pinned him in place. His arms lay limp on either side of him as though offering a silent embrace to an invisible lover. He breathed into the airbag's puffy fabric and Kit saw blood. She flailed her right arm and thudded her fist against his shoulder. "We need to get out!" she shouted. Her voice sounded overloud in the eerie silence. "Wake up now! We need to get out!"

Panic drove her actions as she scrabbled at the gap created by the broken side window. Her body hung at an awkward angle as she shifted sideways, half on the seat with her shoulder leaned against the door. Blood stained her fingers as she searched for an escape through the remains of the glass. The driver stirred next to her and issued a mumbled curse.

A face appeared at the window, the sunglasses discarded and flecked brown eyes peering back at her. Kit released a cry of dismay at the sight of the familiar red beard. The last thing she remembered was blinking and seeing the lube turning red in front of her eyes. Then her mind filled with the unmistakable sound of running water.

CHAPTER 34

Curly Breaks

The next few hours were a blur as Kit realised the full extent of her own stupidity. She slumped on the hospital bed as her single visitor contemplated her from a hard-backed chair at the end of her cubicle.

"A broken nose. Wow!" Piper blinked, creating the effect of a rabbit facing oncoming headlights. Her swollen eyes and the hitch in her chest revealed a woman on the edge. "You and Alec will match now." She swallowed and her chin wobbled.

Kit groaned and exercised all her self-restraint not to touch the tight dressing covering the bridge of her nose. It hurt enough the first four times. "Does it dook bad?" she asked, her voice distorted by the swelling occupying the space beneath her eyes.

"I don't know." Piper sniffed and wiped her nose on her sleeve. "He only punched him once. I forgot what a great left hook he had. It's how we met in the first place, he defended me from a drunk kid at a university disco."

"Dot him! Be!" Kit jabbed a finger at her face, and Piper made a show of collecting herself.

"No. Not bad at all. A little black under your eyes, but the doctor said you won't need surgery. It should heal without scarring."

"Fine!" Kit grumbled. She huffed at the thin sheet covering her legs and stared at the patients gathered in the small bay which made up the temporary ward. A range of mysterious ailments lurked in between the effects of drunken brawls, minor car accidents, a broken arm and Alec. "Pull de turtain," she demanded, making a tugging motion with her hand. "I don't dant to dook at him."

Piper rose and swished the curtain closed against the sight of Alec's pitiful expression. Pure rotten luck sent him staggering into the emergency room at the same moment as the ambulance delivered Kit. As blood trumped pain, he'd jumped the queue and ended up on the other side of the thin curtain material.

"I'm pressing charges!" he called through the fabric. "I'm having your husband arrested."

Piper gasped and pressed her knuckles into her eyes. She took a giant inhalation and Kit thought she might explode. "Oben it!" Kit snapped. She flapped her hand at the fabric again. Piper obliged, her movements wooden. She didn't once look at Alec but stood with her back to him as Kit swung her feet off the bed and watched the floor rise up and down like the deck of a ship.

She glared at Alec, her vision swimming and producing four of him. They were all dicks. Kit lifted a blood-stained finger and jabbed it at him. "You dust dry it!" she snarled. Her voice sounded throaty and venomous, tiredness and pain dragging out the vowel sounds. "You dink your reputation can stand another dock, do you?"

"Huh?" Piper squinted at Kit for a second before the realisation sank into her brain. Then she seized on the weapon handed to her. "Yeah!" She raised her shoulders and straightened her spine, losing the victim's stance and mentality. "That's right. Roy's Motors took a terrible hit with the auction rigging scandal." She gave a disgusting sniff, which made Kit wonder why anyone in their right mind would ever want to kiss her friend. "I wonder how a sexual harassment claim might look in the media."

"Do smoke widout fire," Kit chimed in, her voice containing a sing-song element. "I'd have to dell my dory too. Dat's real bad dews."

Alec swallowed and pulled the blood red wadding away from his top lip. "Dou douldn't!" he gasped. He sounded genuinely shocked.

"Dep!" Kit narrowed her eyes as much as she dared without intensifying her incredible headache. "I dould!"

Alec huffed as Piper swished the thin curtain closed again. She slumped back into the visitor's chair and buried her face in her hands. Kit settled back on the bed and played with the controls for a while, sitting herself up and then laying down again. It seemed impossible to find a position where she didn't feel like her nose might burst off her face.

A nurse discharged Alec with a leaflet and a prescription for mild painkillers. Kit heard her warning him about concussion. The soles of his shoes tapped past the end of her bed and she heaved a sigh of relief.

Piper gave her a sad smile. "It was as much my fault as his," she conceded. "It's not fair to let him take all the blame."

Kit nodded, suspecting Piper's husband might have more to say on the matter. She imagined things evening up somehow. "Where de baby?" she asked.

"Still in day-care." Piper gave her a wan smile. "Things were just kicking off at work when you called me. I'll fetch her soon." She sighed. "I'm looking forward to not having to leave her tomorrow. Even if I end up divorced."

"Do should dalk dore." Kit gave a knowing nod. "But dankoo for doming."

Piper grinned from behind her tears. "You sound so funny," she said. "Can you get paid leave? I can't imagine Mr Rashid wanting your panda-face standing next to him dribbling for the next few days."

Kit leaned her head back against the crinkling pillows and closed her eyes. The movement provided a little welcome relief and she managed a weary sigh. The swish of the cubicle curtain made her jump and a male nurse appeared next to the bed. "Ouch!" she groaned as her nose throbbed.

"Right, Miss Maguire. You're good to go home now. Is there someone who can look after you for the next twenty-four hours? They need to watch you for the effects of concussion because you lost consciousness. Can someone do that?"

Kit blew out a breath and sized up her options. The hospital hadn't been able to reach Marian and she groaned at the thought of staying with her. In between her mother's fussing, Steph's curiosity and Kenny's indifference, she reasoned she'd rather take her chances at the flat.

Piper winced. "Sorry, Kit. I need to go home and sort my life out."

"It's okay. I was only out for a dupple of deconds."

"Oh, excuse me!" The nurse jumped as the curtain at the end of Kit's bed swished open and a crowd piled into the cubicle. "You can't come in here." He raised a hand in protest before registering the collective uniforms which encircled Kit's bed. "Sorry, Vicar," he said to Langdon. His eyes took in the black shirt and pristine white dog collar. A surprised blink acknowledged the power of two as Jerry strode in behind him. Jackson slid through after them and the tiny space became crowded.

"I'll take her home," Jackson said. His chest swelled beneath his Kevlar vest as the vicars flexed their muscles and faced him. Kit closed her eyes as her stupidity magnified itself in Jackson's presence. She knew he wanted to talk about it. She didn't want to discuss it anytime soon.

"We're taking her home," Jerry asserted. His previous life as a defence barrister had given him a wariness of police officers and he glowered at Jackson through unveiled dislike.

Piper rose and pushed her way through the gathered testosterone to plant a gentle kiss on Kit's sore cheek. She wrinkled her nose. "You're sticky," she commented. "I'll call you when I know what's happening."

Kit shook her head and shrugged. "Dow phone," she replied, her tone sad. "It bashed in de car." She pointed to her cheek. "De Dube exploded."

Piper shook her head. "I wish I knew what you were saying."

"Call me instead," Langdon suggested. His trademark smile warmed the frosty atmosphere. Deft fingers yanked his phone from his trouser pocket and activated the screen. "We can swap numbers and I'll pass on any messages if you like?" He jerked his head at Kit. "Her boss keeps texting me, anyway. Something about not being able to get his cash register drawer out of the toilet. I'll go outside to return his call."

"Thanks." Piper gave a feckless wave over her shoulder and ducked under Langdon's arm as he held back the curtain. He followed her out and his voice rumbled along the corridor.

Kit released a groan and watched the nurse as he sized up the remaining rivals for custody of his patient. She gave him a wry smile, which involved more teeth than she would have liked. "Dey're fine," she murmured. "Dey'll duke it out."

The nurse's eyes widened with an expression which suggested he rather hoped they didn't. He pressed a slew of paperwork into Kit's hand. "A prescription for painkillers and a leaflet about concussion," he said. His gaze flicked from Jerry to Jackson and then back to her. The men had stopped their silent show of aggression and waited for the nurse to finish.

Jerry's phone trilled into the heavy silence and he drew it from his pocket and glowered at it. "Damn!" he growled. "I just need to nip to the geriatric ward. Shouldn't take long."

"Somebody died?" Sarcasm laced Jackson's tone and Jerry lifted a hand and touched his clerical collar as though seeking divine guidance.

"Not yet," he snarled in reply. Turning his back on Jackson, he studied Kit with an intensity in his brown irises. "I wasn't far away," he said, lowering his voice. "When you texted me, I turned around and I shouldn't have. I should have ignored you and just come to the shop, anyway."

Kit frowned and the action hurt. She released a sigh and waved away his guilt. "Dot your fault," she said. "Only byself to blame."

Jerry tutted and his kiss grazed her forehead. "You're a worry, Kit Maguire," he whispered. "A real conundrum." Giving her a wink which held affection and gratitude, Jerry followed the nurse through the lifted curtain.

"And den dere was one." Kit sighed and lifted herself off the mattress. The tiled floor seemed a long way down. Jackson smiled and the action changed his face, shining light into dark corners of his soul and crinkling the skin next to his eyes.

"So, there was," he agreed, holding out his hand.

"I dow." Kit nodded and the action set off the pulsing behind her eyeballs again. "I dow you dant to dalk about it. Dot yet, okay?"

"Too bloody right I want to talk about it." Jackson interpreted Kit's jumbled speech with an exaggerated eye roll. He shook his head. "But I think I'll wait until I can get the full effect of your discomfort before I put the boot in properly." His eyes crinkled at the edges as he pointed to her face. "I want to appreciate the exotic blush of your embarrassment and the puffiness and the gauze means I might miss some of it." His sigh spoke more than his words. "And then there's the full apology you'll make. I don't want it garbled. I want to understand what you're saying. So you'll keep, Maguire. You'll keep."

CHAPTER 35

Curly Confusion

Everything hurt. From fitting her feet into her trainers and waiting for Jackson to tie the laces, to sitting in the passenger seat of his police car and noticing every bump and pothole on the way home. Exhaustion snatched at Kit's consciousness, rendering her incapable of anything more than existing. Jackson had snagged her house and shop keys from the tiny pile of belongings remaining in her possession. Her handbag still sat on the shoe rack upstairs in Mr Rashid's apartment and her phone lay in smithereens on the floor of the wrecked vehicle. He unlocked her front door and helped her inside, letting her pick her own route across the lounge until the backs of her legs hit the comfy cushion of her reading chair.

"I'll be fine," she said, leaning her head back and closing her eyes. "De boys don't be dong."

Jackson inhaled a sigh and squatted down in front of her. His gentle fingers clasped hers. His next question surprised her, asked with gentleness but laced with irritation. "What part of 'Don't hang up,' didn't you understand?" he demanded. The dent from a healed scar on his left cheek widened into a dimple as he frowned. "And why would you think that guy was an undercover cop? How many cops do you know wearing Armani?"

Kit blinked and forced herself to face his question. Her vision blurred and separated him into two cross police officers. Both had dimples. "Can dust one of you ask de questions?" she replied.

"It won't be me, my little black-eyed pea," he said with a smirk. "This one is way above my pay grade. The big guns will want to see you soon and take a formal statement."

Kit groaned and squeezed her eyes shut. She pretended to fall asleep, hoping Jackson might take the hint and leave. But the ruse turned into reality as the pain medication took over and plunged her into a dreamless sleep.

Kit woke to the sound of male voices. The words echoed in the narrow hallway and she recognised Jackson's steady cadence. Every bone in her body seemed to lock when she tried to move and her head felt like a bowling ball resting on her skinny neck. "Ooof," she managed. Her fingers strayed to the source of the most pain. As pure agony blossomed out from the gauze across her nose, she wished she'd left well alone. She wished she'd left a lot of things alone.

Jackson's face appeared in front of her and he squatted down on his haunches. He winced and his brown eyes reflected an apology. "The detective sergeant would like to speak to you now," he said. He looked conflicted, his desire to care for her clashing with his responsibility as a police officer. Kit pushed herself upright and nodded her acceptance. She'd been dreading the moment and knew she should get it over with soon. She'd gain nothing by delaying the inevitable.

"I'll do it," she murmured. The smile she tried to give him failed as her lip cracked. Jackson frowned and scouted around for a tissue. He settled on a fresh piece of gauze and dabbed at her lip with gentle fingers.

"Okay?" he whispered. At Kit's wavering nod, he rose and returned to the hallway.

Kit tried not to focus on the detective as he followed Jackson across the lounge. "Miss Maguire?" he said, as though unsure the swollen face in front of him belonged to Kit. She nodded in reply, not wanting to waste words but finding the action equally painful. He looked smart in black jeans and a white buttoned shirt. It seemed incongruous; the difference neat attire made to her perception of him.

Even his straggly red beard looked more under control than the last time she saw him.

"Senior Sergeant Delaney has explained that you were aware of my presence." He glared up at Jackson and a raised eyebrow projected his displeasure. "That was not my intention. I won't bore you with the details, but my department have been tracking the movements of a drug syndicate for quite some time. It seems they discovered a way of administering narcotics without the usual paraphernalia. I witnessed you meeting with their primary researcher who has been on our radar since he linked up with a known drug supplier. We believe your flatmate's disappearance relates to his research. I'd like you to consider your answers to my questions with care. Please understand that I may put you under caution at any point during our discussion if I deem it necessary."

Kit's eyes widened and she stared up at Jackson, seeking his guidance without words. He winced and swallowed once before replying. "Just tell the truth, Kit," he urged. "Do you want me to get you a lawyer?"

"Do!" She stressed, trying to shake her head at the same time.

Jackson tilted his jaw and his eyes narrowed. "Is that no?" He demanded. "Or do you mean that you want me to get a lawyer?"

The detective with the red beard frowned. "She doesn't need a lawyer, Delaney!" he hissed. "I just need her to know her rights." He took a seat on the sofa opposite Kit. His short fingers pulled a voice recorder from his top pocket and Kit's eyes widened when he balanced it on his knee and leaned forward without touching the buttons. It was already running. She stole a glance at Jackson and saw the slightest shake of his head.

"It's dot what you dink," she began. "It's about a barriage, a bissing scientist and some Bineapple Lumps."

CHAPTER 36

Curly Horsing Around

Jerry arrived home to find Kit sitting in a kitchen chair in the middle of the paddock. Jackson had wrapped a tea towel around a packet of frozen peas. She held it to her forehead and tried to ignore the water dripping down her face. Bouffant grazed nearby, his body language relaxed as he gave a giant, grass filled yawn.

"What now?" Jerry demanded. "Why is that man pointing a handgun at our shed?"

The undercover detective wore a Kevlar vest over his white shirt. He stood by the front corner of the rusty structure and reaching forward, rapped three times in quick succession on the shed door. "Come out with your hands in the air!" he shouted. "Armed police! Come out and throw your weapons on the ground! Then lie face down in front of us!"

His hastily summoned colleagues tensed. Positioned around the shed, they wore black balaclavas, body armour and carried heavy duty firearms.

"I think the Armed Offenders Squad might be overkill." Jackson stood next to Kit with his thumbs tucked into the armpits of his Kevlar vest. "I think he'll feel a bit of an idiot in about ten seconds."

Kit murmured something which sounded like agreement, although she suspected ten seconds might be too long. Bouffant emitted a protracted sigh and shot grass seed from his nose. Unconcerned by the unfolding drama, he edged nearer the little group and nuzzled Jerry's shoulder.

"Can someone tell me what's happening?" Jerry demanded. His body jolted as Bouffant's nuzzling grew over enthusiastic. "If they fire those guns, this horse will go nuts."

"Dey don't dire de duns," Kit said.

Jerry peered at her in confusion. "Sorry, what?"

Jackson rested a hand on the back of Kit's chair and leaned forward to regard Jerry with a raised eyebrow. "She said, they won't fire the guns," he replied.

"How do you know?" Jerry glanced at the horse and then back at the police officers gathered around the shed.

Jackson grinned. "Because we know what's in there," he said.

"There's nothing in there!" Jerry protested. "It's rusted rotten. That's why all the horse stuff is in the garage." He reached out a hand and scratched Bouffant's tousled forelock. The horse rewarded him by snorting grass seed over Jerry's smart trousers.

The little group heard the shed door creak before they spotted movement. A raised hand appeared from the gap and then another. "Don't shoot!" a voice pleaded. "I live here. Don't shoot!"

Jackson tensed and rested a hand on Kit's shoulder as the door pushed wider and a foot emerged. Then a body and last of all a head. The face wore a frightened expression and Jerry released a gasp of surprise as the figure dived headfirst into the long grass.

"Are you kidding me?" he demanded.

Jackson glanced down at Kit and his expression held a glimmer of pride. "Kit worked it out," he said. "Apparently, it was the Pineapple Lumps."

"He ate them, didn't he?" Jerry rolled his eyes and shook his head. "I should have guessed. They're his favourite." Bouffant nudged his shoulder and he acknowledged the horse with a scratch to his poll. "Yeah, you tried to tell us too, didn't you?"

"Hey guys!" Raki waved at his little audience as an officer wearing a balaclava pushed his head down to the floor again. They cuffed him on the ground with his hands behind his back. He staggered a little as they hauled him onto his feet and the undercover detective took a firm hold of his elbow.

"Send the others in for the equipment," he snapped at Jackson as he passed. He jerked his head back towards the shed. "I want that data intact."

Raki stumbled as he reached Jerry and he raised a speculative eyebrow. Jerry nodded. "See you soon, mate," he called. "I'll follow you to the station. Say nothing until I get there."

"Dy does dat dop dant Daki's data?" Kit enquired. "Her eyebrows puckered into a frown and the gauze over the bridge of her nose twisted. She winced in pain and held her hands out on either side of her body to express her confusion instead.

"Why does that cop want Raki's data? Evidence?" Jackson shook his head, although he didn't sound too sure. His eyes narrowed as a team of officers wearing street clothes dashed past them and into the shed.

Jerry glanced at Kit and his eyes twinkled. "I don't think that's gonna go quite how they planned then," he whispered, intending the comment for her ears only. She nodded in reply. Some scientific advances were better left undiscovered. Raki had gone to impressive lengths to guarantee it.

CHAPTER 37

Curly Conclusions

"Most people have no reason to consider the toxicity of drugs absorbed through the skin." Raki leaned forward and rested his elbows on the dining table. The front of his tee-shirt bore grass stains from his tussle with New Zealand's finest constabulary. His eyes misted as his mind escaped into his scientific heaven. "Just contemplate all the helpful patches created to help with addictions or pain. Nicotine patches help with cravings for a smoking addict wanting to quit. Fentanyl patches provide constant, lower doses and bypass the harmful effects caused by administering oral opiates. They have a good purpose." Raki flapped his hand. "Science has made a difference to peoples' suffering. But there are other issues, which is why the drug squad wear hazard suits when investigating a clandestine drug manufacturing lab. Officers have almost died from touching drug substances with their fingers or breathing it in by accident."

Kit made a sound like a groan and heard it emerge as more of a hiss. Her body ached from being flung around the vehicle like a rag doll. Sitting on the stiff dining chair didn't help her comfort levels. Jerry rested a hand on her shoulder and gave it a gentle squeeze. "Maybe get to the crux of the story before Kit passes out," he suggested.

"Sorry." Raki exhaled and the huge breath blew his fringe into a crest over his left eye. His hair had grown during his time hiding in the shed and a scrubby black beard coated his chin. Never able to grow decent facial hair, his chin resembled a mange infested cat. "Drugs can pass through the skin and affect us. We've always known that. A tiny amount of a drug can cause an overdose leading to death and that's the part which has limited the pharmaceutical industry." He paused. "I thought I'd cracked it with my formula. I believed I'd controlled the way different drugs absorb through the skin." His eyebrows creased into a line and he ran a hand over his face. "I honestly assumed we'd found the code for administering heavy duty drugs to people who'd run out of options. It offered a whole other way of treating health issues."

Langdon scratched his head and looked confused. "But that's not what your PhD is about, is it?" he said. "We've talked about your research at length and that's not it."

Raki sat back and stared at the ceiling. His shoulders slumped. "No. It isn't. I allowed a researcher to distract me. He painted this amazing picture of us being able to save the world together, one cancer drug at a time. He just needed me to do the chemistry component and promised to give me credit as a co-author of his research and a share of the royalties."

"Kasouf!" Kit spat. She discovered she could speak through gritted teeth and reduce the use of her more painful facial muscles.

Raki turned to her and nodded. "Yeah. And the English guy. The company in India sent him as a kind of enforcer to keep Kasouf on track. The ethics committee weren't happy with his proposal and pulled the plug."

"Why didn't he go to Otago University or Auckland?" Jerry asked. His fingers rubbed a gentle circle over Kit's shoulder. "Didn't he need medical students and the benefit of qualified doctors?"

Raki shook his head. "No. Because he wasn't looking to help cancer patients or anyone else. He wanted a carrier substance for narcotics and opioids."

Jerry frowned. "Easy. Rub cocaine on the inside of your cheek or the membrane of your nose and ride the waves."

"No, no, no." Raki waved his arms like a mini windmill. Kit's lips curved upward. She'd missed Raki's exuberance and characteristic flair. "He wanted more control than that, something less haphazard and risky. He'd got part of the way, but he needed a chemist to tidy up the formula. Me."

"Professor Kirke?" Kit said the woman's whole title, amused that her difficulty speaking didn't extend to any of the letters in the woman's name.

Raki's eyes widened and he nodded. "I'm sure she was onto Kasouf. She came into the lab asking questions and he got very skittish. I overheard her telling him that the ethics committee had turned down his application for animal trials." Raki's lips twisted into a pout laden with guilt. "She didn't know he'd come to me for help. I got a massive scholarship which put me under pressure and I also have a journal publication due before the end of this month. She would have flipped out if she'd known Kasouf had sucked me into his scheme."

Kit's eyes widened in horror. Professor Kirke with an 'e' had blocked her every move. She closed her eyes against the pain of her shaking head as disappointment surged through her. A twinge of conscience told her she'd already decided the woman was guilty just because she didn't like her. "She wouldn't let be speak to the other students!" Kit attempted to infuse her comment with pique and failed.

Jerry cocked his head and offered her a benevolent smile like a proud parent. "That works," he said. "We can understand you if you grit your teeth."

"Yeah, she wouldn't let you anywhere near the students." Raki repeated. "She's protective over the department's reputation. I could tell from the tone of the conversation I overheard that she suspected something. She wouldn't risk it. You could have been a journalist or an undercover cop."

Kit groaned and closed her eyes. "Dey already had one of dose," she said with a sigh.

Raki's head bobbled up and down and his hair wobbled. He tucked a loose strand behind his left ear. "Yeah. I know about the undercover cop. Red beard, dressed like a student?" He acknowledged Kit's nod of agreement with a wince. "He tried to speak to me the night

I drove down to uni. Kasouf rang me and let slip that he was working at a beauty clinic giving massages. He said he'd run out of the carrier product. I realised what he was doing and needed to destroy the data. The English guy had turned up the day before and I panicked. Kasouf seemed terrified of him. So, I destroyed what I could and went into hiding."

"In the shed." Jerry sat back and his chair creaked.

"You cabe into the house, didn't you?" Kit asked. "And dook the Bineapple Lumbs."

"Yeah. Sorry for scaring you." Raki reached over and patted Kit's knee. "I needed to charge the laptop. I came in at night while everyone slept and left it charging in the lounge on the spare cable. The Wi-Fi doesn't quite reach the shed, so I checked stuff online and logged into the university system." His lips pursed and he winced. "I hope you didn't mind me borrowing the laptop, Kit."

Kit swallowed and avoided Jerry's gaze. She twisted her lips and focused on Raki. He smiled and stared through the kitchen window towards the paddock. Bouffant rolled in a patch of sand, his legs waving in the air like bent antennae. "The new flatmate is a bit over affectionate though," he mused. "I made the Pineapple Lumps last for a few days. They were my reward for getting my work done. But I made the mistake of giving the horse a taste and then he wouldn't leave me alone."

"What?" Jerry looked affronted until he realised Raki meant the horse.

"Wasn't the university system monitored?" Langdon asked. "Wouldn't the professor check that first?"

"I didn't log in as myself," Raki scoffed. "I'm not an idiot. A mate left two years ago and the IT department forgot to delete his details. I log on as him if I'm doing something that I don't want traced back to me."

"So, what have you been doing in Kit's shed all this time?" Jerry asked. His eyes narrowed. "Apart from raiding the fridge and eating Pineapple Lumps."

Raki's eyes sparkled. "Thanks for those. I've been writing my doctoral thesis. I've also finished the publication chapter the professor wanted. It's been great with no distractions. Like a writing boot camp."

"What did you eat?" Langdon demanded, his thoughts never far from his next carbohydrate free meal.

Raki shrugged. "Pizza mainly. I used burner SIM cards in my phone, walked along the gully to the back road and got dinner delivered straight to me." He winced. "I'm gonna have a big credit card bill at the end of this. And I'm fed up of pizza, although sometimes I mixed it up with garlic bread or fries." He paused and chuckled. "I've had a lot of fun watching you two clowns though. The boredom tempted me to join in with you."

"What?" Jerry stiffened and shot a look of pure angst at Langdon. "What do you mean?"

"Watched us?" Langdon gulped. "Doing what."

"Don't answer that." Jerry lifted a cautionary hand and pursed his lips. "Just shut up, please. It's embarrassing."

"I dow." Kit shrugged. "I dow adout it." She tried to frown at Raki and formulate a suitable rebuke. It wasn't like him to make a lewd suggestion about joining in with someone else's relationship.

"What's she saying?" Raki cocked his head. "Oh. She knows about it. See, it's fine."

"We kept it secret." Langdon folded his arms and pouted. "Nothing seemed enough, so I figured this might work. It doesn't seem to have made much difference."

"I believe it has." Jerry squirmed in his seat. "Some days, I find it quite hard to sit on my bottom."

Kit's eyes bugged and she pressed a finger over the gauze on her nose. She gave herself a shake and cleared her throat. Jerry gave her a sideways look. "It's the downward facing dog that gets me. Maybe it's my long torso. What do you think, Kit? You do it, don't you?"

"Huh?" Kit blinked.

Langdon threw his hands in the air. "Fine! Tell everyone. Put it in the church bulletin. See if I care!"

"I don't know why you're so secretive about it!" Jerry grumbled. "I'm not sure I want to do it anymore. The gym is better."

"Huh?" Kit repeated.

Raki gave her a quizzical look, accompanied by a frown. "Hot yoga. You said you knew."

"Oh." Kit swallowed and closed her eyes. A clandestine gay vicar relationship seemed so much more likely.

"Hang on a second." Jerry wagged a finger, his quick ex-lawyer's brain sifting through the information as he tried to ignore Kit's discomfort. "Kit said you took the laptop the night she saw you on the porch."

"Na." Raki dismissed the notion with a wave of his hand. "I took it when I first moved into the shed." He looked at Kit. "I guess you didn't miss it. I also dismantled my PC after wiping the data. It's hidden in the attic. I destroyed the backup drives; took them apart and smashed the disks inside them. Kasouf has obviously adulterated the prototype and started using it on clients in his massages. He can't make any more now without the original recipe."

Kit sat up straight and made flapping motions with her hands. Her eyes widened. A numbness began in her chest and spread outward as fear engulfed her. "Oh dow!" she wailed. "Oh dow!"

"What's wrong?" Jerry's brown eyes widened and the surrounding conversation ceased. "Are you sick?"

Kit shook her head and her chin wobbled. She changed the motion to a nod, which sent a searing pain to the bridge of her nose. "He bassaged be!" she whispered. "Bith dugs." Her mind scrabbled back in time to the fated appointment and she tried to place herself back there. A series of pictures flipped through her inner vision like disjointed images in a child's book. The broken blind. How great Kasouf was at foot massages. The soothing scent of lavender. She blinked, no nearer to finding what she needed.

"Oh!" Jerry understood her meaning and his arm closed around her shoulder. "He massaged Kit. She's worried he might have drugged her."

Raki's gentle hands formed into fists and his jaw hardened. "I'll kill him!" he snarled.

CHAPTER 38

High as a Kite

Tired, overwrought and in pain, Kit snivelled into her pillow. She'd locked the door on her self-imposed exile, much to the boys' frustration. "Beave be!" she begged as Jerry rapped on the bedroom door. Her words sounded pitiful and upset her further at her inability to make herself understood.

"Should we break it down then?" Raki's voice echoed in the hallway, and Kit groaned and wondered how she'd ever missed his scatter-brained suggestions.

"No!" Langdon intervened. "We will not break down the door! This is Kit's house. Let's give her a little space." He herded the other two away from the door and their laboured footsteps tracked down the stairs.

She spent the next half an hour practising yoga breathing, although the inability to use her nose hindered the process. But it served as a distraction and exhausted her enough to let the painkillers do their job. She slipped into a fitful sleep occupied by exploding lube and men in smart suits who weren't really cops. A strange sensation woke her as her legs sank lower on the bed. In her dream, she tripped over the edge of the pavement and woke with a start. And a groan of pain.

"Sorry." Jackson sat on the edge of her bed, his head bowed and his thumbs pressed against the bridge of his nose. "Didn't mean to scare you."

Kit pushed herself in the general direction of her pillow and ended up slumped sideways. She muttered something unintelligible and Jackson raised a hand. "Don't speak. I can't really understand you. Let me do the talking, okay?" He raised a dark eyebrow but didn't wait for an answer. "Kasouf didn't drug you. I spoke to the detective who has him in custody. He didn't drug you because he wanted something different from your association."

Kit nodded. "Barriage."

Jackson flattened his lips. "I wanted to reassure you. We can organise a blood test as part of the case if that would satisfy you, or you can visit your doctor. It'll be negative."

Kit closed her eyes and released a sigh. "I dow. It was a dood bassage. I felt fine."

Jackson smiled and it reached the corners of his eyes, crinkling them into laugh lines. "You knew that," he whispered. "But your flatmates didn't." He replied to Kit's questioning look. "They phoned me. All of them," he said. "On speakerphone. They all care about you, don't they?"

Kit nodded and rested a hand over her chest. Sleep had taken the tightness away. She glanced at the door and then raised an eyebrow at Jackson. He smirked. "Takes a thief to catch a thief," he said. He raised his right hand in a universal stop sign. "I didn't break the lock, so don't worry."

"Danks."

"Oh, the little guy asked me to give you this." He leaned back and retrieved her phone from his trouser pocket. "They used it to call me."

"On beakerbone." Kit sighed. She imagined the scene; two vicars and a scientist choosing the less destructive options to navigate life. She gave a painful nod of approval and accepted her phone, dropping it next to her on the bed.

Jackson clicked his fingers as he remembered something else. "Oh, yeah. He said you should check your emails."

Kit ran a hand through her hair and frowned at the knots she found lurking beneath a mat of frizz. Extracting her fingers with difficulty, she reached for the phone and tapped the screen. It flickered to life and displayed a flashing, unopened envelope. Kit jabbed at it and the email opened.

'Dear Miss Maguire,' it began.

Kit pushed herself upright and her eyes widened. Jackson frowned and shifted on the bed. His Kevlar vest creaked as he turned to face her, a hand resting over her shin in concern. "Bube!" she hissed. "De bube."

Jackson swallowed. "I won't pretend I understood that."

Kit jabbered as she read and Jackson shook his head. She finished and handed the phone to him. "Dook!" she insisted.

Jackson inhaled and skipped through the email before reading the conclusion aloud. "Faulty machine in the packing area ... some tubes didn't receive enough product ... explosions ... partial refund." He looked up at Kit and released a low whistle. "Aaaahhh, that's what that stuff was." A grin broke across his face. Then he laughed, a deep, pleasant sound. "It will devastate the Clandestine Drug Team when they get the test results back from the English guy's car. They thought they'd scored the product in its raw state. Kasouf told them he'd used the last of it before they raided the clinic." He laughed again as though the thought tickled him. "Didn't the officers who attended the scene ask what it was?"

"I dried to dell dem!" Kit flapped a hand at her nose and almost smacked herself in the face. She blinked at the near miss. "It dot by dault!"

Jackson sniggered again. "Oh, Maguire. You crack me up for sure." The smile remained in his eyes. He opened his mouth to speak and Kit held her breath.

Her phone rang, the sound loud and intrusive. Jackson almost dropped it and glanced at the screen as he juggled it. "Oops, it's your mother," he said reading the name out loud.

Kit accepted the phone and braced herself. She paused while trying to find words which didn't sound muffled by her nose injury. If she gritted her teeth, her mother would read into it. She almost got the phone to her ear when Marian's wailing began. "It's a disaster, Kit!" she screeched. "I can't believe it."

Kit bumped the phone with her cheek and pain ricocheted across the bridge of her nose. She released a groan and stared at the screen in accusation. Marian continued to rage, increasing in volume so that even Jackson quirked an eyebrow. Kit stabbed a finger at the speaker button and her mother's voice split the air molecules in the bedroom. Jackson reared back and alarm flitted across his dark eyes. "What the heck?" he asked.

Marian's tirade halted. "Is that a man, darling?" she demanded. "Is that him? Is that my masseur?"

"Dooo!" Kit grumbled. She flopped backwards into her pillows and jammed her hands over her ears.

Jackson cleared his throat and lifted the phone nearer his lips. "Er, hello Kit's mum," he said. "I'm Senior Sergeant Jackson Delaney. There's something you should know." He opened his mouth to continue, but Marian unleashed a volley of high-pitched squeals.

"You!" she yelled. "I recognise your name! You're the reason our chairwoman is in a police cell."

"What?" Jackson's politeness slipped and degenerated into surprised officialdom. "I'm sorry, Madam, I don't understand what you mean."

"Oh, yes you do!" Marian railed. "Her husband just phoned me to ask if I knew any good lawyers. You're listed as the arresting officer. It's all a lie! Our entire crocheting group is baying for your blood!"

Jackson ran a hand through his hair and shot Kit a sideways glance. He shrugged and tried to hand her the phone. She closed her eyes and pretended not to notice as he fumbled through placating her mother.

"This isn't ringing any bells," he said, tapping Kit's shin with his other hand.

"We'll ring your jolly bells!" Marian raged. "Poor Maude had a little moment on her way back from the beauty clinic this morning. She had a tiny lapse of concentration at the roundabout and ran up the back of another driver. She's ninety-two! Ninety-two! And you arrested her like a common criminal!"

Jackson mouthed a curse and his eyes widened in alarm. "Oh, her. I'm sorry, but I'm not allowed to comment on an active case." He shoved the phone into Kit's lap and stood, putting distance between himself and the apoplectic Marian. He spread his hands and mouthed, "The woman was as high as a kite. Her eyes were pointing in different directions!"

Kit bucked and the phone flipped onto its screen. Marian's yells still issued from the speaker. Kit rolled onto her side and squeezed her eyes as tightly closed as her poor nose would allow, before the threatening pain blossomed into her head. A text pinged and curiosity nagged at the last of her resolve. She picked up the phone and groaned at Debbie's latest communication. Another tube of purple-willy-shaped lube had exploded in another Curly's bathroom on the other side of the city. She dropped the phone back onto the bed and shoved her pillow over it.

Marian continued to shout into the bedding, listing all the terrible things the Catholic Ladies Crocheting Guild intended to inflict on Maud's arresting officer. Outside, Bouffant neighed and flicked his scrubby tail, missing the company of his special friend in the shed.

PLEASE HELP ME BY LEAVING A REVIEW

If you've enjoyed Kit's quest for Curly Approved products and laughed out loud at her antics, then please leave a review saying so.
I will be eternally grateful because I really need your help.

About the Author

K T Bowes is a bestselling teen and women's author. Her novel A Trail of Lies was the winner of the genre award for Author's Cave in 2014.
The New Du Rose Matriarch has consistently been an Amazon Bestseller.
K T Bowes is an Englishwoman in exile in New Zealand, swapping rugged cosmopolitan for mountain ranges and terrifying rivers. She lives in the same street as the Māori king and the culture around her is infused into most of her novels.

You can find her hanging out on social media in the following places.
Check in and say hello. Maybe suggest she gets back to writing and stops watching cat videos.

FACEBOOK
https://www.facebook.com/NZauthorKTBowes/

TWITTER
https://twitter.com/ktboweswrites

INSTAGRAM
https://www.instagram.com/k_t_bowes

PINTEREST
https://www.pinterest.nz/hanadurose/

LINKEDIN
https://www.linkedin.com/in/ktbowes/

GOODREADS
https://www.goodreads.com/author/show/7212024.K_T_Bowes

OTHER NOVELS

BY K T BOWES

The Hana Du Rose Mysteries:
Logan Du Rose
About Hana - FREE digital copy
Hana Du Rose
Du Rose Legacy
The New Du Rose Matriarch
One Heartbeat
The Du Rose Prophecy
Du Rose Sons
Du Rose Family Ties
Du Rose Vendetta
Tama Du Rose

The Calculated Risk Series:
The Actuary - FREE digital copy
The Actuary's Wife
The Actuary in Trouble

Troubled Series:
Free from the Tracks -FREE digital copy
Sophia's Dilemma
A Trail of Lies
Gone Phishing

New Zealand Soccer Referee Series:
All Saints

Escaping the Back Country NZ Series:
Pirongia's Secret FREE to mail subscribers
Deleilah

A Keeper's War Fantasy Trilogy:
Perpetual Winter
The Bee Queen
Hive

UK based mystery/romances:
Artifact
Demons on Her Shoulder

The Curly Fan Club
Dead Straight
Bad Hair Day